The

BAD
MOTHER'S
DETOX

SUZY K QUINN

Lightning
Books

Published by
Lightning Books Ltd
Imprint of EyeStorm Media
312 Uxbridge Road
Rickmansworth
Hertfordshire
WD3 8YL

www.lightning-books.com

British Library Cataloguing in Publication Data
A catalogue record for this book is available from the British Library

Printed by CPI Group (UK) Ltd, Croydon CR0 4YY

ISBN 9781785631573

Yay!

You picked up my book.

Which at least means the cover is good.

I still cant believe so many people read my books.

Each and every day, I am humbled by this fact.

I cant thank you enough.

Im a chatty sort and I LOVE talking to readers.

If you want to ask me any questions about the books

or chat about anything at all, get in touch:

Happy reading, gorgeous

Suzy xxx

Email: suzykquinn@devoted-ebooks.com

Facebook.com/suzykquinn

(You can friend request me. I like friends.)

Twitter: @suzykquinn

Website: suzykquinn.com

Sunday, 1st January
New Year

A time to take stock.

Last January, I was living with Nick in London.

We were engaged.

Things weren't perfect.

Nick's mum was always letting herself into the apartment, criticising my parenting and eating fishy salads at the breakfast bar. Nick was drunk half the time, and panicky when left alone with Daisy.

Also, getting Daisy's pram into the tiny executive lift was a nightmare.

But I honestly thought Daisy would grow up with two parents living together.

I was wrong.

Now I'm staying at my parent's pub in Great Oakley, with Daisy in a travel cot, while Nick plays happy families with my former best friend, who will give birth to their child any day now.

Last year, Nick and Sadie's affair felt awful. I wallowed. But then I got on with it. I even ran a marathon. Now I'm stronger. I've learned that life doesn't end because your ex-boyfriend and ex-best friend are shitheads.

And now Alex and I…well, things are looking up.

Can't stop thinking about the Dalton Ball.

What a night.

Nick was SO shocked when Alex and I headed upstairs together. *'Julesy. Babe. Please. You can't leave with him. Come on. We have a baby together.'*

Hilarious that after getting my best friend pregnant, Nick thinks he can have a say in my love life.

Nick STILL hasn't paid any maintenance for Daisy.

And it's been six months since we split up.

BLOODY Nick.

I suppose I shouldn't be surprised.

Everyone warned me not to settle down with a charming, bit-part actor. But pre-Daisy I was young and stupid.

In my early twenties, Nick's puppy-dog eyes and charismatic personality felt romantic. Then Daisy came along, and I realised charm means nothing. Responsibility is everything.

Nick's new baby is due any day, so it's not a great time to talk finances. But that's not Daisy's fault.

Sent Nick a text message:

Hope you are well. We need to sort out maintenance.

If you keep sidestepping this, I'll have to take you to court.

Sorry.

The text message wasn't strictly true. I don't hope he's well, and I won't be sorry to take him to court. But social nicety is hard-wired into me.

Nick hasn't replied yet.

Knowing him, he probably won't answer.

Denial is his favourite way of dealing with problems.

Monday, 2nd January

Alex Dalton called late last night.

'How are you?' he asked. 'Did you catch up on sleep after New Year's Eve?'

I pictured Alex in one of his marble-floored hotel lobbies, black suit and white shirt, jet-black hair, gleaming jawline. Like an aftershave model, but a heterosexual one.

'I'm OK,' I said. 'Just a bit of family drama.'

'Is Daisy all right?'

'Fine.'

Silence.

Then Alex said, 'I want to see you. But I'm flying out to Tokyo for work. I'll keep the trip as short as possible. I hate leaving, but a lot of people are relying on me.'

'How can you be working already?' I asked.

'There's no such thing as a holiday in the hotel trade,' said Alex. 'We have big plans for the Dalton Group this year. Do *you* have any New Year's resolutions?'

'Just one,' I said. 'I want to stop Daisy eating biros.'

'Come on now, Juliette,' said Alex. 'There must be something you want.'

Yes – many things.

+ Unstained clothing.
+ Leaving the house before 9 am.
+ Eight hours' uninterrupted sleep.
+ Financial support from Daisy's father.
+ And a lovely cottage with roses around the door.

But I'd count myself very lucky just to have unstained clothing.

Tuesday, 3rd January

Mum's been arrested again.

It was the usual charge – disrupting the peace.

She was drinking tea with the policemen, playing cards and sharing out her sausage rolls when I picked her up.

The police were cheerful too, letting Daisy crawl into the empty cells and jangle their handcuffs.

Mum asked me about the Dalton Ball on New Year's Eve.

Under different circumstances, I would have shared my evening of drama. However, the police station wasn't the place to relive a romantic encounter, so instead I lectured Mum about proper grandmother behaviour while she signed her release papers.

I could tell she wasn't really listening, because when I'd finished the lecture, Mum said, 'Can we stop at the Co-op on the way home? I fancy some Findus Crispy Pancakes.'

Wednesday, 4th January

Visited Nana Joan this afternoon with the shopping she wanted – bacon, pork chops, frying steak and beef kidneys.

Her care home has a strict vegetarian policy these days, so Nana makes a little on the side selling contraband meat.

Nana took one look at my tired face and fired up her portable grill to make bacon sandwiches.

She's not supposed to have Calor gas in her room, but the staff let her get away with it because it saves arguments at meal times.

Daisy got really excited about my bacon sandwich and kept making grabs for it. Foolishly, I let her have a bite, and she crammed half the sandwich in her mouth before I could stop her, then clamped her little lips closed and stubbornly refused to let me pry them open.

Was concerned about salt content, choking, etc., but Nana told me not to worry.

'Our family are born with unusually large gullets,' she said. 'Your mother used to scoff whole Eccles cakes, and no harm ever came to her.'

Cleaned Nana's portable grill in the en-suite shower room, using Fairy Liquid from the shower rack.

Then I helped Nana with her mobile phone. 'It doesn't ring any more,' she complained. 'There's something squiffy with it.'

It turned out to be an easy problem to solve.

Nana had confused her phone with the temperature controller. The diagnosis was a relief for Nana because she'd been sweating at night for months.

Told Nana I'm a bit worried about Daisy re walking.

The NHS website says babies start walking *around* the age of one, but Daisy hasn't even taken her first step yet.

'Daisy is fifteen months old,' I said. 'Surely she should be able to walk by now.'

Althea's little boy, Wolfgang, walked at eight months – although it proved to be a nuisance. Althea was forever arguing about the price at soft play and eventually resorted to bringing Wolfgang's passport everywhere.

'But Daisy is walking right now,' Nana insisted. 'Look at her go.'

'She's not walking,' I said, as we watched Daisy pull herself up on the rise and recline chair. 'She's cruising.'

'Cruising?' said Nana. 'Isn't that something you do on a ship?'

'It's when children hold onto furniture,' I said. 'But it's not the same as walking. I wish she'd take a few steps.'

'She's probably just lazy,' Nana reassured me. 'Your mum was the same. She only bothered walking if there was cake to be had. The rest of the time she'd sit and whack your Uncle Danny with her rattle.'

Nana asked if I'd seen Nick recently.

'I saw him on New Year's Eve,' I told her. 'He asked for a second chance.'

'Steer well clear,' said Nana. 'He's a good-looking waster, that one. Has he paid you any money for Daisy yet?'

'No,' I said. 'Not a penny.'

'Better sort that out,' said Nana Joan. 'He'll have another baby soon, won't he?'

'It's not that simple,' I said. 'As far as Nick's concerned, Daisy and I are staying with Mum and Dad, so he doesn't need to take care of us.'

'Don't the government just *take* money from absent fathers these days?' Nana asked.

'Not in our case,' I said. 'Most of Nick's earnings are undeclared. And he gets pocket money from his mother – there's no tax bracket for that. If he doesn't pay up, we'll have to go to court.'

Nana asked about the New Year's Eve Ball. 'I hope you wore something that showed off your figure,' she said. 'I used to have a natural cleavage like yours. These days, I need yards of sticky tape.'

Nana is what you call a 'glamorous granny'. Even in her eighties, she wears leopard print, Lurex and Wonderbras.

Told Nana that Alex Dalton and I 'got close' at the New Year's Eve ball.

I don't really know how else to describe things with Alex.

I mean, I suppose we were already 'close'. Alex trained me for the Winter Marathon last year. And we had a few romantic moments while that was going on. But now…it feels like we're sort of, possibly, seeing each other.

'About time,' said Nana. 'Look at you. All your own curly hair and a lovely bosom. It's no wonder you've been snapped up.'

'Our lives are different, though,' I admitted. 'Alex is a Dalton. His family owns half of London.'

'Opposites attract,' said Nana. 'Your grandad liked wholemeal bread. Whereas I stick to white sliced.'

But the truth is, I have baggage with a capital B.

Actually, a capital N.

Nick.

Thursday, 5th January

Nick phoned at midday, sounding terrified.

Sadie is in labour.

Nick and I aren't exactly on friendly terms, but I sensed he was desperate for support, so I let him rattle on.

'How long does it last?' Nick asked. 'Sadie's going mental, and we're only an hour in.'

'Don't you remember my labour?' I said. 'It was over twelve hours.'

'Twelve *hours?*' Nick screeched. 'Daisy didn't take that long to come out, did she? That's *all day.*'

I couldn't help adding, 'You know my friend, Althea? Her labour took five days.'

To be fair, I think Althea strung her labour out a bit.

She had a big hippy love-in with candles and hummus and cushions, and shouted down any midwife who talked about 'speeding things along'.

Also, a yogi came to bend Althea's womanly figure into 'baby-friendly' positions, and weave her thick, curly black hair into 'love braids'.

Baby Wolfgang was 'breathed' into the world, with the occasional bellow of 'Om Shanti'.

'They won't let Sadie into the hospital yet,' Nick sobbed. 'I can't handle this shit, Jules. You know how sensitive I am.'

'Funny to hear you describe yourself as sensitive,' I said.

'Immature and self-absorbed are the words I'd use.'

In the background, I heard Sadie screech, 'Put on my Ellie Goulding album, you *useless twat.*'

Felt a bit sorry for Nick then, but not that sorry.

When Nick got Sadie pregnant, my world fell apart. But like Althea said, 'Karma will get him. Wait and see.'

She was right.

Friday, 6th January

Nick and Sadie have had their baby.

A little boy.

Actually, *really* little – only 5lbs 10oz.

Daisy was 8lbs, and the midwives said things like, 'big strapping legs' and 'a great pair of lungs'.

Daisy has a half-brother. Such a weird thought.

I wonder if the baby looks like Nick, with dark, flirtatious eyebrows and blue eyes. Or like Sadie, with a big moon face and porcelain skin.

Nick and Sadie's baby was born last night by C-section.

Nick phoned in the early hours of the morning to tell Daisy about her new brother. He was glowing with new fatherhood, telling me about little baby Horatio and his massive balls.

'You've called him Horatio?' I said. 'Like Penelope Dearheart's dog?'

Nick went quiet for a moment. 'Well we can't change the name now,' he said. 'Mum's ordered an engraved silver tankard.'

Sadie's doing well apparently (not that I asked) but has got a bit possessive – hissing at anyone who comes near 'little Horry'.

Nick sounded slurred, so I'm guessing he'd managed to sneak some whisky into the labour ward.

No surprises there.

At Daisy's birth, Nick won the prize for worst birthing companion ever, drunkenly screaming, 'What the fuck is that?' at all the wrong moments.

Even the midwife asked if I'd prefer he waited outside.

Saturday, 7th January

Nick phoned at 3 am, asking if I could put his 'little girl' on the phone.

'I'm not going to wake Daisy,' I told him. 'It's the middle of the night. Why didn't you ring in the daytime?'

'Come on, Jules,' said Nick. 'The baby wants to say hello. He's Daisy's *brother*.'

Wow.

Brother.

'Did you get my text message about maintenance payments?' I asked.

Nick didn't answer, which I took to mean yes.

'Sort it out,' I said. 'Or I'll take you to court.'

Sunday, 8th January

Alex just called.

He's cutting his Tokyo trip short and flying back next weekend specially to see me.

And in possibly the weirdest post-coital conversation ever, he asked if I would attend Mass with him and his mother at Westminster Cathedral.

Once I'd ascertained Alex wasn't trying to purge me of sin, I asked why he wanted me to meet his mother.

'Because you're an important person in my life,' said Alex.

'OK,' I managed to say. 'Yes. I'd love to come.'

Hung up before I started blubbing girl tears.

Think I must still be tired from New Year's Eve. That's the trouble with having children. You never get a chance to catch up on sleep.

But I felt so emotional. *Meeting Alex's mother …*

Nick *never* introduced me to his mother.

I met Helen by accident when she let herself into our apartment to give Nick a pair of Gucci loafers she'd picked up at Selfridges. Helen screamed in shock when she saw me, having had no idea I'd moved in with her son.

Not *totally* happy about Westminster Cathedral as a venue.

I might spontaneously combust at the door.

Need to sit down with Dad for a quick Christianity recap.

He has rubbings from all the famous cathedrals and can recite great chunks of the King James Bible by heart.

I haven't been to a proper church service since mine and Nick's wedding-day fiasco. And before that, not since school when we all used to snigger at Mrs Blowers, singing in her funny falsetto voice.

Monday, 9th January

Just phoned my old employer, Give a Damn, to find out when I can start work again.

Left a message, but got the distinct feeling it had fallen into a black hole of messages that will never get listened to.

Will keep trying.

Like the idea of using my brain again, but feel guilty about Daisy.

Then again, I feel guilty about living with my parents, and I need a job to solve that problem.

I suppose guilt and motherhood go hand in hand.

Tuesday, 10th January

My adopted cousin, John Boy, turned up on the doorstep this morning, wearing a huge military rucksack.

He left the army last year after losing half his leg in Afghanistan, and said he'd come to 'learn the pub trade.'

John Boy has gelled, black hair, a pencil moustache and lots of tattoos – plus Harley Davidson stickers over the fibreglass part of his prosthetic leg, and a Nike trainer on his metal foot.

Technically he's a war hero, although he didn't lose his leg in combat – it got blown off when he jumped from the tank for a roadside wee.

Still. We're all extremely proud of him.

After losing his leg, John Boy spent a long time in hospital, having fistfights with anyone who used bad language in front of the nurses.

Mum ushered John Boy into the living room, where he pulled out presents from his rucksack:

+ A jumbo tin of Quality Street for 'the ladies' (Mum, Brandi and me).

+ Army-ration lamb-stew sachets for Dad's countryside hikes.

+ Twenty Afghani pirated DVDs for Daisy and Callum (most of which contained moderate to frequent bad language and violence).

Once he had distributed gifts, John Boy started doing push-ups on the floor, clapping his hands between each one. For more of a challenge, he made Callum sit on his back.

After eating all the green triangles, Mum asked, 'Are you glad to be out of Afghanistan, John Boy?'

'Not really,' he said, switching to one-handed push-ups. 'I miss the lads. The punch-ups. The ten-mile desert runs. Staying awake all night on watch. But it wasn't meant to be. The physio said sand

and prosthetic legs don't mix.' Then he looked sad and said, 'They won't have me back now anyway. Not with half my leg missing.'

'You've been living with Trina, haven't you?' said Mum. 'What happened? Did she kick you out again?'

'We had a bit of a barney,' John Boy admitted, grabbing Callum in a headlock and ruffling his hair. 'You know what Mum's like.'

We all exchanged 'yes we do' looks.

Aunty Trina works in a hospital laundry and is obsessed with germs. She has cleaning products to clean cleaning products. Also, she's deeply religious and carries three different bibles in her handbag.

These days, Aunty Trina wouldn't be allowed to adopt, but she and Uncle Danny got John Boy in the 1980s before psychological evaluations came into it. All they had to be were homeowners and non-smokers.

'What did you fall out over this time?' Mum asked.

John Boy said Aunty Trina had thrown away his special-edition, luminous-orange Adidas trainers.

'I admit, I shouldn't have retaliated,' he said.

Apparently, John Boy phoned the local curry house and told them Aunty Trina wasn't really an OAP.

'She won't get free papadums with her main any more,' said John Boy. 'I'm not sure she'll ever forgive me.'

Wednesday, 11th January

Just had a heated phone call with Nick re maintenance.

'Daisy and I can't live above Mum and Dad's pub forever,' I said. 'I'll be going back to work this year, and it's time you supported your daughter.'

Nick said he was *trying* to be a better dad, a better *person*.

'Why don't we just get back together?' he said.

'Jesus Nick, you've just had a baby with someone else,' I said. 'What on earth are you talking about? Think of your son. And *Sadie*. Cut the bloody theatrics and send me some money.' 'I can't do that Julesy,' he replied. 'It has to be legal and shit. We need to come to a proper adult agreement.'

'But only one of us is a proper adult,' I said.

'I *am* an adult now,' Nick insisted. 'Living with Sadie has changed me. You can't have two irresponsible people in the same house, or there would never be any toilet paper.'

Agreed to meet in person tomorrow to 'sort things out'.

I know exactly how the meeting will go.

Nick will try and charm his way out of paying up.

I will shout at him.

Then we'll have to go to court.

Thursday, 12th January

Met Nick in Hyde Park.

It was FREEZING.

Luckily, I'd bundled Daisy into a snow romper suit, ski gloves and boots, thermal hat, and scarf. She was more padding than baby.

For a change, Nick was on time. He swaggered into the park wearing tight black jeans, Ugg boots, a leather jacket, Afghani scarf and sunglasses.

Baby Horatio was with him, wearing tinted sunglasses and tucked under a Mulberry blanket. He was held aloft in one of those futuristic pod prams, like an offering to the gods.

'You've dyed your trendy beard,' I said.

Nick stroked his facial hair. 'Oh. Yeah. Someone said it looked ginger, so I used Just for Men.'

'Where's Sadie?' I asked.

'Doing Instagram shots back at the apartment,' said Nick. 'You know – trying to get into mummy modelling.'

'Doesn't she need Horatio for that?' I asked.

'He throws up too much to get a good picture,' said Nick. 'We've nicknamed him Regurgatron.'

'How can Sadie do mummy modelling without a baby?' I asked.

'She Photoshops him in afterwards.'

Nick looked so tired. Drained. Like life had beaten him. He certainly wasn't glowing with new fatherhood, and the excitement of Horatio's massive balls had obviously worn off.

I suppose anyone would be tired, living with Sadie.

'How's your mother?' I asked. 'Slaving away over a hot witch's cauldron?'

Nick said he didn't know.

Apparently, Helen isn't talking to him right now.

'She keeps going on about a credit card bill, but I don't know what she's on about. I hardly ever go shopping in Sloane Square.'

Had a quiet smirk to myself, remembering my Sloane Square shopping spree last year courtesy of Nick's 'family' credit card.

Serves Helen right.

Anyway, as Althea said – Nick did offer to buy me clothes if I ran the marathon. So it was only fair.

Nick watched Daisy with tears in his eyes.

'She's walking,' he whispered. 'And I missed it. Daddy wasn't there.'

'She's not walking,' I corrected. 'She's just hanging onto the pram. It's called cruising.'

'Isn't that what gay men do outside nightclubs?' said Nick.

Daisy took one look at Nick's brown, beardy face and started crying.

'I love you, Daisy boo,' Nick simpered. 'It's *Daddy*.'

'Nick, you're a stranger to her,' I said. 'You hardly ever visit. How would you feel if a beardy stranger picked you up?'

'That's very hurtful,' said Nick. 'There's no need to knock the beard.'

Then Horatio started crying and threw up cottage-cheese sick over his Mulberry blanket.

Nick went white. 'Christ,' he said. 'Sadie's going to kill me.'

He ran off in search of a dry cleaners.

I told him I'd text over my bank details.

Friday, 13th January

Woke up this morning to find little Callum hiding under my bed wearing a gremlin mask.

I nearly screamed the house down.

I have a love-hate relationship with my mischievous nephew.

Callum is a great kid, but he can also be 'challenging'. In other words, a little shit. Some people say he lacks a father's firm hand, but my little sister Brandi is pretty strict, screeching at him morning, noon and night.

Anyway, Callum said he was playing a 'Friday the 13th trick'.

'You're getting confused with April Fool's Day,' I told him when my hysterics had worn off. 'Friday the 13th is just unlucky.'

Callum thought about that. 'I won't bet on the footie today then,' he said.

'You're betting on football matches?' I asked. 'How? You're five years old.'

Apparently, Callum's primary school has its own highly sophisticated bookmaking system, using Match Attax cards and keepie uppies as gambling currency.

Saturday, 14th January

Told Dad I'm meeting Alex and his mother at Westminster Cathedral tomorrow.

Dad's eyes filled with happy tears and he said, 'I always dreamed you'd discover the *true* meaning of love.'

Mum said, 'I'll say this for religion. It wears you down the nearer you get to dying. But if it's Mass, at least you'll get free biscuits.'

Daisy perked up at this. 'Biscuit! Biscuit!'

Dad looked stern. 'It's not only about biscuits, Daisy. It's about Jesus. Anyway, you get *wafers* at Mass.'

'Jesus biscuit?' Daisy asked.

Mum said, 'They probably sell Jesus biscuits at Aldi, Daisy. You get all sorts of weird confectionery there.'

Sunday, 15th January

Mass at Westminster Cathedral.

Managed to get Daisy into a nice dress, but she ruined the look by demanding her black swimming cap.

After half an hour of screaming, scratching and biting, Mum said, 'Oh let her wear it, love. She's going to church. Judge not lest ye be judged.'

So, I took Daisy to our nation's most famous cathedral dressed like a lunatic.

Met Alex outside Westminster Cathedral at 10 am, in a swirling crowd of well-dressed Londoners and wide-eyed tourists.

Alex wore his Sunday best, which was basically the same crisp, black suit and white shirt he wears all the time, teamed with a wool coat and leather gloves.

He pulled me into a long, serious hug, and told me he'd missed me. Then he held my face and looked right into my eyes with that intense stare of his.

When Alex noticed Daisy, he smiled and knelt down to the Maclaren.

'That's a very fetching cap you're wearing,' he said, shaking Daisy's hand. 'My mother always says that ladies should wear hats to church.'

Daisy said, 'Biscuit?'

'Well I don't have any biscuits,' said Alex. 'But I did bring you one of these – if it's OK with your mummy.'

He pulled a packet of fruit yoyos from his suit pocket and turned to me for approval.

'She loves those,' I said. 'How did you know?'

'I asked,' said Alex. 'My PA has young children. Come on. Let me introduce the pair of you to Anya.'

'Anya?' I said. 'Your mother's called Catrina, isn't she?'

'Anya is what Zach and I call her,' Alex explained. 'It's the Hungarian word for mother.'

He stood then and pushed the Maclaren towards the cathedral.

Catrina Dalton was by the steps, laughing gaily and shaking hands with tourists like she was a visiting dignitary.

She wore a fitted pencil skirt, black high heels and a ruffled white blouse with a jewelled brooch at the collar.

Her white-blonde hair was in its usual French pleat under a swooping black hat, and her gleaming skin was stretched tight over sharp cheekbones. Heavy kohl lined her eyes, and her lips were bright pink with gloss.

I must admit, Catrina looks great for fifty-something, even if she does dress like someone out of Dallas. But then, she's had a lot of work done – including a fairly disastrous nose job that's given her Michael Jackson nostrils.

Alex waved at her. 'Anya. This is Juliette. The girl I've been telling you about. And her daughter, Daisy. You've probably seen her at our New Year's Eve balls and around the village.'

Catrina gave me a celebrity smile and a little gloved wave then turned on high heels and glided into the cathedral.

I felt like a rejected autograph hunter.

'I wouldn't swap her,' said Alex, 'most of the time. Come on. Let's get you two inside – it's cold.'

Alex parked the Maclaren, then led us into the magnificent cathedral.

I ended up squeezing onto a pew beside Catrina Dalton, hemmed in by Alex on the other side.

Catrina gave me another benevolent smile, eyes glazed and unseeing.

I smiled back, clutching Daisy.

Soon, the singing started.

I mumbled along where I could.

Alex didn't sing at all, which made me feel better.

'Why aren't you singing?' I whispered. 'Don't you know the words either?'

'I don't sing in public,' Alex said, taking my hand and squeezing it.

'Do you sing in private then?' I asked.

'No.'

'But you have a piano at your house.'

'I haven't played that in a long time.'

After the singing and some prayers, everyone lined up for wafers and Ribena from the priest.

I blurted out to Alex, 'We're not baptised or anything.'

Alex laughed. 'Nor is Anya. You don't have to go up if you don't want to.'

Behind me, I felt Catrina Dalton bristle. 'Alex! *What* are you saying? Of *course* I am baptised.' She pushed past us then and joined the sacrament queue.

Alex whispered, 'I shouldn't have said that. Anya has a certain image to uphold. It doesn't necessarily link to reality.'

Daisy noticed the wafers in the golden communion bowl then, and pointed excitedly at the priest, shouting, 'MUMMY! BISCUITS! BISCUITS!' Then she tried to clamber over Alex.

Alex held Daisy to stop her falling. 'It looks like Daisy wants to take the sacrament. Shall we go up?'

'OK,' I said. 'But we've never been blessed before.'

'You're blessed every day of your life,' said Alex, handing me Daisy. 'You have this little one. Look – just bow your head, hold out your hand and say Amen, then take a wafer for Daisy. It's not strictly allowed, but otherwise, I think you'll have a riot on your hands.'

'OK.'

As we approached the huge-nostrilled priest, I threw on my best religious smile. 'Good morning, Father.'

The priest looked down at Daisy. 'What colourful clothing!'

I bowed my head and held out a hand for the wafer, but while my attention was on the stone floor, Daisy grabbed five wafers from the priest's golden bowl and stuffed them into her mouth.

Then she reached for his giant cup of Ribena.

'Oh no, little one,' chuckled the priest. 'You can't have that.'

'Mine?' Daisy enquired.

'No, my child.'

'Mine,' Daisy decided, clamping both hands around the cup.

'Daisy!' I said. 'Daisy! NO Daisy! Naughty!'

'MINE!' Daisy shouted, so the word rang around the stone walls.

The priest pulled.

Daisy pulled.

Then Daisy, sensing she was losing the battle, sank her teeth into the priest's kindly fingers.

In slow motion, the chalice shot up into the air, splashing vivid purple Ribena over the stony floor.

The cup rolled noisily down the stone steps, coming to a stop by a frightened-looking old lady.

There was a stunned silence.

Beside me, I noticed Alex holding back a smile.

Then I heard Catrina Dalton's distinctive Hungarian accent: 'Good God.'

Daisy erupted into angry tears, landing a few well-aimed punches on the priest's arm before I could carry her away.

'NO man. OLLOCKS (bollocks) man!'

I hurried down the aisle and out of the cathedral, with Daisy howling over my shoulder.

On the hard, grey steps, I sat Daisy on my lap and dabbed her teary cheeks.

Then I heard Alex's leather shoes hitting concrete, and felt him sit down beside me.

'Juliette,' said Alex, eyes twinkling with amusement. 'How was your first holy communion?'

'Awful,' I said. 'I'm so embarrassed.'

'Don't be.' Alex took my hand. 'You were wonderful.'

'Something tells me your mother doesn't think I'm wonderful.'

'My mother doesn't usually pay much attention to other people. But I think you've made your mark.'

'By bringing a swearing child into her place of worship?'

'Anya's not as devout as she makes out. She wasn't brought up Catholic. She converted when she met my father. Come on – let me take you for lunch.'

After sandwiches and soup at a nearby deli, Alex bought us takeaway coffees, and we pushed Daisy along the Thames.

Late afternoon, as darkness fell, Alex called a driver to take us home. He spent ages checking Daisy's car seat and even made sure

I was strapped in properly too.

'It's OK,' I said. 'I know how to work a seatbelt.'

Alex looked serious. 'I like to make sure. I'd hate it if anything happened to you.'

We held hands the whole way home.

When we reached Mum and Dad's pub, Alex kissed me goodbye.

'We'll try again with my mother another time. OK?' he said.

'OK,' I said. 'Thanks for today.'

We smiled at each other.

Then Alex kissed me again and said, 'See you soon.'

Monday, 16th January

Just checked my bank account.

Predictably, there was no money from Nick.

Have arranged a 'last chance' meeting with him.

Alex has been texting from New York.

I get all giddy and excited when a new message arrives.

Alex always asks questions:

Where are you? What are you doing? Are you OK?

So different from Nick's former 'romantic' messages, which were usually pictures of himself in various 'amusing' poses.

Alex isn't happy that I'm meeting Nick tomorrow. He referred to Nick as 'Nick Spencer' and wrote he was 'disappointed' with my choice of companion.

But what can I do? I don't *have* a choice of companion. I'm stuck with Nick, for Daisy's sake.

Can Alex and I really work past one amazing night? I mean, really? I suppose anything's possible.

Will have to reread *Cinderella*.

Tuesday, 17th January

Met up with Nick again, this time at Taylor St Baristas near our old flat in Canary Wharf.

Correction, *my* old flat.

Now Nick and Sadie's current flat.

Nick started with the usual theatrics – sobbing that Daisy barely recognised him.

'If you want Daisy to recognise you, make a proper visitation schedule,' I said. 'No more of this "as and when" business. Think of your daughter for a change.'

'And how do I do that?' Nick demanded. 'Sadie keeps my balls in the bedroom drawer. The only reason she let me out today was because I'm wearing a geo-tracker.'

'Let's talk about maintenance,' I said.

'I offered you fifty quid a month—'

'No,' I snapped. 'You can afford more than fifty quid a month.'

'My income is complicated,' Nick wheedled.

'We can always prove your income in court,' I said.

'Can't we just get back together, Jules?' said Nick, sounding tired. 'I know I screwed it up. But I can't turn back the clock.'

'Forget it,' I said. 'Your focus should be on Daisy and your new family.'

'It *is*,' he insisted. 'But paying money is so final, isn't it?'

Then Nick tried to cuddle Daisy in her big snowsuit. She looked like an alarmed starfish.

'Look, Nick,' I said, taking Daisy before she cried. 'I'm being more than reasonable. I just want you to start paying up as of now. That's it. No back payments or anything.'

Nick got all actor-teary then, and said, 'You're right. I'm no good at being an adult. I fucked up…'

Blah blah blah.

Asked if he still had my bank details, and he said, 'Yeah, yeah. I'll sort it, OK?'

Wednesday, 18th January

Alex took me to the cinema last night in Leicester Square.

He was very gentlemanly, sending a driver to pick me up and helping me out of the car when I reached the busy city.

As we walked through the crowds, Alex held me tight and glared at anyone who jostled me.

'Did you wear your seatbelt in the car?' he asked as we headed into the cinema.

'Of course I did,' I laughed. 'What is this obsession with seatbelts?'

'Sorry,' said Alex. 'It's to do with my mother. She never wears one. It used to worry me to death as a child.'

'And now?'

'Now I know my mother is a law unto herself. So, I just have you to worry about. And Daisy.'

As we took our seats, Alex grilled me about meeting Nick. He wanted to know every detail – if Nick had arrived on time, what was said, if Nick had done anything 'inappropriate.'

I told him that Nick was his usual sidestepping, feckless self.

Alex said, 'I don't like you seeing him.'

We were silent for a bit after that.

Then my phone rang.

It was Mum.

I'd asked her only to call in an emergency, but our ideas about emergencies are different.

She rang three times during the film to ask:

+ Where I'd last seen Daisy's sleep blanket.
+ If I could sing Daisy a bedtime song down the phone.

• If I wanted to do Facetime, and see Daisy 'sleeping like an angel'.

The other cinema goers got a bit fed up with me – especially when I sang a whispery lullaby.

There were a few exaggerated huffs and sighs, and someone whispered, 'For goodness sakes!'

I felt I couldn't go to the toilet after causing so much disruption, even though I really needed to.

It got quite uncomfortable by the end because the film was nearly three hours long and had lots of underwater scenes. Plus, the man next to me had a particularly large slurpy drink.

Thursday, 19th January
Fucking bloody bollocking NICK!

OH, MY GOD, I was so blind with fury this morning that I put my dress on backwards.

Have just received a signed-for letter from Nick's solicitor, saying he is applying for RESIDENCY of Daisy.

This is absolutely outrageous.

After being absent for the best part of a year, not paying maintenance and getting my bridesmaid pregnant, Nick now thinks Daisy should live with him.

Why? WHY? What is he playing at?

He must know there is no fucking way ON EARTH he'll get residency.

The letter said that, prior to any court hearing, Nick and I must attend a Mediation Information and Advice Meeting (or MIAM).

MIAM looks a lot like 'maim', as in, to hurt or cause harm.

Couldn't those mediators have thought of a better acronym?

After mediation, Nick will apply for a Child Arrangement Order.

I'm so FURIOUS.

How DARE he?

Friday, 20th January

Rang Nick twenty times, but he didn't answer – the cowardly little shit.

I marched around to Helen and Henry's house with Daisy in tow.

Normally, I'd rather lick rats than visit my ex-mother-in-law, but I needed someone to shout at and decided she'd have to do.

Helen was on her way out, pulling red-leather driving gloves onto her sinewy hands. Her manic blue eyes looked startled when she saw me, and she tipped her head back to look down her long, bird-beak nose.

'I was just going into town,' she said. 'Whatever it is, can't it wait?'

I told her that no, it bloody well couldn't wait. And how dare Nick apply for residency when he's been an absent father and not paid a penny in maintenance.

Helen gave a patronising smile and patted the ends of her wiry black bob. 'He wants you *back*, Juliette. And a chance to father his daughter. How long are you going to humiliate him like this?'

'Humiliate *him*?' I exclaimed.

'Neither of you is perfect. You're both still *learning* to be parents.'

'Fuck off, Helen,' I said. 'I'm with my little girl EVERY DAY. Every single day. What does your son do?'

'Nicholas hasn't had a *chance* to be a father,' said Helen. 'You've kept his daughter from him.'

'What a load of bollocks,' I said. 'Nick didn't ring me for months after the wedding. And he hasn't paid a penny towards Daisy.'

'I'm not going to talk about finances,' Helen snapped.

'He's just doing this to dodge the maintenance issue, isn't

he?' I shouted. 'He lives in *London* for Christ's sake. What court would give an absent father residency *and* move a child from their location?'

Helen raised an eyebrow. 'As a matter of fact, Nicholas is moving closer to home. We're investing in a proper *family* home for him. Somewhere near Henry and I.'

I said a lot of bad words then.

Henry lumbered into the hall in his tweed jacket, buttons straining over his large belly, gingery-grey hair in strands over his bald head. 'What's all this?'

I said a cheery hello to Henry, then barked at Helen: 'You should be ashamed of yourself. AND your son.'

'I don't have time for this, Juliette,' said Helen, pushing on unnecessary sunglasses and strolling towards her Land Rover.

'Tell Nick he'll never get residency of Daisy,' I shouted after her. 'NEVER.'

Helen turned, gave me another patronising smile and said, 'Perhaps if you want to rethink your behaviour – these maintenance threats – then Nicholas will rethink his position too.'

Saturday, 21st January

Finally got through to Nick.

Asked him what the hell he was playing at.

'Desperate men do desperate things, Juliette,' he said.

'No one's stopping you seeing your little girl,' I shouted. 'But how on *earth* can you think this could be in Daisy's best interests? Putting us through a custody battle?'

'I want my family back,' he said.

'This isn't about what *you* want,' I said. 'Think of Daisy, for goodness sake. What's best for *her*?'

'When Daisy grows up, she'll thank me,' Nick insisted. 'She'll say, "Clever Daddy! Mummy was being silly, but you made me live with you, and then Mummy came back." You'll see.'

Ugh!

'You're a spoiled child, Nick,' I said. 'WE'RE NOT GETTING BACK TOGETHER!'

Sunday, 22nd January

Alex called.

He was in the First-Class lounge at Heathrow airport, about to jet off to Dubai, and wanted to tell me how much he was going to miss me.

Aw.

Told him about Nick wanting residency, and he was suitably disgusted.

'The man can't even dress his age,' said Alex. 'Why is he trying to play the father all of a sudden? He can't look after himself, let alone a child.'

'*Another* child,' I said. 'Sadie's had her baby.'

'Did the hospital check it for horns and claws?' Alex asked.

Which I thought was pretty funny.

'Why would Spencer want residency?' said Alex, in a pondering voice like a murder-mystery detective.

'He says he wants his family back,' I said.

Alex was silent for a long time. Then he said, 'I suspected as much.'

'Nick's a lot of hot air,' I said. 'You can never trust what comes out of his mouth.'

'You shouldn't see that man any more,' said Alex, his voice low. 'He's not to be trusted.'

'*What?*' I said. 'I have to see him. He's Daisy's father.'

Silence.

Then Alex said, 'I hate that he's in your life.'

More silence.

'Alex?'

'I have to go. It's getting busy here.'

It *did* sound a little noisy at his end. Someone was kicking off about the buffet lobster tails being 'F-ing tiny' and the caviar trough running dry.

Monday, 23rd January

Nick asked if he could come to the pub today to see Daisy.

Although I'm still furious with him, I agreed for Daisy's sake.

He is already over an hour late.

Just left an angry message saying that if he can't turn up on time, he shouldn't bother.

Have got the tea mugs ready for when Nick finally shows up. His tea will be in a rather rude mug.

Evening

Two hours late! AND Nick brought Helen with him.

I had to physically restrain Mum when she saw Helen on the doorstep. She wanted to squirt her with Callum's Super Soaker.

I screeched at Nick about responsibility and timekeeping and HOW DARE HE TAKE ME TO COURT, then slammed the door in his beaten-puppy face.

Oh god! I was SO FURIOUS!

Helen tapped softly on the door. 'Juliette. Be reasonable. Nick wants to see his daughter.'

'You'd never be late for a business meeting, Helen,' I shouted. 'What's your excuse about this one?'

'Good news,' said Helen brightly. 'Your joint bank account has been unfrozen and put into your name. So, you have access to funds. Can't you see how reasonable we're being?'

I shouted back: 'That's my own bloody money Helen – NOT A PENNY OF IT WAS NICK'S. TELL HIM TO PAY ME MAINTENANCE AND DROP THIS BLOODY COURT CASE!'

Silence.

Then I heard Helen mutter, 'She's obviously not seeing reason. Let's go and see if the café still has that nice soup on.'

Tuesday, 24th January

Alex called this evening from a balmy balcony in Dubai.

'I miss you,' he said. 'I hate being so far away.'

Told him I missed him too, then filled him in about yesterday.

'Well what did you expect?' said Alex. 'Nick Spencer didn't treat you respectfully before. Why would he start now?'

'Nick's just Nick,' I said. 'He's a mess – it's nothing personal.'

'Getting your bridesmaid pregnant isn't personal?'

'You don't have to be brutally honest all the time,' I said.

'Sometimes, the unvarnished truth is a kindness.'

'I'm fully aware I had a baby with the wrong person,' I said. 'You don't need to rub it in.'

'I'm not rubbing anything in. The last thing I want to remember is a woman I…care for deeply…is saddled with Nick Spencer for the rest of her life.'

Wednesday, 25th January

Met with super-solicitor Jeremy Samuels today to discuss residency.

Jeremy is still on Alex's payroll, which I feel awkward about. But am planning to pay Alex back with interest as soon as I start work, and will get legal aid soon.

'The courts usually favour the mother,' Jeremy assured me. 'But they also take into account lifestyle, the child's physical and moral well-being and so on.'

He asked about my living arrangements, income, lifestyle etc.

I have to admit, my life doesn't look good on paper.

Told Jeremy that I'm still living above the Oakley Arms.

'How many people live at your parent's residence?' Jeremy asked.

'Seven,' I told him. 'Me, Mum, Dad, Daisy, my little sister Brandi and her son, Callum. And my cousin has come to stay.'

'Mm,' said Jeremy. 'Rather crowded.'

He seems confident that I'll get sole residency, though.

'This is nothing more than official unpleasantness,' he said. 'And at the very least, it'll firm up visitation for you.'

So, every cloud, and all of that.

Thursday, 26th January

Finally got through to the Give a Damn HR department.

They offered me an interview.

For my own job.

Was a bit taken aback.

'I've been on maternity leave,' I said. 'Why do I have to interview for a job I already have?'

Julie in HR told me, quite bitterly, that lots of things had changed.

Some staff have been 'let go'. And the old coffee machine has gone, replaced with one that doesn't give the right change.

'I've lost five pounds forty so far,' said Julie. 'And the vending machine company never answers their phone.'

The interview for my own job is this Monday, which feels soon, but I suppose that's not a bad thing.

Am pretty keen to get back to work.

Aside from the 'getting my own place' issue, using my brain again (what's left of it) will be nice. There are only so many *Teletubbies* episodes you can watch without thinking you've taken LSD.

Texted Nick again demanding maintenance payments.

No reply.

Friday, 27th January

Feel oddly nervous about the interview on Monday. It's been ages since I've been in a professional environment.

Let's just hope my body behaves itself.

Since Daisy, my intestines have never been the same. They make odd 'wheee!' noises for no reason at all. Sometimes, going to the toilet is like a machine-gun going off.

Being around noisy children, you don't notice your bodily noises. But offices are so still and quiet. The slightest stomach gurgle and heads turn.

Still no maintenance from Nick.

Saturday, 28th January

Told Mum that Nick still hasn't paid maintenance.

She was outraged.

'His mum earns a fortune,' she said. 'A couple of hundred quid a month is nothing for her.'

'But it's not Helen's responsibility to pay for Daisy,' I said.

'She brought up that feckless excuse of a son,' said Mum. 'Who else is to blame?' Then she offered to slash Nick's tyres.

Nana Joan, who'd come round to watch *Game of Thrones* on our big telly, offered to put shit through Nick's letterbox. Possibly her own – she wasn't specific.

Why are the women in our family so prone to anger and violence? I must take after Dad because the Scottish side of my family is very calm. Perhaps because they live in a village with more sheep than people.

Sunday, 29th January

Ugh, just bumped into Helen, while helping Daisy cruise around the village streets on her VTech walker.

Helen looked like a velociraptor, wearing a hat reminiscent of a Mr Kipling's fondant fancy.

She turned pointedly away from me, and told Henry in a loud voice,

'I'm so *pleased* for Nicholas. After so many false starts, this little house will be perfect for him. And so *close* to us too!'

Pretended not to hear her. If Nick, and presumably Sadie, really are moving nearby, I just want to pretend it isn't happening.

Henry smiled apologetically and gave Daisy a little wave.

I feel sorry for Henry being married to Helen, and inheriting Nick as a stepson. Henry's all right, really.

I said to Daisy in an equally loud voice, 'Mind the dragon, Daisy. It's over there, wearing that stupid hat.'

Helen pursed her lips and dragged Henry into the church.

I hope she spent time reflecting on what a terrible person she is.

Monday, 30th January

Got fined £50 on the train for 'failure to possess a valid ticket.'

Burst into silly woman tears when the inspector read out the charges.

'I have a baby,' I sobbed. 'I honestly meant to buy the right ticket. I didn't realise my railcard had expired.'

The inspector crossed his arms and said, 'I've heard all the excuses, love.' Like I was some sort of criminal.

I asked where Railway Bob was – the ticket inspector who lets you travel on yesterday's ticket and prints off blanks for the kids to play with.

The inspector sneered, 'Bob's too soft for the metropolitan route.'

So, all in all, the interview for my own job cost me £90.

Plus, lunch.

Being in London during rush hour was full-on. People had one agenda – to get somewhere quickly. And if that meant stamping on someone's foot, so be it.

Give a Damn has changed a lot since I went on maternity leave.

The old 1970s brown offices have been painted electric blue, and there's a trendy brushed-metal logo.

My old boss, Alan Bender, has suffered a nervous breakdown, and been replaced by Hari Khan, a floppy-haired thirty-something who wears loose jeans and Adidas trainers.

The old marketing department has been 'revamped', meaning it's not there any more. And there is a 'Street Collection Team' – a gang of twenty-somethings who bother shoppers for money.

Hari took one look at me in my new Whistles suit and said, 'You look the part. Like a curly-haired Lois Lane.'

I made sure I didn't turn around at that point, knowing there was a play-dough stain on the back of my skirt.

'How about you be my new head of training?' Hari continued. 'You can start this Thursday.' Then he turned to the office and said, 'Team. Hasn't Juliette done well today? Can I get a whoop whoop?'

A muted 'Whoop whoop' rang around the office.

I said, 'Head of Training? What's that?'

Hari said it was an exciting opportunity, with a solid baseline pay and excellent bonus structure – including a free cinema ticket and standard-sized Starbuck's drink 'each and every week'.

'You won't ask me to wear a neon tabard and harass strangers for money, will you?' I asked.

'Of course not!' Hari laughed. 'The streets are a young person's game. You'll stay in the office with me and manage the new recruits. We have a high turnover here. Street monkeys leave every day, so we need new faces. That'll be part of your job. Bringing in the new faces.'

'In what way?' I asked.

'It's not difficult,' said Hari. 'Just never use the word "begging".'

I don't have a good feeling about my new boss.

Alan Bender wanted to do something good for the world.

Something tells me Hari doesn't share those values. Although I'll admit, I'm pretty happy about the free Starbucks.

Got home at gone seven, due to train delays.

Thought Daisy would be upset when I got back, but she was fine.

She'd had a great afternoon with Mum, eating nearly-out-of-date crisps and playing with the pub optics.

Tuesday, 31st January

Alex phoned again to see how I am.

He's STILL in Dubai but says he'll try and cut the trip short so we can see each other.

Told him about Give a Damn.

'If you needed a job, why didn't you say so?' Alex said. 'There's a new position opening up in my Chelsea office. Events manager. Part-time. You'd be perfect.'

'Most people would say congratulations,' I said.

'Then most people wouldn't have listened correctly,' said Alex. 'Because quite clearly, you're starting a job you don't want.'

Alex can be quite perceptive at times.

'It's OK for the time being,' I insisted. 'Anyway, I couldn't work for you. It would be weird.'

'You shouldn't have to work at all,' he said. 'Not now you're a mother.'

I laughed. 'Welcome to the twentieth century, Alex.'

'It's the *twenty-first* century, Juliette. And whatever century it is, a man should be responsible for his children.'

'You have met Nick, haven't you?' I said. 'When it comes to being a responsible adult he falls well short.'

Alex was silent for a moment. Then he said, 'Have you seen him again? I find it *extremely difficult* when you see him.'

'I know, Alex,' I said. 'But Nick is just someone you'll have to accept.'

Wednesday, 1st February

I'm having mum-guilt about work.

Told Dad today how *awful* it felt leaving Daisy for the job interview. Like a part of my body was missing.

'I'll have to do that three times a week from now on,' I said.

'I know exactly how you feel,' said Dad, who'd just come back from his allotment and was hanging up his bobble hat. 'It was the same when you were growing up. You don't want to miss a moment, do you?'

'Dad,' I said. 'What happened to your hair? You look like a scarecrow.'

'New Year's resolution,' said Dad, admiring his badly chopped brown-grey hair in the hall mirror. 'I'm cutting it myself to save a fortune at the barbers.'

I wish I could say I didn't want to miss a moment of Daisy. But actually, there are some moments I'd be happy to miss. Daisy threw up on my face yesterday.

Alex didn't call today. I get the feeling he's angry about our Nick discussion.

I miss him. Will it always be like this?

Thursday, 2nd February

Alex surprised me at St Pancras station on the way to work this morning.

I was running past the Meeting Place statue with a hot coffee in one hand and croissant in the other, when I heard someone call out: 'Slow down, Juliette, you're spilling your coffee.'

I turned around, and there was Alex – hands in his suit pockets, smiling with his dark brown eyes, but not his mouth.

It was good to see him. And very romantic too, by a statue of two travellers embracing.

'Did you wait by this statue on purpose?' I asked, smiling.

'Which statue?' said Alex.

'*This* statue,' I said, gesturing to the metal man and woman, caught in a passionate clinch.

Alex turned. '*This* statue? You mean the Meeting Place statue? No, I most certainly didn't wait here on purpose. I've actually *complained* about this statue before. It's nauseating.'

'It's *lovely*,' I said. 'Two travellers meeting after being apart.'

'It's sentimental nonsense, and everything art shouldn't be,' said Alex. He looked up. '*That* piece up there – *that's* art.'

I followed his gaze. 'It's a clock.'

'No. The black clock is a work of art by Cornelia Parker. A reflection about time, reminding us to live in the moment. Hang on to every precious second. Like the precious seconds, we've spent together. Which I treasure.'

'You don't strike me as a live-in-the-moment sort of man,' I observed. 'More like plan every second.'

'That's where you're wrong. I know about moments.' Alex gave me that intense stare of his. 'I've missed you. You know that, don't you? Not being able to see you…to make sure you're OK… It's been hard. Are you ready for your first day back at work?'

'Not in the slightest,' I admitted.

Alex escorted me downstairs, past cafés and a pianist playing, 'The Entertainer'.

'Christ, he's massacring that,' said Alex.

'Could you do better?' I asked.

'I should hope so. I used to play for the National Youth Orchestra.'

A typical Alex response.

'Can you play the theme from *Game of Thrones*?' I asked.

'Four notes, repeated? I think I could manage it.'

'What about "Somewhere Only We Know" by Keane?'

'Yes. But I wouldn't.'

'What about—'

'I don't do song requests.'

When we reached my workplace, Alex was all frowns again.

'You work here?' he said, looking over the electric-blue walls.

'Yes.'

'It looks bloody awful.'

'Just because it's not part of London's regal past, doesn't mean it's not a nice place to work,' I insisted.

'You make some interesting choices, Juliette,' said Alex. Then he kissed my forehead and said, 'I'll meet you after work.'

'I can't,' I said. 'I have to get back for Daisy.'

Alex's expression darkened. 'Are you meeting Nick Spencer?'

'No,' I said. 'Alex, you need to stop this. It's ridiculous.'

'Will you tell me if you meet up with him?'

'OK,' I said. But as I said it, I thought, *Am I really going to do that? Report back to Alex whenever I see Daisy's dad? That doesn't sound very healthy …*

'I'll take you to lunch tomorrow,' Alex said. 'Will St Pancras do you? I have to catch the Eurostar, mid-afternoon.'

I said it would do me just fine.

Then Alex asked about Daisy, and I told him I was worried about her walking.

'She's cruising,' I said. 'But she won't take a step.'

'Cruising?' said Alex. 'Isn't that something you do in a large car on the American freeway?'

Friday, 3rd February

First day back at work was...not great.

Give a Damn doesn't feel like a charity any more.

I mean, yes – some profits do go to charity. But everything is run like a business. There are bonus schemes and shareholders and fabulous prizes for staff who bring in big profits.

Helping third-world countries is sort of an afterthought.

Hari Khan's background is in credit-card sales, and he thinks asylum seekers are 'scroungers'.

My shifts are all over the place too, and I have to work bank holidays.

'Can't I just do the same days each week?' I asked Hari.

But he said no. Apparently, recruitment is 'unpredictable' on the Street Collection Team. Meaning you never know who'll quit and when.

On the positive side, I did manage a nice lunch with Alex before he left for Paris.

We met at St Pancras and ate at an expensive salad bar.

Alex took my hands over the table and said, 'I feel very protective of you. And Daisy.'

It was just like that scene in *Twilight* when Edward says more or less the same thing to Bella. Minus the child reference.

Would have been a lovely, romantic moment, except an old lady behind us shouted, 'It's a bloody disgrace! Nine quid for a bunch of lettuce leaves.'

Saturday, 4th February

Brandi has bought a huge flat-screen TV for her bedroom.

Why do people keep giving her credit?

Probably flirtation has something to do with it. My little sister is extremely appealing to the wrong sort of man, with her spray tan, fake eyelashes and acres of blonde hair extensions.

Since starting her beauty course, Brandi looks more like Barbie every term. Albeit a Barbie with heavily pencilled eyebrows.

The new TV covers half of one wall and can be seen flashing away from the village play park. It's extremely loud too, which adds something else to my long list of reasons to move out.

Brandi is delighted with the TV and so, of course, is little Callum.

His favourite thing is trying to kick Power Rangers in real life.

Game of Thrones is now absolutely terrifying.

Was relieved when the final credits came up, and the announcer said, 'If you've been affected by the issues in *Game of Thrones*, call this number.'

Brandi snorted, 'What is that announcer chatting about? Oh yeah – I've been affected by *Game of Thrones*. I just found a White Walker in my garden.'

Sunday, 5th February

Nana Joan visited the pub today.

She'd made a dress for Daisy at her Singer sewing club. It was as long as it was wide and made Daisy look like Mr Strong.

After a cup of tea and a Blue Riband biscuit, Nana fell asleep on the sofa, sitting upright with her mouth open.

She looked like she'd been unplugged.

Monday, 6th February

Went to the sexual health clinic this morning to discuss contraception.

Things haven't moved on with Alex and me since New Year's Eve, but I want to be prepared, contraceptive-wise.

The nurse presented me with some options – a diaphragm, a coil and a vaginal ring.

Why are all vaginal devices so massive?

The medical profession seems to think vaginas are large enough to hold a mug of tea.

When the nurse showed me the digestive-biscuit-sized vaginal ring, I asked, 'How on earth will that fit around my cervix?'

'Oh, it doesn't have to fit exactly,' said the nurse. 'You just shove it up there.'

'And what about this?' I asked, picking up the equally large diaphragm.

'You'd be surprised how accommodating the vagina can be,' said the nurse. 'It can manage a baby's head. So theoretically it could fit a watermelon.'

It's always fruit, isn't it?

I am considering the vaginal ring, but the diaphragm is a definite no. I could imagine Callum using it as a mini trampoline for his action men.

Tuesday, 7th February

I really miss running. But Dr Slaughter says I should give my ankle a rest this year. It's still not quite right since I hurt it in the marathon.

I mean, I can run if I really need to. Which is lucky, because I'd never catch the train otherwise. But I won't be doing any long-distance jogging for a while.

I bet Alex still runs every day.

Maybe we can start running together again next year. On the understanding that it will be purely recreational, and that I am never, ever training for another marathon.

Wednesday, 8th February

I thought the pub was crowded before, but with John Boy sleeping in the lounge, we're bursting at the seams.

Also, all the landings now smell of Lynx deodorant.

On the positive side, John Boy and Callum are getting on well. They did an assault course together this morning, jumping over the sofas and running up and down the stairs. Then John Boy pulled down the loft ladder and did pull-ups from the top step, while Callum hung off his foot.

John Boy has been sensible with Callum and 'laid down some ground rules'. The key one is 'don't punch me in the balls'

Thursday, 9th February

Work.

Tired.

Friday, 10th February

Ugh.

Letter from the Family Mediation Council.

They've requested I arrange a MIAM session at my soonest convenience.

The letter came with an accompanying leaflet, advertising the services of Fiona Skelton – my nearest mediator.

There were directions to a mediation centre in Great Oakley, which is ironically the church Nick and I nearly married in.

Under the map were instructions:

We understand this is a sensitive time but kindly request no raised voices in the car park either before or after the session.

Have managed to book in for next week, because Fiona Skelton had a cancellation.

'It will be just you at first,' Fiona told me, in a dreamy voice. 'I give women their own session, to begin with. That way they can speak freely, without being intimidated or talked down.'

Assured Fiona that I wasn't a downtrodden, broken ex-girlfriend and that Nick was far more scared of me than I was of him.

Saturday, 11th February

Clarke from Belle Homes told me, over his lunchtime rum and coke, that the Jolly-Piggott family would soon complete on a Great Oakley High Street property.

It's a big double-fronted house called the Gables and has 'perfect family home' written all over it.

I'm guessing Helen is buying the home for Nick and Sadie, and am extremely jealous. Not to mention mortified that they could be living down the road.

Feel especially bitter, because my own living situation is becoming increasingly difficult.

The pub feels *really* crowded.

Nana came for tea, and there weren't enough seats.

Dad was happy to stand, though.

'In our day, sitting was a luxury,' he informed us. 'I stood every Christmas day from 1955 to 1969, until your granddad made me a stool from the stair banisters. I counted myself a very lucky boy that year!'

Sunday, 12th February

Facebook-spied on Nick today, to see if I could work out if he's moving house or not.

No clues about that, but there were lots of pictures of Horatio.

Daisy has a stepbrother.

SUCH a weird thought.

How on earth is Nick going to handle another baby, when he hardly ever sees his first one? And what on earth makes him think he should have *sole residency* of Daisy? ALSO, what does Sadie think about him seeking residency? Surely, she can't be happy.

Baby Horatio does look like Nick – he has the same dramatic eyebrows. But then again, Sadie has slept with a lot of men with dramatic eyebrows.

So, you never know.

Monday, 13th February

Alex phoned from Paris to wish me an early happy Valentine's, and invite me for 'elevenses' this Wednesday at the Bond Street Dalton.

Not entirely sure what elevenses are in a hotel setting, but I'm guessing it won't be a two-finger Kit Kat and a cup of tea, like at Nana's.

Am praying Daisy behaves herself.

She is a liability around china these days.

Told Alex about the upcoming mediation session with Nick.

He seemed annoyed. 'Why don't you just go to court and be done with it?'

Explained that's not how things work these days.

You must pretend to be civil first before the courts let you legally beat the hell out of each other.

Tuesday, 14th February
Valentines Day

Aw...got fifty red roses from Alex, and a four-leaf-clover pendant necklace in a velvet jewellery box.

The pendant leaves are, according to Nana Joan, solid platinum and set with real diamonds and emeralds.

None of our family knew the jewellery brand, so it must be very expensive.

Alex phoned in the afternoon, apologising for not being with me in person.

Thanked him for the gifts and said, 'It's OK that you're not here. I know you have a business to run.'

'I hate being away from you,' said Alex. 'I have nightmares. That something has happened. That you've had a car crash or...' He gave a curt laugh. 'I dreamt last night that Nick Spencer kidnapped you.'

'Nick isn't capable of organising a kidnapping,' I said. 'And if he ever tried it, I'd break his nose.'

Alex laughed too. 'I believe you. I just...my mind plays tricks.'

'Well tell it to stop.'

'Easier said than done. This is new for me, having someone to lose. I mean, obviously, I have my family. But this is different. There's a song, isn't there? Freedom means having nothing to lose. Now I have something. Well, someone. It's an adjustment.'

I found myself smiling at the phone then. 'You won't lose me, Alex.'

'Tell that to my subconscious.'

Wednesday, 15th February

Alex's driver took Daisy and me into London this morning.

Very thoughtfully, there was a new child seat in the car. It looked unnaturally clean, but Daisy soon got to work grinding oatcakes into the mesh fabric and making spitty trails on the straps.

When we arrived at the Bond Street Dalton, Alex was waiting by the revolving doors. He had a bunch of giant daisies in his hand.

'You're on time,' said Alex, cantering down the hotel steps to kiss me on the cheek. 'I'll remember to tip my driver.'

We smiled at each other.

Then he plucked a giant daisy from the flower arrangement, knelt down to Daisy's pram and said, 'This is for you.'

Daisy chewed the flower thoughtfully, then gave little coughing retches and regurgitated a few stiff white petals.

Decided I'd better hold on to the bouquet after that.

Thanked Alex again for the Valentine's gifts.

The doorman helped lift Daisy's pram into the lobby, setting the muddy tyres on the sparkling marble floor. Then a caretaker appeared with a golden dustpan and brush.

'Well done, Philip,' said Alex, clapping him on the back. 'Fastidious as always.'

The caretaker told Alex about the new floor polish he'd been using – which had some sort of special sealant. He eyed the Maclaren wheels again and said, 'I'll follow you through to the sitting room. Just to be on the safe side.'

'Your staff are very diligent,' I said, as we were shown to a table.

'Yes,' Alex said. 'And loyal.'

Alex poured tea and told me about a function this week – some black-tie thing at the Mayfair Dalton.

'I can't get out of it,' he said. 'But I wondered if you'd come as my guest. A driver can pick you up.'

'Are you sure you want me there?' I asked. 'Won't you be doing business stuff?'

'Yes,' said Alex. 'But I'm sure we can snatch a few moments. Your sister is going, by the way. With Zachary.'

Ah, my beautiful big sister Laura. Coming to the party on the arm of Alex's dashing younger brother.

When Laura and Zach got together last year, I was so happy for her. To think! Laura Duffy, going out with a *Dalton*. And now I am too. Crazy!

I adore Laura, but life can be hard living in her shadow. She inherited Dad's straight hair, meaning she's one of those polished blondes who look effortlessly classy. And she keeps healthy like Dad but has inherited Mum's boobs, meaning her figure is perfect and amazing.

I, on the other hand, am a mess of browny-blonde curls and have inherited both Mum's boobs *and* her bad eating habits.

Alex didn't mention staying overnight or anything, but…maybe things will happen.

Thursday, 16th February

Mediation session.

Very weird, having it in the village church.

You'd think a holy place wouldn't allow separated partners to slag each other off. But I suppose Christianity has to move with the times.

Was surreal, walking down the aisle again.

Fiona Skelton waited in a side-room by the altar – a sad-faced woman in loose, grey wool clothing. She stood by a whiteboard and welcomed me with a floppy handshake.

The whiteboard had faded writing on it:

'Ten Reasons Why We Love Jesus.'

The reasons only went up to eight.

'Shall we get started?' said Fiona, cleaning the whiteboard.

'Yes,' I said eagerly. 'Do you want to know why Nick and I broke up?'

'I don't feel we need to look backwards,' said Fiona. 'Let's look to the future.'

Felt cheated.

If you can't slag off your ex-partner in mediation, where can you?

Fiona neatly sidestepped all my attempts to badmouth Nick and his family and stuck to her own list of stupid questions.

Answered them easily:

+ Yes, I am happy to undergo mediation.
+ No, I won't drink or take drugs during the sessions.
+ No, I won't raise my voice in the car park.

Then Fiona looked over my financials, benefits, child tax credit stuff, etc. and signed forms for legal aid.

Nick will be at the next mediation session.

Oh, joy.

Friday, 17th February

Why is sending a text message so difficult when you have kids?

I suppose it's all the distractions.

NO Daisy, you can't play with the toilet brush. OR chew the toilet brush! OR clean Mummy's clothes with it!

Meant to message Laura SO many times today re Alex's black-tie thing, but she'll be asleep by now.

Laura goes to bed early, so she can jog at 5 am before pollution levels rise.

She runs ten miles most mornings, then eats raw vegetables for breakfast.

Saturday, 18th February

Finally sent a message to Laura.

She's worried about the black-tie thing too – specifically what to wear/say/do around Zach's business associates.

Ridiculous for Laura to worry. She'd make a tracksuit look classy and never says the wrong thing or drinks too much.

I, on the other hand, have a phobia of an empty glass – especially when I'm feeling nervous.

Should probably set a phone reminder – *Don't drink too much.*

Messaged Alex to hint about possibly staying overnight, but I don't think he understood because he texted back, 'If you need an early night, I can have a driver take you home.'

Sunday, 19th February

Lovely Alex.

He's just sent me a dress with a note saying, 'A late Valentine's gift from Paris, for the black-tie event.'

It's a ball gown, which I wasn't expecting.

The skirt is very full, and the corset top makes my boobs look massive, but there's a chiffon shrug to cover them. Well – one of them.

Have chosen the left.

Daisy is fast asleep in the travel cot, sucking her thumb.

Am getting a bit worried about her thumb-sucking now. It's definitely pushed her teeth into different shapes, and I think she has a lisp. Although Mum says, it's a rare one-year-old who pronounces 'Ribena' properly.

Monday, 20th February

Black-tie thing was OK.

Didn't get to see Alex much, but that was to be expected.

On arrival, he took me on a tour of the canapé tables. He shook hands with lots of people and talked about hotel finance, then asked Zach and Laura to take care of me while he had a 'quick meeting' in the conference room.

Was nice to see Zach and Laura.

Zach was his usual charming, friendly self, guffawing at things that weren't very funny and patting people on the back. He'd shaved his blond beard off, and looked very grown up in a black suit and tie.

Laura was elegant and serene, gliding around on Zach's arm and smiling at all the right times. She remained beautiful and poised all evening, not a hair or word out of place.

I dropped a smoked salmon canapé down my dress within a minute of arriving and felt the need to repeatedly explain that it wasn't baby vomit.

Then my alarm went off just as I was showing off pictures of Daisy, and the words 'Don't drink too much' flashed on my iPhone screen for all to see.

Asked Zach when Alex would come back.

'If they've got him in the conference room, you won't see him for the rest of the evening,' said Zach. 'There'll be some crisis or other he has to deal with.'

Most of the women at the party were in their early twenties, and evidentially childless by their flat stomachs, stain-free clothing and carefree laughter.

'I don't have anything in common with these people,' I told Zach and Laura. 'This is business land. And I'm from mother world.'

'There must be someone here who has a baby,' Laura soothed.

'I know!' Zach announced, clapping his hands together. 'Joanna Mittal has *several* children. She's right over there.'

He led me to a twitchy, blonde woman in a sleek, black trouser suit.

'Joanna,' Zach said, pushing me forward. 'Allow me to introduce a friend of mine. Juliette Duffy.'

'Hallo,' the woman announced, shaking my hand with urgency. 'Joanna Mittal. Where do you work?'

One of Joanna's fake eyelashes was slightly loose, and she didn't seem to have noticed, so I had high hopes she might be just as exhausted as me.

'This is Juliette,' said Zach. 'A friend of Alex's. Juliette has a baby. So, we thought the two of you... well, ah. You might have things to talk about.'

Then Zach melted into the crowd.

'So, you have a baby?' Joanna enquired, holding out her champagne glass for a refill. 'How old?'

'Eighteen months,' I said. 'She was a bloody nightmare this evening. I had to rock her to sleep in front of *In the Night Garden*. How many children do you have?'

'Two,' said Joanna, eyelashes twitching. 'Twin boys. Full of energy. But they haven't changed me.' She pulled a business card from her suit pocket. 'This is what I do.'

I took the card and read: 'Show me the Mittal – for all your PR, marketing, social media, consultancy, design, web, PowerPoint presentation, Excel spreadsheet and Word document needs.'

'You do a lot,' I remarked.

'We're expanding this year,' Joanna said, eyelashes still flickering. 'So, what *do* you do? Where do you work? Do you work?'

'I've just gone back,' I said. 'I work for a charity. Give a Damn.'

'Who does their PR?' Joanna asked. 'Do they have a Facebook page?'

'Um…not sure,' I said. 'By the way, how did you manage to dress and leave the house with twins at home?'

'There are sacrifices,' said Joanna, taking a rapid gulp of Champagne. 'Sleep. Birthdays. School holidays. But THE REWARDS ARE WORTH IT! So, you're Alex's friend, did you say?'

'Sort of a friend,' I mumbled. 'Kind of a…girlfriend sort of friend.'

That got her attention. 'His *girlfriend?*' She scrutinised my tired face. 'You're…so he's a…you have a *baby* together? Catrina would have…was there a christening?'

I was forced to explain, red-faced, that the baby didn't belong to Alex.

'Oo-oo-oh,' she said, still studying my face.

'Alex doesn't seem to mind.' I reddened. 'Actually, he's very good with Daisy.'

'But she's not his?'

'No.'

'Who'd have thought!' Joanna gave a sharp laugh.

I tried to change the subject. 'So, tell me about—'

Then Alex appeared.

'Juliette, there you are,' he said. 'Hello, Joanna. How's the family?'

'They're ABSOLUTELY fine,' said Joanna. 'Don't listen to Deepak. He's never back more than five minutes. How he can criticise…now listen – you'll have to fill me in. This young lady tells me she's your *girlfriend*. And yet I've never met her before! How can this be?'

Alex gave a half smile. 'Juliette is mercifully different from my usual acquaintances. So, she doesn't know many people at a Dalton launch party.'

Joanna looked startled. Then she gave a high, fake laugh and said, 'And she has a *baby*.'

'A beautiful baby,' said Alex. 'Whom I love very much. And see rather less often than I'd like.'

'Oh Alex,' said Joanna, blinking rapidly at him. 'Come off it. Don't tease the poor girl. She must know it's business first with you. Just like Deepak. Ha ha! Well – I should get back. There's a new au pair due at Heathrow any minute, and Deepak *refuses* to pick her up. And he *knows* I need to get to Manchester tomorrow.'

After Joanna had stridden away, I said to Alex, 'Different from your usual acquaintances?'

Alex kissed me on the forehead and said, 'Exactly right. You're the most genuine person I know. And funny too. Often without meaning to be.'

'Thanks.'

'You and Joanna seemed to be having a nice chat,' Alex continued. 'I was worried I'd left you stranded.'

'You did leave me stranded,' I said.

'I warned you it was a work thing. You didn't mind, did you?'

He did warn me. But I did mind.

'Listen, are you staying?' Alex asked. 'Did you bring your overnight things?'

'I wasn't sure if you wanted…I didn't bring anything for overnight,' I said.

'I can have things brought for you,' he said. 'If you want.'

'I'm not sure I can now,' I said. 'I have mediation with Nick tomorrow.'

Alex frowned. 'Why didn't you tell me?'

'I haven't seen you all evening.'

'I'm assuming you found out *before* this evening.'

'Yes, but—'

'Juliette, you said you'd tell me. If you were seeing him.'

'I know I sort of said…but Alex, I don't have to check in with you every time I see Nick.'

56

'I'll have a driver take you home.'

He didn't kiss me goodbye.

Tuesday, 21st February

Mediation session with Nick.

Poor timing meant we bumped into each other in the car park.

Nick looked vulnerable, an oversized scarf wrapped over his leather jacket.

He gave me a subdued, 'Hi.'

'How's Horatio?' I asked.

'Still vomming all the time,' said Nick. 'I've got a new name for him now. Hurl-ratio.'

'And how's Sadie?' I asked. 'What does she think about you trying for residency?'

'She doesn't know,' said Nick. 'And I'd like to keep it that way. No sense rocking the boat before I need to. Horry's at a sensitive age. I mean, I may not even *get* residency.'

'God, Nick.' I shook my head in disgust. 'Of *course* you won't get residency. You've been absent for months. You're not paying to support your daughter, and you're in a volatile relationship with a fellow actor.'

As we walked towards the church, an old lady opened her back window and shouted, 'Don't start f-ing and blinding you two – I've got *Poldark* on catch-up.'

Fiona Skelton was waiting for us at the altar, wearing her usual grey robes and pitying smile.

She had the whiteboard and pen ready.

Today, the faded writing said, 'What does God *really* look like?'

'We're going to do some groundwork,' said Fiona. 'And hopefully set the stage for some positive changes. Today is all about understanding what the two of you want from each other and for

57

Daisy. Maybe we can avoid court, after all.'

Then Fiona asked questions, nodding sympathetically at the answers and throwing in an occasional, 'How does that make you feel?' and, 'Mmm'.

The best part of mediation was when Fiona told Nick to get a stable job.

'That's definitely top of my agenda,' Nick said. 'I'm hoping to show Juliette she can trust me again.'

Fiona gave a tired smile. 'Oh, that's wonderful, Nick. Trust is crucial.'

I laughed. 'Nick hasn't paid a penny in child support and had a baby with my bridesmaid. Would *you* trust him?'

'Mmm,' said Fiona. 'How does that make you feel?'

Nick and I disagreed for the next hour, with Fiona looking on sympathetically.

I don't know if Nick was trying to impress Fiona or make a point for court, but he *kept* going on about us getting back together.

Anyway, of course we couldn't agree on anything, so Fiona signed the Child Arrangement Order papers.

Surprised Nick hasn't backed off yet, but I'm sure he will. As soon as he works out this tactic won't win me back or get him out of maintenance payments.

Wednesday, 22nd February

'Official' training at work today in the 1970s conference room.

Tried to stay awake, but it was difficult.

On the positive side, there were bottles of fizzy mineral water, silver flasks of coffee and little packets of caramelised Biscoff biscuits.

Had a discussion (row) with Hari about morality.

It got quite heated at one point. I had to stand up and wave my finger.

Hari seems to think charities are all about avoiding taxes.

Ended up angrily Googling statistics about mosquito nets and holding my phone inches from Hari's face.

I don't think it made any difference.

Hari is still convinced that some third-world children catch malaria to get free trainers.

Thursday, 23rd February

Finally!

A call from Alex.

But not a good call.

'I thought you'd forgotten me,' I said.

'How's the job going?' he asked.

'Not great,' I admitted.

'I don't like the sound of your boss,' said Alex. 'He has all the makings of a scam artist.' Then he said, 'Listen, I was thinking about you and Daisy's father. This mediation business. You should have some space. Work out what you really want.'

'I know what I really want,' I said.

'Are you sure about that? You and Nick Spencer clearly have unresolved issues.'

'Of course we do,' I said. 'We probably always will. But he's Daisy's biological father, Alex. And he loves her in his own way.'

Silence.

Then Alex said, 'There are things you need to think about. I have to go now. Goodbye Juliette.'

Friday, 24th February

Daisy has hundreds of beautiful soft teddies, but her bedtime comforter is a frayed, smelly old blanket.

I have to put her to bed with it every night, or she screams, 'Manket! Manket!'

Then I have to do the funky chicken dance (I should NEVER have got into that habit) and sing all five verses of the Hokey Cokey before she'll let me leave the room.

Saturday, 25th February

Althea and I took Daisy and Wolfgang to Queen Victoria Park today, just outside the village.

It's a bit more of a trek, but worth it because the play equipment is made from very sturdy plastic and Wolfgang hasn't broken anything there yet.

We were sawing up homemade spelt bread on a picnic bench when Althea grabbed my arm.

'Jules,' she said. 'Your worst nightmare just arrived.'

I turned to see Nick's mum, pushing baby Horatio into the play park.

Beside her was Penelope Dearheart, carrying a wriggling, redheaded toddler who I took to be her granddaughter.

Penelope's two huge dogs bounded into the play area and began head-butting swings and chewing at the shredded bark.

Since that awful lunch at the Dearheart's house last year, Penelope has pretended not to know who I am. I suppose cleaning poo off your conservatory leaves bad memories.

Helen and Penelope wore identical black sunglasses and displeased expressions.

Penelope spotted me first and tapped Helen's arm. Then Helen's witchy face turned in my direction. Her bony shoulders shot up.

'Juliette.' Helen looked momentarily flustered. 'You're here with Daisy?'

'Yes,' I said. 'She's right there. You've probably forgotten what she looks like by now.'

'I do *try*, Juliette,' said Helen, putting on her serious, business voice, and throwing an embarrassed glance at Penelope. 'You don't make it easy.'

'*I* don't make it easy? The last time I came round your house, you tried to blackmail me into dropping maintenance requests.'

Helen reddened at this, her role as doting grandmother challenged.

'You were using terrible language,' said Helen. 'And you never *trusted* me with Daisy, Juliette. Sadie is always asking for help.'

Helen turned to Penelope. 'Of course, I can't babysit as much as they'd like. You know those two – always being pulled back to London for one reason or another. And Horry isn't the best of sleepers. Very hard to settle. So sometimes I just have to tell them, it's your turn now! Ha ha!'

Penelope forced a grin.

'You know Nick won't get residency of Daisy,' I said. 'Why are you putting me through this? After everything Nick's done?'

'As a matter of fact, we're getting a strong case together,' said Helen. 'We're hoping *character* will win the day. And lack of it... Nick is *determined* to win his daughter back.'

'If he's so bloody determined, how come he didn't see her for nearly half a year?' I shouted.

Helen danced awkwardly and turned to Penelope. 'Perhaps... shall we head to the café?'

Penelope gave a strained nod.

They turned and scurried off.

'That's right, fuck off back to your Land Rovers,' Althea shouted after them.

Sunday, 26th February

Sunday lunch at the pub with the family.

Especially nice to see Laura, who came down especially from London.

Mum did her special, extra-crunchy roast potatoes, which are essentially scoops of buttery mash dropped into the pub-kitchen deep-fat fryer.

Told everyone about bumping into Helen.

'Nasty old cow,' Mum said.

'Do you think Nick *could* get residency?' I asked.

'No way,' said Laura. 'The courts almost always favour the mother.'

'But will it *actually* go to court,' I asked. 'Nick might back off now things are getting serious. What do you think?'

The room went silent, except for the awkward munching of Mum's extra-crunchy roast potatoes.

Monday, 27th February

Still no maintenance from Nick.

He hasn't responded to my phone calls or messages.

Sent a text message, threatening to phone the HMRC tax-dodger hotline if he didn't call back.

Tuesday, 28th February

Nick just rang, begging me not to phone HMRC.

I could tell he was stressed – his voice had gone all high and wobbly.

Horatio was screaming in the background.

'Look, I'm about to have a nervous breakdown,' he screeched.

'You can't call HMRC. The tax people will be after me for years of back pay. I don't know how you can be so vindictive. You've already got your revenge. I'm fucking miserable, and Sadie is too.'

'I'm not being vindictive,' I told him. 'I just want what's best for my daughter. START PAYING MAINTENANCE.'

'How can I send money when I'm not working?' said Nick. 'My skin is terrible. I'm getting no sleep. No one will hire a spotty actor with bags under his eyes. Just give me time, Jules. Give me time.'

'Take a non-acting job,' I said. 'You have two kids to support. Playtime is over.'

'The country is in crisis. There *are* no jobs.'

'Rubbish. Give a Damn is always looking for new street collectors.'

Nick gave a hysterical laugh. 'What – join those limp-faced, twenty-something drama students crawling around Oxford Street, begging for money? No thank you.'

'There's work out there if you look, Nick,' I said. 'You're just going to have to swallow your pride and take what you can get. It's time to grow up.'

'Can't we get back together, Jules?' Nick whispered. 'You have no idea how sorry I am.'

'No,' I said.

'Listen,' said Nick. 'I *will* pay for Daisy, just as soon as I get my act together. But I haven't seen her in weeks. Jules – can you bring her over? At least to see her brother?'

I agreed, for Daisy's sake.

She *does* have a brother now.

Whether I like it or not.

We're meeting tomorrow at the old apartment.

Sadie will be out.

Nearly texted Alex to tell him I'm seeing Nick, and then thought – no. That's not healthy. He's jealous, and he'll have to get over it.

End of story.

I'm not sure how we stand right now, anyway.

He hasn't phoned since telling me he thought I should have some 'space'.

Wednesday, 1st March

It felt really weird going back to the old apartment.

Daisy probably doesn't remember living there, but for me, it was like yesterday – forcing the pram into that tiny elevator and jabbing Nick's date of birth into the security door lock.

Nick appeared at the apartment door looking shifty.

'Sadie hasn't left yet,' he whispered. 'Her facial was moved. Don't say anything about the residency stuff, yeah?'

Suddenly, Sadie appeared wearing a black-fur hat and puffy jacket. She pushed haughtily past us and headed towards the elevator.

Her large, pale face was expensively made-up with big eyeliner swoops, and her brown-blonde hair was shiny under her hat. She was carrying a bit of baby weight but had squeezed herself into leather trousers and her old red soldier coat.

I glared at her as she walked out.

'Bye bye, my love,' Nick called out.

Sadie didn't reply.

'We'd better go inside,' said Nick, running a stressed hand through his hair. 'Horatio's probably vommed again by now. He can't keep anything down.'

Was pleased to see the apartment was a total pigsty. Not so pleased to see a great big pile of moving boxes by the panoramic window.

'Take a seat,' said Nick, clearing piles of baby clothes and junk mail from the sofa.

Horatio was in a vibrating baby chair, drooling.

'Oh, thank fuck for that,' said Nick, unstrapping Horatio and putting him against his shoulder. 'He hasn't thrown up. Jesus. I can't go on like this. Two actors together are like an explosion. A bad explosion. A terrorist bomb.'

Seeing Horatio dangling over Nick's shoulder, wide-eyed and innocent, I felt so sorry for him.

'Sadie's probably just stressed with the new baby,' I said. 'You should try and work things out.'

Nick gave a hysterical laugh. 'Work things out? Have you *met* Sadie? You should know that's impossible, Julesy – *you* were friends with her.'

'Maybe it's her hormones.'

'Oh, come on. You know what she's like. And now we're on this crazy fucking family rollercoaster, and I can't get off. Mum has bought us a house. We're moving back to Great Oakley in like a *week*. It's like no one is listening to me. I'm drowning.'

That hit me like a bullet.

'You and Sadie are moving to Great Oakley in a *week*?'

'It was a stupid idea,' said Nick. 'I thought it might fix everything. Happily ever after, and all of that. But now I'm more trapped than ever.'

He patted Horatio frantically on the back, and a plume of white vomit exploded over Nick's AllSaints jumper.

'*Christ*,' said Nick.

'You can't seriously want residency,' I said, watching Nick dab at sick with a Heal's tea towel. 'You can barely cope with one.'

'I reckon I can manage,' he said, a fierce expression in his eyes.

'*Manage?*' I said. 'Jesus, Nick. Think about what's best for Daisy.'

Thursday, 2nd March

Have been contacted by Cafcass – the child-welfare organisation, who get involved in 'more conflictual' child-centred court cases.

'We don't judge or take sides,' said the Cafcass lady. 'We just make sure parents remember that the child is at the centre of everything.'

In other words, Cafcass think Nick and I are at risk of fucking up Daisy's life with our inability to cooperate.

I'll be contacted shortly by my local Cafcass officer. He wants to meet me prior to the first court hearing, which is another way of saying, 'assess'.

So, I will be tested as a parent.

I'm way too tired to be perfect. But I try my best – surely, he'll see that?

Friday, 3rd March

Work again.

VERY tired.

Saturday, 4th March

Letter from family court.

They've asked me to submit documentation re why Daisy should continue living with me full-time.

There's also a date for a First Hearing Dispute Resolution Appointment at county court.

It's 5th April, just one month away.

I honestly thought Nick wouldn't go through with this, but it looks like he's not backing off.

Wanted to crawl back into bed, but couldn't because Daisy pulled the duvet off and force-fed me plastic hotdogs.

Decided to phone Nick instead and shout at him.

Sadly, he won't answer his phone.

Sunday, 5th March

Have just seen a removal van outside the Gables.

Am praying that it's nothing to do with Nick and Sadie. Maybe the Jolly-Piggott house purchase obscurely fell through. Or something.

But I'm not feeling that lucky because there were at least twenty boxes labelled 'wardrobe' in the back of the van.

Monday, 6th March

Fucking hell.

Have just seen Sadie in the Co-op, complaining about the lack of guacamole.

This has forced me to accept a horrifying truth – Nick and Sadie have now moved to the village.

MY village.

Tried to sneak out of the shop without Sadie seeing me, but unfortunately, Daisy had shoplifted a bunch of bananas, so we had to come back.

Daisy spotted Horatio's evil-genius pod pram while I was apologising to the check-out lady.

She shouted, 'My bugger. My bugger, Mummy.'

Sadie saw us then. She was dressed in skin-tight jeans, brown riding boots and a navy kind of shawl-jumper-polo-neck thing.

'Jules!' she said, startled.

'Bugger, bugger!' Daisy shouted, pointing to Horatio.

'Is she…calling him a bugger?' Sadie asked.

'She means brother,' I said, through gritted teeth. 'Come on

Daisy, let's go.'

Horatio made grunting noises.

'Oh *god*,' said Sadie. 'He's going to puke again.' Her eyes went wild. 'It's never-ending. Jesus, can't he just give me *five minutes?* We haven't even unpacked yet.'

'This is motherhood,' I said, pulling Daisy out of the shop. 'Putting someone else before yourself. I'm not surprised you're struggling.'

'Wait!' said Sadie, suddenly tearful. 'Who'd have thought, the two of us in the countryside with babies, hey? Do you remember when we used to go for cocktails? You know, you should come over sometime. For wine or…something.'

'Jesus, Sadie, you must be kidding,' I said. 'Daisy. Come *on*.'

'But Jules, I've really missed you.'

I laughed. 'I haven't missed you. Actually, it's been brilliant – not having a great big bucket of shit tipped over my head every day.' Was very tempted to add, 'By the way, Nick's seeking residency of Daisy because he wants his family back. HA! How do YOU like THAT?' But decided to be grown-up about things. No sense stirring – there are two little children involved in all of this.

I'm going to bump into Sadie all around the village now. And Nick too.

This is an awful development.

Tuesday, 7th March

Alex called.

He didn't mention our last 'you need some space' conversation, which was sort of weird.

In the background, a waitress said, 'There's your steak, Mr Dalton. Would you like more red wine?'

After the usual pleasantries, Alex asked if I had any plans to see

'Nick Spencer'.

'You don't make plans to meet Nick,' I said. 'He turns up when you don't want him to, and when you do want him, he's late.'

'You visited his apartment recently,' said Alex.

I went quiet. 'How did you know that?'

'A member of my staff saw you at Canary Wharf.'

I felt angry then. 'Are you spying on me?'

'Why didn't you tell me you'd seen him?'

'I already told you – I don't have to report back. Anyway, it's not exactly news, is it? I'm bound to see him from time to time. And the last time we spoke, you said I needed some space.'

'But why at his apartment?'

'Alex, me meeting up with my daughter's father is none of your business.'

'I'm sorry you see it that way.'

He's in Edinburgh at the moment, due to some Amtico flooring crisis.

Feel our relationship is too early and uncertain to moan about wanting to see him more – especially after the oddness of our last phone conversation.

But I want to see him more.

Realise I've seen Nick more than I've seen Alex this year.

Not a good sign.

Wednesday, 8th March

Mum's just come back from the doctors, moaning because Dr Slaughter has put her on a diet.

'He says I have to cut down on sugar and attend some sodding NHS healthy-eating class,' she complained. 'And right before Easter, too.'

I asked her why Dr Slaughter had got so strict, and she admitted she might have to start injecting insulin for her diabetes.

'What do you mean, *might?*' I asked.

'If I don't start taking better care of myself,' said Mum.

I told Mum that insulin injections were serious, and she'd have to make some major lifestyle changes.

Dad and I are worried.

We spent the evening Googling health sites and diabetes blogs.

I don't think Mum quite understands how serious this could be because she's feeding herself up in preparation for the diet class tomorrow.

'I'll need some reserves if they're going to make me live on lettuce leaves,' she said.

Why do people my parents' age always think of diets in terms of lettuce leaves?

I told Mum I'd go to diet classes with her for moral support.

'I don't want some skinny cow going with me,' she complained. 'It's humiliating enough already.'

'This could be good for you, Shirley,' said Dad. 'A re-education.'

'But I always hated school,' said Mum.

Thursday, 9th March

Mum has bought herself the 1970s version of health food:

+ Cottage cheese
+ Nimble bread
+ A bag of baking potatoes
+ Three different flavours of Cup-a-Soup
+ Butterscotch Angel Delight and low-fat squirty cream
+ A lettuce

Laura came over this evening and lectured Mum about the sugar in powdered soup.

'Packet food is a nutritional void,' she said. 'If you're cutting back calories, you need to pack every meal with vitamins and minerals.'

She presented Mum with a bag of shopping she'd brought from her local organic health-food shop.

I have to admit, it didn't look very appetising, and everything *was* brown.

Laura wrote a diet plan, which included organic vegetable broth, mung-bean biscuits and hummus.

The thought of mung-bean biscuits threw Mum into a depression, and she barred one of the regulars for putting Take That on the jukebox.

A change of diet will be tough for Mum, but ultimately, it's about time she took care of her health.

Her cure for colds is a double shot of tequila or, in severe cases of flu, WKD blue and port.

Friday, 10th March

Mum has ripped up Laura's diet plan, complaining the mung-bean biscuits have caused constipation.

Dad wrote her a new plan this morning.

He's eaten healthily for years and baked his own seeded wholemeal bread before it was readily available.

The plan includes things Mum absolutely won't eat, like vegetables. But Dad is determined.

'It's about time your mother treated her body better,' he said. 'She owes it to her family. I don't want to be a widower.'

Then he had a bit of a cry.

I put my arm around him and said Mum would be fine.

He gave a sad laugh and said, 'She seems like a tough old soul. But only I know how fragile she is.'

I'm worried about Mum too, but it's very hard to think of her as fragile. She's the only person I know who's ever frightened a traffic warden into removing a ticket.

Saturday, 11th March

Just found Dad in the garden, watching the stars with tears in his eyes.

I asked if he was thinking about Mum.

He nodded and said, 'But I'm trying to stay positive. When you look at the world, there are so many miracles.'

'Diabetes isn't cancer,' I said. 'You never know. If she loses weight, she might be healthier than before.'

'I don't want her having injections from now until forever,' Dad said. 'And she doesn't *need* to lose weight. I love her the way she is.'

But the truth is, Mum's weight puts a lot of stress on her body. Even holding in a fart gives her backache.

'Weight loss will do her the world of good, Dad,' I said.

'But she'll be miserable,' he argued. 'Your Mum lives for a good meal.'

'She'll just have to start liking healthy food,' I said.

Dad pointed to the sky and said, 'I suppose if God can make stars burn bright like that, anything is possible.'

I wish I were Christian, like Dad. It must be very reassuring.

I blame my primary school for making us sit cross-legged on a hard floor while we sang hymns. Also, cold churches with their wooden pews. Why not move with the times and get sofas?

Sunday, 12th March

Call from my Cafcass officer today – an upbeat man called Johnny Jiggens.

He's threatened to visit soon with puppets and 'feelings' emoji

72

cushions.

'I want to find out about Daisy and her living environment,' he said. 'And how you and Nick work things out.'

'*We* don't work things out,' I said. '*I* do. Nick is irresponsible.'

Johnny said, 'Fathers have a very hard time these days. We want to be involved. But society has expectations. I do a lot of work with Fathers for Justice, and there are so many dads who are great guys just trying to get it right... I mean, are you sure you're not just *perceiving* your partner as irresponsible? Just because he's a man? Sexism works both ways.'

Am not looking forward to the meeting.

Monday, 13th March

Work training has finished, so tomorrow I'll be doing my job for real.

Want to make a good start, so am getting the 7.30am train.

Mum has agreed to childmind, as long as Daisy is handed over fed and dressed.

Want to arrive on time, so have bought an instant porridge pot to speed along Daisy's breakfast.

The only trouble will be getting her into her clothes.

Daisy is getting very wilful and refuses to wear certain items – usually clean, pretty dresses that make me look like a good mother.

Her favourite outfit is a black swimming cap, felt-tip stained dungarees (which she calls 'dunga jeans') and a pair of spotty tights – the last one not on her legs, but worn around her neck like a scarf.

It's all very creative – Althea heartily approves.

Told Althea I was still worried about Daisy's walking.

'But she's holding onto stuff, isn't she?' said Althea. 'And pulling herself about.'

'Yes, she's cruising,' I said. 'But not walking.'

'Cruising?' said Althea. 'Isn't that something middle-aged men do in Amsterdam's red-light district?'

Tuesday, 14th March

Work.

Because training is over, I had to bring in my own biscuits and coffee.

Spent the day getting to grips with my new job.

Hari told me I'd be working closely with deputy manager, Lloyd – a nineteen-year-old, shaven-headed lad in a shiny nylon suit.

'Lloyd fires up our cash tractors every morning,' Hari explained, giving the teenager a proud shake of the shoulders. 'He turns the ignition key and sends them out to harvest all that lovely money. Lloyd – tell Juliette how it's done.'

Lloyd fiddled with his overlong shirt cuffs and said, 'Well…uh, I just sort of hand out cans of Red Bull and play really loud house music.'

'The team are due any minute,' said Hari, throwing Red Bull into the fridge. 'Better put their petrol on ice.'

Lloyd cranked up the Ministry of Sound album and shouted, 'Woo! Yeah!'

Wednesday, 15th March

Yay!

Alex is back tomorrow. He's catching the overnight train from Edinburgh, and has a 'quick meeting' in the morning, but will take me out during my lunch break.

Managed an early breakfast with Daisy before work today.

She's really babbling now, saying all sorts of half-words.

Unfortunately, those half-words often sound like swearing.

She calls yoghurt, 'buggert', and for some reason has picked up the phrase 'fucking about'.

Callum is being very patient with her, explaining what she can and can't say. 'No Daisy. Only Nana and Mum can say "fucking about".'

Thursday, 16th March

Lunch with Alex.

He took me to a posh Spanish restaurant near King's Cross, with ham hanging from the ceiling.

All the staff knew Alex by name.

Halfway through lunch, the manager came over to greet him personally, and the two of them spent the next twenty minutes talking about the best mosaic for swimming pools.

When the manager finally left, I said, 'I thought we were having lunch together.'

Alex said, 'We *are* having lunch together.'

'No,' I said. 'I've been sitting here smiling like an idiot, while you talk business.'

'I have a lot on this year.'

'That's fine,' I said. 'But do it in the other twenty-three hours of the day, when we're not having lunch.'

Alex frowned at his plate. 'I don't respond well to orders.'

'And I don't respond well to being ignored.'

'Perhaps you can arrange to meet Nick Spencer again,' said Alex. 'He seems to be paying you *plenty* of attention.'

We ate in silence for a moment.

Then Alex said, 'I'm sorry. You're right – I haven't seen you in weeks. I should have told Emilio to leave us in peace. How's the job going?'

'It's OK. The training has finished now. I'm finally seeing what

I've got myself into.'

'And what have you got yourself into?'

'I don't like my boss,' I admitted. 'He's morally corrupt.'

Alex's lips tilted up. 'No surprises there.'

Friday, 17th March
St Patricks Day

Nick texted, wishing me a happy St Patrick's Day and asking if things were 'cool' between us.

Was a bit taken aback.

Said I wasn't thinking about killing him right at this moment if that's what he meant.

Nick texted smiley faces and a knife emoji. Then he asked if he could see Daisy tomorrow.

I hate how he does that – just assumes Daisy will be waiting around, dressed in bows, ready to see him.

Told him no.

Saturday, 18th March

A sobering thought – court isn't far away. Have never been to court before. Will have to ask Mum and John Boy what to expect.

Sunday, 19th March

Too tired to write today.

And stressed.

Keep thinking about court.

Monday, 20th March

Oh my god. OH, MY GOD!

Laura is PREGNANT!!!

She's eight weeks gone, so Zach must have knocked her up in February.

I'm delighted.

Laura told us the news over lunch with the family.

I should have known something was up. She never usually eats Mum's Yorkshires.

We all bombarded her with questions.

Would she and Zach get married? (me)

Had they 'done it on purpose'? (Mum)

How about Star or Blue for names? (Brandi)

Can I buy the baby pick-and-mix sweets, and eat the foamy strawberries? (Callum)

Can you get Adidas tracksuits for babies? (John Boy)

Would Laura *please* now consider buying a sensible family car with a tow bar? (Dad)

Tuesday, 21st March

Phoned Alex about Laura's pregnancy.

He didn't seem surprised.

'Did you know?' I asked.

'I had an inkling.'

'Why didn't you tell me?'

'Didn't *you* have an inkling?'

'No,' I admitted.

Feel a bit upset, actually. That Laura didn't tell me earlier.

'Imagine how my mother is going to feel,' said Alex. 'She has a certain opinion of you Duffy girls.'

'Which would be?'

'That you're all vixens out to trap her innocent boys. She won't be cracking open the Champagne, put it that way.'

God!

'How can you put up with that?' I said.

'I can't change her,' Alex replied. 'It's just how she is. She's one of the two people in my life I have no control over. But in your case, I live in hope.'

'Can't you tell your mum how nice Laura is?'

'It won't make the slightest bit of difference,' said Alex. 'I doubt she'll even come to the wedding.'

'What wedding?'

'Zachary and Laura's wedding.'

I nearly spat out my tea. 'They're getting *married*? Since when?'

'With a baby on the way, I'm assuming it won't be long.'

'You can have children without getting married,' I said.

Alex snorted. 'I'd think you of anyone would be championing marriage *before* babies.'

'It's the twentieth century, Alex.'

'As I said before, it's the twenty-first century, Juliette. And human nature doesn't change. Tradition is there for a reason. You should have married Nick Spencer before Daisy came along.'

'Nick would never have married me before we had Daisy,' I said. 'He's not the marrying type.'

'Exactly. That should have been your first warning. You're now tied to a feckless layabout for the rest of your life. And if our relationship continues, so am I.'

'Thanks, Alex.'

'It's the truth, Juliette.'

'Sometimes the truth hurts,' I said.

'If you don't like the truth, I'm the wrong person to spend time with.'

He had to go then. Another typical Alex emergency. Three crates of Scottish smoked salmon were stuck in traffic and needed airlifting to the Chelsea Dalton.

Wednesday, 22nd March

Johnny Jiggens visited today, armed with cushions and puppets.

He was a 'hippy-turned-corporate' sort, with a blond ponytail, patchy beard and the kind of ill-fitting, found-it-in-a-sale suit you knew he'd only bought for work.

'I'm here to make sure Daisy's needs are being considered,' Johnny explained, arranging his cushions on the corduroy sofa. 'Often parents get so wrapped up in their own needs, they forget about the children.'

The cushions were primary colours, with different emojis sewn onto them to represent emotions.

'How are you feeling today, Daisy?' Johnny asked, gesturing to the cushions. 'Can you choose a face to show us?'

Daisy grabbed her favourite colour.

Red.

The angry emoji.

'You're feeling angry today?' Johnny said, making a note.

Daisy nodded happily. 'Hungry. Hungry. Biscuit?'

'She's a bit young for this, don't you think?' I said.

'Oh, you'd be surprised how these cushions help children express themselves,' Johnny replied.

Then he asked Daisy how she liked living at the pub.

She grabbed the sad and scared emoji cushions and tried to build a house with them.

'Anxious,' said Johnny.

'But she loves it here,' I said. 'Honestly. She doesn't even wake up at kicking-out time.'

Johnny made another note. 'What about Daddy's house?' he asked Daisy.

Daisy picked up the smiley face cushion.

'She's never been there,' I said. 'At least, not to his new house.'

'That must be very *painful* for Daddy,' said Johnny. 'I don't get to see my little girl very often. Her mum thought life would be better in Australia. No consideration for *Daddy's* life. Or the extortionate cost of airfares...'

'Baddy! Baddy!' Daisy shouted, cuddling the smiley face cushion.

Johnny said, 'Sometimes children tell other adults things they can't tell their parents.'

'But she doesn't even know what these cushions mean,' I said. 'Look – she's using them to beat up her toys.'

We watched Daisy, chattering away. 'Naughty Spiderman. You get hit now.'

Johnny made a note.

'It's her cousin, Callum,' I explained. 'He has all these violent games.'

'Callum bollocks,' Daisy agreed.

Johnny made another note. 'If you can lessen her contact with aggressive children ...'

'We can't do much about that,' I said. 'Callum lives here.'

'Here?' said Johnny. 'With you and Daisy? And...so his mother... How does that work?'

'His mother lives here too,' I said. 'She's my little sister, Brandi.'

'Right,' said Johnny, making a note.

John Boy swaggered into the lounge then, shirt off, scouting around for his baccy pouch.

'Hello,' said Johnny cheerfully. 'Who are you?'

'Jules's cousin,' said John Boy, looking Johnny up and down. 'Who are *you*?'

Johnny stuck out his hand. 'Johnny Jiggens, Cafcass Officer. Just here to find out more about Daisy. Do you live here too?'

'At the minute,' said John Boy, shaking Johnny's hand.

'So that's...' Johnny started counting his fingers. '*Seven* of you? Is that right?'

I glared at John Boy.

'What?' said John Boy, holding up his hands. 'What did I say?'

After an eye-watering puppet show, during which Johnny put on pretend mummy, daddy and child voices, he packed up his bag of tricks and left.

God knows what he made of us.

Probably best not to think about it.

Thursday, 23rd March

Met Althea for lunch in Shoreditch today.

She chose a Mexican canteen where you could serve your own margarita from a glass soda fountain.

Foolishly, she let Wolfgang try her margarita, so he could 'learn about flavours'. But then he wanted the whole thing, so she had to wrestle him to the floor shouting, 'No Wolfgang! Mummy's booze!'

Wolfgang's hair is extremely long now – it's practically down to his shoulders. If he were one of those pretty little boys with rosy cheeks, he could get away with it. But teamed with those ferocious eyebrows, long hair gives him a wild, feral edge.

In honour of the Mexican theme, Althea had dressed Wolfgang in a 'Day of the Dead' shirt, complete with black-and-white sombrero.

Wolfgang kept pulling at the hat and blurting out 'Arg! Arg!', but Althea wouldn't let him take it off. She's child-led about most things, but when it comes to fancy dress, she's very strict.

Over lunch, I told Althea about the Cafcass visit, and how worried I am about the court hearing.

'You don't need to worry,' she said. 'The courts always favour the mother. Unless she's a drug addict or something. It's still sexism, but for once it's in our favour.'

Then she talked about a *Big Issue* article she'd just read that mentioned Give a Damn.

'It's a shameless capitalist enterprise,' she said. 'Only 5% of last year's profits went to charity.'

That didn't surprise me.

To be honest, I'm amazed any money goes to charity, now Hari is at the helm.

Friday, 24th March

First Hearing Dispute Resolution Appointment on Monday – aka court.

The fact it has the word 'first' in the title suggests there will be a second court hearing. Which bothers me. Although Jeremy says that if I'm lucky, everything could be 'wrapped up' first time.

We'll see.

Saturday, 25th March

To cheer me up about the court hearing, John Boy has bought Daisy a pair of fluorescent-yellow Nikes.

At £50, the trainers are a very generous present – meaning I can't really tell John Boy how hideous they are.

They're so bright that the lady next door thought her two tropical Macaws had escaped onto our trampoline.

Daisy loves them and refuses to take them off.

'Shoe! Shoe!' she shrieks, whenever I stoop down to undo the Velcro. 'MY shoe! MY SHOE MUMMY!'

I nearly lost my temper at bath time, but we compromised –

Daisy could keep her shoes on in the bath if she let me cut her fingernails.

Sunday, 26th March

Little family get together, to celebrate Laura's pregnancy.

Nice tea at the pub with fizzy wine, triangular sandwiches, crisps, nuts and fresh fruit.

Of course, Mum complained about it 'not being a proper bloody meal'. But she's doing quite well at cutting back. Ordinarily, she would have slapped a microwave lasagne between two slices of bread to 'pad things out a bit'.

Laura only drank Cranberry juice, despite Mum's chiding that 'one glass of fizzy won't do the baby any harm. I drank *pints* of Guinness when I was expecting you...'

Everyone is reassuring me about court tomorrow.

But am still worried. I mean it's *court*.

Monday, 27th March

First Hearing Dispute Resolution Appointment.

Because it was a first hearing, things were supposedly informal, and we all sat together in a sort of classroom at county court – me and Jeremy Samuels, Nick and his solicitor Penny Castle, Johnny Jiggens and an elderly judge with a walking frame.

The jolly old judge asked if anyone wanted 'a nice cup of tea', but we were all too nervous or professional to say yes.

Then the judge asked about Daisy and the nature of mine and Nick's relationship, where we were living and so on.

After that, Johnny Jiggens was called upon to dish the dirt re living arrangements. He spoke about the crowded nature of the pub, and how people seemed to be 'coming and going'. He also talked about Nick's new home and how 'Mr Spencer' offered 'exceptional' living arrangements.

'And what about the best needs of the child, Mr Jiggens?' the judge asked. 'What's your opinion there?'

'In my opinion, the child's needs will be best met with joint residency,' said Johnny. 'I think spending an equal amount of time in each residence would be ideal at this moment in time.'

Felt like I'd been punched in the stomach. Expected Jeremy to say something, but he was frowning and making notes.

'Mr Spencer owns a spacious, family home and is committed to Early Years learning,' Johnny Jiggens continued. 'He's even built a bee hotel in the garden. Once Nick – I mean Mr *Spencer* – can bond with his daughter again via a joint residency arrangement, I suggest residency is reviewed and Mr Spencer is allowed to reapply for full custody.'

Oh my *god*.

I couldn't believe it.

Nick gave Johnny a thumbs-up.

Jeremy said, 'Miss Duffy's residence is temporary, following her separation from Mr Spencer. She is committed to finding her own home. And I should remind you that Mr Spencer has been absent for much of last year.'

'Mr Spencer visited when he could,' said Penny Castle. 'Miss Duffy refused him visitation on many occasions, and has continued to do so this year.'

The judge said, 'Thank you, Mr Jiggens, for your appraisal. As a Cafcass Officer, you are the eyes of family court and I pay close attention to your views. However, I don't feel confident awarding joint residency at this stage. Miss Duffy has only recently started work again. She needs more time to find a permanent home.'

Then he gave us our court orders.

Nick and I are to attend an online 'parents' separation course'.

We have to go to more mediation, and there will be another court hearing – 'prior to which Miss Duffy is urged to find more suitable accommodation.'

On the way out of court, Jeremy Samuels said, 'Juliette. A quick word.' He gave me serious eye contact and said, 'If it wasn't clear enough in there, let me summarise. Get your own place sooner rather than later. We don't want to leave any gaps.'

Everyone *said* this was just a formality. That Nick had no chance.

Am now extremely worried.

Bloody Nick.

Tuesday, 28th March

Have spent all day looking on Rightmove, while trying to stop Daisy prodding sticky little fingers on the iPad screen.

In the end, I did what I swore I'd never do – Mum's 'keep 'em quiet' trick of feeding her Jammie Dodger after Jammie Dodger.

It sort of worked, except for occasional jam smears across the iPad screen – which sent Rightmove into shock and churned up homes in Birmingham.

Have found a big problem, though.

Rental prices have skyrocketed since they extended the local university. The most I can afford is a bedsit, and I don't think the court will look upon that as a decent family home.

'But interest rates are very low, love,' Dad pointed out. 'Mortgage repayments will be a lot less. Why not think about buying?'

He's right, but this comes with a whole host of new problems – i.e. getting a mortgage. I suppose I do have a wage now. So, you never know.

Told Mum I needed to find my own place 'sooner rather than later'.

'I don't see why a court would have an issue with you living here,' she said. 'Four solid walls and a fridge full of cheese. What's the problem?'

But Mum is very prone to delusion. She thinks a Jaffa Cake is a healthy snack because it's fruit-flavoured and full of air.

Wednesday, 29th March

Phoned five different banks and got told the same bad news five different ways – you can't get a mortgage within the first six months of a new job. The fact I don't have a deposit doesn't help either.

'I was on *maternity* leave,' I kept saying.

But apparently, because I have a new job title, this doesn't matter.

Was very frustrated. Tried to be polite, but by the last phone call, I lost my temper.

'I can afford the repayments,' I said. 'And it's *not* a new job.'

'I'm sorry, Mrs Daffy,' said the squeaky-voiced mortgage advisor. 'You're seen as high-risk.'

There are some positives if I'm prepared to wait six months. I have a good wage, no childcare payments (thanks to my amazing family) and no debt.

So I can afford a nice flat around here, or a maybe even a very small terraced house.

I asked if paternity payments from Daisy's father would help, but he said no. Apparently, very little counts as a source of income. Not even employment.

Why are banks so strict? I know loads of people reneged on their credit in the 1990s, but I WASN'T ONE OF THEM.

People like Brandi have a lot to answer for.

Thursday, 30th March

Visited Althea in Bethnal Green today, and told her my stresses over a big pot of camomile tea and soapy-tasting lavender biscuits.

Althea was outraged that I can't get a mortgage. 'That's against European Human Rights law,' she ranted. 'You need to contact Brussels and start banging heads.'

After a lengthy chat (moan), Althea came up with a neat solution to my mortgage application problem.

'Just lie and tell them you've been in your job for more than six months.'

It sounds so simple.

But I'm one of those ridiculously honest people who go bright red at the slightest untruth.

When I told Althea I valued honesty, she snorted and said, 'If you value honesty, stop dying your bloody hair.'

'But this is a BIG lie,' I said. 'You know I'll go all red.'

'Oh yeah,' Althea laughed. 'Like that time you used my VIP pass. And the White Stripes thought you'd done amyl nitrate.'

Friday, 31st March

Arranged a mortgage appointment with the only high-street bank I haven't tried.

Wanted to apply over the phone, but they had some policy about meeting in person. So, I'm going into the bank on Monday.

The thought of being scrutinised face-to-face made me even more nervous.

I'm seeing someone called Kelly Borstal.

She sounds tough. Unyielding. The sort of person who'd make lengthy eye contact.

Saturday, 1st April

One of our cash tractors got sacked today.

It's a rare occurrence because usually they're the ones who leave. Within hours sometimes. It was a fair sacking because the cash tractor had been stealing from the collection bucket.

It's pretty much the only thing a collector could be fired for.

Street collectors arrive late, drunk and, in some cases, on Grade A drugs. But Hari is happy as long as they're bringing in the cash.

After the sacking, Hari sent the other collectors out with their buckets and clipboards, giving them high fives and hearty pats on the back.

'There they go!' he said, eyes moist with excitement. 'Going out to harvest all that lovely money.' He turned to Lloyd and whispered, 'That guy I just sacked. What's his name?'

'Terrance,' said Lloyd.

'Give him a ring next week,' said Hari. 'If he says sorry, he can have his job back.'

Sunday, 2nd April

Told Dad about mortgage woes.

'Keep trying, love,' he said. 'There's nothing like owning your own home. I remember when your mum and I bought this place. We were over the moon. Of course, the mortgage payments brought us down to earth a bit. Ninety-four pounds a month! That made our eyes water.'

Ninety-four pounds a month…

I wish I could go back to the Seventies.

Not getting a good night's sleep here, which increases my stress and desperation to move.

Mum snores like a motorbike and John Boy shrieks in his sleep.

Monday, 3rd April

Mortgage appointment.

Kelly Borstal wasn't how I imagined. She was a cuddly, ex-figure skater from Southend who said things like, 'What am I like?' and 'Oh my days!'

She told me, conversationally, that she'd never been able to get a mortgage herself.

'There are so many blimmin rules,' she laughed. 'You get jaded, seeing rejection after rejection.'

I blurted out my carefully prepared lie, red-faced and frantic, but Kelly was barely listening.

'You don't have a deposit,' she lamented. 'So…it doesn't really matter about your job.'

She went through three different mortgage products, then told me why I was ineligible for all of them.

Tuesday, 4th April

Have spent all afternoon calling mortgage companies.

Am now calling obscure banks with weird names like 'Sparrow and Dudley' and 'The Black Bank'.

No joy so far.

The worst part is knowing I can *nearly* get a mortgage. And that I can afford the repayments.

Wednesday, 5th April

Letter from family court.

The next hearing is 10th July. That gives me three and a half months to get a property, and I don't even have a mortgage yet.

Ironically, a salesman called in the afternoon, saying I'd been mis-sold payment protection on my mortgage.

'No one will give me a sodding mortgage,' I barked. 'And I *really* need one.'

Unperturbed, the bright-voiced young salesman asked, 'Are you sure you don't have one? Have a *really* good think.'

Thursday, 6th April

A BRILLIANT day.

Alex turned up at the pub unexpectedly with a big bunch of roses for me and offered to take Daisy and me out.

We went to the village pottery café, so Daisy could smash plates while Alex and I drank coffee.

I had a cappuccino. Alex had an espresso macchiato, which he said wasn't a *real* macchiato but 'would do'.

Then Alex harangued me about my living arrangements.

He'd been talking to Jeremy and was 'alerted to the seriousness' of my current living situation re residency.

'I'm trying,' I said. 'Believe me – I'm bending over backwards to get a mortgage.'

Alex grilled me about my income, forcing me to expose the pitiful state of my finances. Then he sat back and pondered, fingers steepled together.

'I know some banks that might give you a mortgage,' he said. 'Let me call my mortgage broker.'

He strolled outside, and paced back and forth in front of the glass window, frowning and barking into his mobile phone.

When he returned, Daisy had eaten his muffin. She was very sneaky about it, grabbing the bun while I was hunting under the pram for wet wipes, and eating the whole thing – paper and all.

Alex didn't seem to mind. He stroked Daisy's fluffy hair and said, 'You have the right instincts. Maybe you can teach Mummy a thing or two.'

He downed his coffee while standing, then said his broker friend had found me a mortgage.

'The fees are relatively high,' said Alex. 'But you can add them to the loan.'

I stared, a stupid smile on my face. Then I jumped up and threw my arms around him.

'Oh my God!' I shrieked. 'Really?'

'Don't thank me yet,' said Alex, giving me that half smile of his. 'You haven't even filled out the paperwork.'

'Last week, getting a mortgage was impossible,' I said.

'That's my job then,' said Alex. 'Helping you achieve the impossible.'

We smiled at each other, and for a moment it was like all our problems didn't matter.

Friday, 7th April

Long phone conversation with Alex's broker, while pretending to do a spreadsheet at work.

The broker requested all sorts of paperwork, including an employment reference and contract.

Realised I've never actually signed an employment contract.

'You don't have a contract as such, Juliette,' Hari told me when I asked. 'We all work in a far more flexible world these days.'

'Yes, but I need one,' I insisted.

'Let me look into it,' said Hari.

'No, Hari,' I said. 'Don't look into it. Do it.'

Hari said he'd try and 'knock something up'.

Saturday, 8th April

Completed the mortgage application.

Almost.

Sent off bank statements, passport, etc.

The only thing missing is my employment contract and reference.

Had to answer all sorts of unusual questions, like how much I paid in school fees and how regularly I went skiing because the mortgage isn't with a high-street bank.

Sunday, 9th April

John Boy woke at 5am to 'spring clean the house to army standards'.

He worked all morning, only allowing himself a brief pause for five custard creams and a six-sugar tea with condensed milk.

By lunchtime, John Boy's back and legs were giving him trouble. He had to sit down on a hard chair with his prosthetic leg propped up. Of course, he played down the pain, saying he 'just needed a rest', but he winced every time Callum played teaspoons on his metal foot.

I put on a violent computer game for Callum, then fetched John Boy another six-sugar cup of tea.

'Should I book you in with Doctor Slaughter?' I asked.

'No point,' said John Boy. 'He'd only give me painkillers.'

'What's wrong with that?' I asked.

John Boy explained that he never took painkillers during the day, saving them for phantom leg pain at night.

'Why didn't you tell us you were in pain at night?' I asked.

'No point in moaning,' said John Boy. 'It's not going to bring my leg back, is it?'

Monday, 10th April

I've been accepted for A MORTGAGE!!!!

Right before Easter too, so I can stuff myself with chocolate to celebrate.

Keep doing my happy dance (stir the cake bowl, stir the cake bowl!).

Alex was quietly pleased when I phoned him.

I think he might have known already because he mentioned something about his broker calling.

Alex has offered to visit the estate agents with me tomorrow, which I'm excited about.

He's the sort of man who knocks heads together and gets things done.

Tuesday, 11th April

Met Alex at Belle Homes this morning.

He told me off for not bringing a notepad.

'You're in an oversubscribed market,' Alex said. 'If you want to win in any oversubscribed market, you have to be organised. The organised bird gets the worm.'

'I thought it was the early bird,' I said.

'The organised bird is, by default, always early.'

The estate agency staff were terrified of Alex.

It was like watching a shark swimming with goldfish.

Alex introduced himself by barking his own name, then began an aggressive line of questioning:

'What haven't you put on yet? What's on the to-do list today? What's selling? What's not?'

He sorted out viewings on THREE properties tomorrow – two of which haven't even been put on the market yet. AND he's coming to the viewings with me.

Woo!

Things are moving forward.

Wednesday, 12th April

Viewings today.

Clarke Jackson from Belle Homes drove Alex and me around Great Oakley in his fancy silver BMW.

The first place had mould on the walls (which Clarke said just needed 'a bit of bleach'). The next was right by the noisy bus stop where all the teenagers hang out and drink cider (a commuter's dream!), and the last one was miles out of the village (just a quick bus ride to the shops ...)

Alex was tight-lipped and silent throughout.

Back at the Belle Homes office, Clarke made us coffee.

It was instant coffee with powdered milk.

Alex's frown was the deepest I've ever seen it.

'This isn't coffee,' he barked. 'It's synthetic brown water. And when I'm looking for a house, I expect to see something decent. How can you market properties like these?'

Clarke straightened his Armani suit and went on about Great Oakley being a 'highly desirable' area, adding that the coffee was Gold Blend and 'not all that bad'.

Alex demanded to see something decent, and Clarke pulled out another property that hadn't been put on yet.

'We expect this one to sell dead quick,' said Clarke. 'It's called Station Cottage. And it's on cheap because the owners are divorcing. A perfect little starter home, I call it. Two bedrooms, kitchen, lounge – the lot. They're even throwing in the furniture because they can't agree who bought what. It's right near the train station too, so perfect for your fancy London job, Juliette.'

The pictures showed a cosy front room with wood-burning stove. No garden, but that's just one less job to do.

Of course, I've been fooled by pictures before.

Estate agents turn into Spiderman when taking photos, getting spacious-looking shots that can only have been snapped from the ceiling.

'It's right near the railway station,' said Alex, in a way that suggested he didn't approve.

'So?' I said.

'You'll be fighting with high-earning commuters, willing to up the price.'

'This could be a great house for me,' I insisted. 'And it's within my budget.'

'You really like the look of this one?' Alex asked.

I nodded.

'What can you do about that asking price?' Alex barked at Clarke. 'What's the leeway?'

'Two percent,' said Clarke. 'They can't afford to go lower.'

Alex turned to me. 'Well, Juliette. I suggest you set up a viewing. And speaking of viewing houses, would you like to come round *my* house for dinner this Sunday?'

'I'd love to,' I said, surprised by the invitation.

So, will see Station Cottage next week.

And seeing Alex at his HOUSE this Sunday.

Thursday, 13th April

Work.

Spent the day filling in complicated expenses sheets and ordering crates of Red Bull.

Asked Hari about getting time off over the Easter holidays, but he wasn't optimistic.

'Charity doesn't take holidays, Juliette. Christian festivals are some of our best collection times. We don't say Jesus Christ here. We say Jesus ching, ching, ching!'

Got home at 6.30pm, limp and exhausted.

Daisy was already sleeping.

Was awful not to be able to cuddle her or sing a lullaby.

Cried a bit as I looked over the cot.

Mum told me off for feeling guilty. 'Me and your dad used to leave you kids *all* the time. And you turned out just fine.'

Friday, 14th April
Good Friday

Arrived late for work this morning due to train delays. An old lady lost her ticket and couldn't pay the fine, so they held the train while the rail company had her arrested.

Sprinted into the office at 9.30am and got the shock of my life.

NICK was sitting with the collection team, drinking Red Bull and nodding his head to thumping house music.

I have to say he looked the part – dressed in a Florence and the Machine t-shirt and eye-wateringly tight jeans. You wouldn't have guessed he was forty.

'What are you doing here?' I shrieked.

'Taking up stable employment,' said Nick, accepting a fluorescent tabard from a girl with pink hair. 'You heard what the mediator said. I need to show I'm a provider.'

A bearded student type whooped and gave Nick a high five.

'This isn't stable employment,' I told Nick. 'It's temporary sales hell for twenty-somethings who still live at home. There's no way you can earn a proper living—'

'Uh oh!' Hari interrupted. 'Sounds like a neg head. Team, who thinks Juliette should do twenty press-ups for being such a downer?'

'I'm not doing sodding press-ups, Hari,' I snapped. 'Nick, you need to leave.'

'But I've joined the collection squad,' Nick protested. 'And I'm going to give 110% today.'

There were more whoops and cheers.

'There are a million crappy jobs you could have taken,' I shouted. 'Why pick this one?'

'It's not a crappy job,' said Nick, creaking in his skinny black jeans. 'Hari has explained there's an excellent career structure. Look, I'm trying. OK?'

He gave me his puppy-dog eyes, and a pink-haired girl said, 'Aww!'

'Did Hari also tell you street collecting is a cash-in-hand job?' I asked. 'Unless you declare it, I can't touch you for maintenance payments.'

Nick waved his hand airily. 'I don't get caught up in all that tax nonsense. Look – I'll pay you something once I get going, all right?'

'You're a massive shithead, Nick,' I said.

As I was storming off to get a Red Bull, I saw three (female) street collectors putting comforting arms around Nick's shoulders

Saturday, 15th April

Am commiserating with a LOT of Easter eggs today.

Nick did brilliantly yesterday and today.

He was one of the top collectors.

We all had to give the 'new boy' a high five and tell him how well he'd done.

As I left the office, stuffing mini eggs into my mouth, Nick caught up with me.

'Thanks for telling me about this opportunity, Julesy,' he said, bounding along. 'I never considered charity my thing. But Hari has explained it's not all about giving. I can take some for myself too.'

'Just pay some sodding money for Daisy,' I said.

'When are you going to drop all this cash talk, Jules?' Nick asked. 'We're collecting for kids who don't have a thing.'

'Too true man,' said one of the bearded young collectors, cycling past us on a rusty old bike. 'This job isn't about the money. I mean, how can it be? It pays like nothing.'

Evening

Feeling a bit funny about dinner round Alex's tomorrow.

His house is VERY posh, from what I remember of it. And of course, there are bedrooms there. Which invites the question… Are we finally going to sleep together again?

Seems a bit unladylike to ask.

So, will just wait and see.

Mum is very happy to babysit overnight if needs be, saying it's about time I let my hair down.

Sunday, 16th April

Dinner with Alex.

It was a ten-minute walk to Alex's front gate and a further fifteen minutes up the driveway to his front door.

The air was warm, and the sun still bright when I arrived.

Alex was waiting for me on the porch, hand resting casually on a pillar.

He'd made a nod to informality by taking off his tie and loosening his shirt collar.

'You walked,' he said, smiling.

'Why not?' I replied. 'You're only up the road.'

'I thought you'd come in that old car of yours,' Alex said, showing me inside.

'My car isn't that old,' I said. 'It's just not a Rolls Royce.'

'I don't have a Rolls Royce any more. I sold it, remember? One of my better exchanges, as a matter of fact.'

'Well if you ever want to borrow my Fiat...'

Alex's house was immaculate, but there were no personal touches like books or photos. It felt more like a hotel, really.

Lots of things were in pairs, I noticed. Two stone owls on the mantelpiece, next to a pair of brass candle holders and two leather bibles. A pair of tables stood in the hall, with matching flower vases on them. There were even two brass umbrella holders.

Alex had laid out veal steak, fresh pasta, pesto and various French cheeses he'd picked up in Paris ('a light supper') in his showroom kitchen.

Everything was duplicated there too, including two identical vases of white roses.

Alex completed the 'Home and Garden' look by offering me red wine in a huge balloon glass. He had a matching one, of course.

There was a maid to help clear up, but other than that we were totally alone.

'Where's Jemima?' I asked, realising I hadn't seen Alex's cute little sister in forever. 'I thought she came home at the weekends.'

'No. Not this weekend. It's her birthday tomorrow, so she's been summoned to London.' Alex raised an eyebrow. 'My mother is taking her shopping.'

'Won't she have a birthday party?' I asked.

'My family aren't big on birthday parties,' said Alex. 'They always end in arguments.'

'I don't even know when your birthday is,' I said. 'You never had parties when you were at school.'

'It's November the fifth,' said Alex. 'Firework Night. The date my family home nearly burned down.'

I glanced at his arm then, seeing the twisted scar tissue under his rolled-up shirtsleeve. God. For something like that to happen on your birthday…

'We can eat outside,' said Alex, gesturing to the bi-folding doors and extensive grounds.

I was happy with that, knowing that any mess I made would be far less conspicuous.

'It's a massive garden,' I said, helping the maid carry everything outside.

Alex helped too, ensuring everything was arranged symmetrically.

Halfway through our al fresco meal, I dropped the 'Nick working at Give a Damn' bombshell.

The clink clink of expensive cutlery cutting veal steak was chilling.

'Look, it won't last forever,' I said, breaking the silence. 'Nick has no work ethic.'

'How reassuring,' said Alex. 'Perhaps he'll be fired.'

Clink, clink.

'It's pretty hard to get fired from Give a Damn,' I admitted. 'Actually, Nick's doing quite well. He's already been promoted.'

'Every dog has his day,' said Alex. 'It won't be long until he shows his true colours.'

I asked if he had any more clichés to throw on the pile.

He said, 'A person is known by the company they keep.'

Alex called a taxi to take me home.

Mum was surprised to see me back.

'I thought you were staying the night,' she said.

'So did I.'

Monday, 17th April
Easter Monday

Long day at work.

Nick got promoted to 'Gold Collector' because he recruited an eighteen-year-old student girl silly enough to believe she'll make a career out of charity street-collecting.

We all had to high-five Nick, and cheer, 'Nick, Nick, he's our man, if he can't do it, no one can', while Hari played GOLD! by Spandau Ballet.

Then Nick won today's bonus – a Wispa Gold Easter Egg with special-edition mug.

Tuesday, 18th April

Nick has been promoted again.

He's now a 'Platinum Team Leader.' It means he can build his own team of naïve students.

I have to admit Nick *is* doing pretty well. He got thirty sign-ups today (all women), which put him in the top five collectors. And he's recruited two new collectors (both women).

I suppose it's not a bad job for him, really.

Nick isn't afflicted with moral decency.

Wednesday, 19th April

Email from the estate agents. They're doing a 'block viewing' on Station Cottage tomorrow, so I have to see it with a load of other people.

Althea says this is to make the house look popular.

'They did the same thing when my place was on the market,' she said. 'It was like a bloody theme park. Luckily me and the estate agent bonded over Gypsy punk music, so I got first refusal.'

'But what if I don't bond over anything?' I said.

'You'll have to try other tactics,' said Althea.

I think she was hinting at prostitution, but I'm not that desperate. Yet.

Thursday, 20th April

Woke at 6am for house viewing.

Was probably the first time I've EVER woken up before Daisy, and yet I still managed to be late.

Daisy refused to eat porridge, refused to drink water and refused to wear socks.

After breakfast, I wrestled Daisy to the floor, trying to grab her flailing feet.

She wiggled free, flung off her nappy and threw it onto the kitchen lino.

Unfortunately, somewhere in the struggle, she had pooed in her nappy.

I was running late at this point, so shouted, 'Mum! Daisy's thrown poo on the floor, can you help? I have to go out. I'll owe you a massive favour.'

'No, I bloody can't,' Mum shouted back. 'My parenting days are over. I'm a grandma now. My role is provider of ice creams and toys.'

'Dad!' I shouted. 'Can you help? I promise I'll make it up to you.'

But Dad was doing some delicate calculations, on suspicion that the brewery was 'diddling' him out of half a pint per barrel.

So I cleared up the poo and ended up being late.

Station Cottage was lovely – exactly like the pictures.

There were LOTS of people at the viewing, though. Mostly young couples. Double incomes. But I got the estate agent's name (Janice) and mobile number and rang her immediately after the appointment.

'I'd like to offer on Station Cottage please!' I said, breathless with excitement.

Janice was very coy, refusing to tell me if anyone else had made an offer.

She just said, 'I'll put your offer forward.' In the same way she might say, 'Madonna has received your fan mail.'

I'm just going to try and forget about everything now.

Nothing to do but wait.

Friday, 21st April

Launching a new product at work today – Refugee Flash Sale.

Nick turned up late, vaping from a flashing neon pipe.

When Lloyd tried to explain the new product, Nick said, 'Yeah yeah, look I'm an actor, right? I can play any part.'

But Lloyd warned Nick that street collectors get a lot of abuse on refugee projects.

'Why do they get abuse?' I asked.

'Cause refugees take our jobs,' said Lloyd.

'What are you talking about?' I said. 'We're desperate for people to work at Give a Damn. People quit every day.'

'Foreigners take the *good* jobs,' Lloyd clarified. 'And leave us with the shit. We should send everyone who ain't British home.'

'But half our doctors are poached from overseas,' I insisted. 'If we sent foreigners home, the NHS would crumble.'

'Oh, my days,' Lloyd laughed. 'Refugees aren't *doctors*.'

Couldn't be bothered to argue.

Wonder how Nick will cope if he gets abused? He has a very fragile ego.

I suppose we'll find out tomorrow.

Saturday, 22nd April

Nick threw in his tabard before lunchtime yesterday.

He sent Lloyd an email citing 'psychological abuse' and 'corporate bullying' as reasons for failing to complete the afternoon shift. But a friend of Althea's saw him in Soho with a whisky sour, flicking through the pages of *Stage*.

Nick says he'll return to work as soon as we start collecting for third-world children again. So, I have that joy to look forward to.

Am encouraging Hari to run the refugee project for as long as possible.

Sunday, 23rd April

Mum's adopted a mangy cat she found outside the Spar shop.

She's named the cat 'Sambuca'.

I'm pretty sure Sambuca is bi-polar. One minute he's friendly as anything, sitting on your lap and purring. The next, he turns on you, scratching for no reason.

He's the cat equivalent of Sadie.

'Isn't the pub crowded enough?' I asked Mum.

'Rubbish,' Mum said. 'You and Daisy will be off soon. You'll get that nice little house by the station, I'm sure of it.'

The estate agents still won't tell me if there have been other offers on Station Cottage, though.

Mum has a plan to keep other buyers away.

Putting cat poo in the front garden.

Monday, 24th April

WOOOOOOWWW!

Totally unexpected phone call today – my house offer has been accepted.

I honestly can't believe it.

Swung Daisy round and round.

'We're getting a house!'

Feels very unreal. But GOOD unreal.

Have spent the day looking at pictures of Station Cottage,

working out where I'm going to put things.

Daisy will have her own room.

I'll never miss another train.

No garden, but I have to be realistic. Single mums don't live in mansions.

I asked Mum how long it takes for a house sale to go through.

'Will you be using a solicitor?' she asked.

I told her yes, of course. The estate agents recommended a local firm called Badger Partridge.

'Imagine the longest time you can think of, then double it,' Mum advised. 'Solicitors are stuck in the Victorian age. If it were down to them, they'd send their post by horse and cart.'

Phoned Alex, and he gave me muted congratulations. He couldn't talk long – something about the on-going Amtico-flooring crisis.

Tuesday, 25th April

Will be SO good to move house.

Callum has joined the big dining table, and Mum still takes up one and a half chairs, despite her half-hearted dieting. So meal times are a tight squeeze.

But it won't be long before I have a dining table of my own. Well, a half-sized one, anyway.

Wednesday, 26th April

I walked past Station Cottage on my way home.

The SOLD sign is up.

It's sold to me.

ME!

Thursday, 27th April

Badger Partridge Solicitors are doing 'searches' right now.

Asked Mum what that meant, and she said, 'They'll be wasting time, sending letters back and forth to the local council, asking bloody obvious questions and charging you for the privilege.'

Friday, 28th April

Nick was back at work today, downing Red Bull with the other charity collectors.

'Come on, team,' he was shouting. 'Let's give it 110% today. Woo! Yeah!'

I miss Daisy at work. It hurts so much it's almost physical.

If someone had told me how much pain motherhood would bring, I might have thought twice about it.

Saturday, 29th April

Got back from work to see the sweetest thing – Callum and John Boy singing Daisy a lullaby:

Twinkle twinkle little star, my Dad drives a rusty car …

John Boy's voice went quite falsetto in parts.

When he saw me watching, he went all red and said, 'Callum wanted to sing her a song. You know – for a laugh.'

He's a big softy really, despite the Rambo II survival knife he keeps in his underpants.

Sunday, 30th April

Shopping at Lakeside with Mum, Dad and Brandi.

We couldn't all fit in one car, so I took my Fiat and Mum, and

Dad drove their Honda Civic Shuttle.

When we reached Lakeside, Brandi and Mum went straight to New Look and bought as much neon Lycra as they could lay their hands on.

Dad was tempted by a practical outdoor jacket, but it didn't come with enough pockets.

On the way home, we got stuck on the M25.

The traffic crawled along, and Daisy began bashing her head against the car seat cushioning like a zoo animal, going slowly mad in captivity.

Mum kept phoning from the car behind, complaining that she needed a wee.

She can't hold it in for long these days, because of her diabetes.

'Can you see any bushes from where you are?' she kept asking. 'I'm busting.'

When we finally drove past some shrubbery, I phoned Mum and told her she could pull over soon.

'It's OK, love,' she said. 'I went in my lunchbox back at Junction 14.'

Monday, 1st May
Early May Bank Holiday

Cyber-spied on Nick and Sadie today.

I don't know why – I suppose Nick moving to Great Oakley has shaken me up a bit.

There were loads of pictures on their timelines of Horatio dressed up in various pretentious outfits.

In one, he wore gangster gear, stocking cap over his eyebrows, hands arranged in a 'yo yo' gesture.

Then there was a picture titled: 'Our countryside move, innit', with Horatio dressed in a tweed hat, silk scarf and wax jacket.

Sadie was in some of the pictures, pouting. But they're all headshots – so I'm guessing she's still carrying some baby weight.

Pleased about that.

For a moment, I thought – what if Nick and I did get back together? What would that look like?

Then I realised there were no pictures of Daisy on Nick's wall.

Felt furious with myself, both for looking and caring.

Tuesday, 2nd May

There's been a higher offer made on Station Cottage.

The estate agent phoned to tell me.

'But that shouldn't matter, should it?' I asked. 'The sale is already underway.'

'Under English law, the seller can pull out at any time,' said the estate agent. 'They've asked if you can up *your* offer.'

'But I can't,' I said. 'I'm stretched enough as it is.'

What if I lose the house?

Feel sick at that thought. Have already committed thousands in legal and mortgage fees.

Phoned Alex for advice.

He was appalled about the counteroffer. 'The estate agents shouldn't have allowed it,' he said. 'It's called gazzumping. And it's very much against the rules, if not against the law. Are you sure you want this house?'

I told him I was certain.

'Let me look into things,' said Alex. 'I'll see what I can do.'

Wednesday, 3rd May

John Boy brought his new girlfriend round for tea this evening.

She's a sociology student called Gwen Dubois.

They met outside the Co-op while Gwen was studying litter-dropping habits.

John Boy had been dropping litter.

Gwen's hair is a natural colour, her nails are modestly manicured, and she doesn't wear much makeup.

In short, she's way too classy for John Boy.

At tea, she said 'please' and 'thank you' after everything – even when Callum spilt orange squash on her.

Mum fussed over Gwen, piling her plate high and making her endless cups of tea, then poking her ribs and telling her she needed feeding up.

Both Callum and John Boy gazed at Gwen with soppy eyes.

Callum even asked if Gwen would like to go to the cinema with him.

Gwen smiled her nice, gentle smile and said, 'Oh yes. We can all go together.'

Mum said, 'You don't need to be on best behaviour with us, love – we don't stand on ceremony.'

Gwen said, 'Thank you.'

Then Mum and Brandi took it in turns to interrogate Gwen about previous boyfriends, favourite cleaning products and Quality Street chocolate preferences.

Mum said, 'You will be careful in the bedroom, won't you, love? Trina tells me that John Boy's already had one scare.'

Gwen went bright red and said, '*Thank* you.'

Thursday, 4th May

Oh, the relief!

The estate agent rang – they've disallowed the higher offer on Station Cottage.

They didn't say so explicitly, but I know Alex phoned to tell them off because they mentioned a 'third-party objection'.

Called Alex to say thank you.

'You don't need to thank me,' he said. 'Friends help each other.'

'We're friends, are we?' I asked.

'I like to think so.'

'Not anything more then?'

'Of course we're more,' said Alex, sounding annoyed. 'Much more. But there are...issues. Look, I'm struggling with the Nick Spencer stuff. *Really* struggling. When I pictured us together...he wasn't in that picture. I can't stand that you're tied to that man.'

'But what can I do?' I said. 'He's Daisy's *father*.'

'That title is so often bestowed on unworthy people,' said Alex.

But Nick really does love Daisy in his own way. It would be wrong to keep that love from her.

Why can't Alex see that?

Friday, 5th May

Didn't want to leave Daisy this morning.

When I'm at work, I feel like a piece of my heart is missing.

Daisy is my little treasure, my special little girl, my sunshine.

Does this get easier?

Considered pulling a sickie so I could have a mummy-daughter day, but thought it would be bad form since I've only been back at work a few months.

Sometimes, I wish I were irresponsible like Nick. Life would probably be easier.

Phoned Althea to moan about mummy guilt, but she has the opposite problem.

She's still breastfeeding Wolfgang, so sees way too much of him.

Saturday, 6th May

Walked past the Gables and heard Nick and Sadie rowing.

It was hard to determine exactly what they were shouting about, but I heard, 'sneaking around' and 'lying to me'.

I'm assuming Sadie has worked out Nick is doing something behind her back, i.e. seeking custody of Daisy.

Feel sorry for little Horatio.

At least Daisy has one sane parent.

As I was listening, Nick charged out of the front door with Horatio in the pram, looking sweaty and scared. He did a double-take when he saw me.

'Did you hear all that?' he asked.

'Who are you talking to?' Sadie screeched from the hall. 'It had better not be that fucking leaflet girl with the big tits.'

'I'm going OUT,' Nick shouted back, slamming the door behind him. He pushed the pram down the path and said, 'I was just taking Horry for a walk. Which way are you going?'

'Back to the pub,' I said.

Daisy shouted, 'Little bugger, little bugger!'

We walked towards the pub, Daisy holding onto Horatio's pram.

'I'm getting a visitation schedule together,' said Nick. 'It could be a while before the court makes a decision so…I thought Daisy could come once a month to start off with. How does that sound?'

I said it sounded uncharacteristically reasonable.

'I'm growing up, Jules,' said Nick. 'Learning to take responsibility. I have to, living with Sadie.' Then he looked at Daisy and Horatio and said, 'Look how well these two get on.'

I had to admit, the children weren't killing each other.

When we reached the pub, I told Nick I had to go.

'Are you still seeing Alex Dalton?' he asked.

'That's none of your business,' I said.

'It *is* my business,' said Nick. 'I don't want him around Daisy.'

'You don't get to make those decisions.'

Nick looked stoically into the distance and said, 'I do if the courts give me residency.'

'We've got mediation to get through before court, Nick,' I snapped. 'You have to survive *that* without me ripping your head off.'

Sunday, 7th May

Nick texted to apologise for yesterday. He used big words like 'immature' and 'inappropriate', rather than his usual mess of misspelt half-words and random emojis.

He finished up by saying he was trying to be a good father to both his children and that he was finally growing up.

I texted over my bank account details again, and a short message: Actions speak louder than words.

Monday, 8th May

Daisy took her FIRST STEP!!!

FINALLY!

I have Brandi to thank. She came up with the genius idea of luring Daisy across the room with cheesy Wotsits.

Cried tears of joy watching Daisy do one-step, two-step, unaided, on her chubby little feet.

She looked so happy, all smiles and dribbles and cheesy Wotsit powder over her face.

Brandi and I spent the rest of the afternoon helping Daisy walk back and forth across the living room, while I filmed her and clapped with delight.

My phone keeps flashing warning messages about low storage.

Suppose I could get rid of the (very) long video where Daisy spins around fifty times, then falls over. But in its own way, that's a precious memory too.

Sent Alex an edited video of Daisy walking, and he sent back a smiling emoji.

That means a lot coming from him because he's not an emoji sort of man.

Tuesday, 9th May

Bumped into Dr Slaughter in the supermarket today, while stocking up on three-for-two Wotsit multipacks.

He told me Sadie had been in the surgery yesterday, asking for anti-depressants, and that she suspected Nick was cheating on her.

Now Sadie is in the village, I'm particularly glad that Dr Slaughter ignores the Hippocratic oath and doesn't 'hold with' patient confidentiality.

He's the biggest gossip in Great Oakley, after Mum.

Felt a bit sorry for Sadie. But not that sorry.

It's Horatio I really feel sorry for.

Wednesday, 10th May

Got a phone call from Badger Partridge Solicitors today.

The searches have come back on Station Cottage.

They show contaminated land, flood risk and potential subsidence.

'So, you're nearly good to go!' said the cheery solicitor's assistant.

Freaked out and said I couldn't buy a house that might flood, sink or make us ill. But the assistant said it was OK.

Apparently, the searches are carried out by paranoid council workers who have to cover their backs and cite everything as a risk.

'I can't remember a property that *didn't* come back with a risk of something or other,' she assured me.

Phoned Alex, and he confirmed this was true.

'Half my properties are at severe risk of flooding, and they're nowhere near the river. Don't pay any attention.'

'And the contaminated land?'

'There's a train station nearby.'

'And subsidence?'

'A plot in the village had subsidence once. It was built on an old rubbish dump, but that's miles away.'

Buying property is SO stressful!

Thursday, 11th May

Good news – the sellers have agreed on a 'provisional completion date' for Station Cottage.

It's not until mid-June because the sellers are in long negotiations over who gets the eco light bulbs. But we'll complete way before the next court hearing, so it's all good.

Feels great to have a moving date in sight.

Having my own place will relieve a LOT of stress.

Althea visited today to congratulate me on my impending house purchase.

We took the kids to the freezing cold play park.

Spring seems to have forgotten Great Oakley right now.

The play park was so cold that we were in danger of frostbite from the swing chains, but that didn't stop Wolfgang putting his beefy hands on the swings and trying to chuck them over the metal frame.

Althea was very proud, saying, 'He really sets high goals for himself. Most two-year-olds would give up, but look...he keeps trying.'

An old lady near us said, 'The terrible twos, eh?'

'Oh yeah,' Althea replied nonchalantly. 'I'm so lucky. I mean, you read about kids going mental at this age. But Wolfgang hasn't changed a bit, bless him.

Friday, 12th May

Just got a call from Alex.

A gold-leaf paint disaster has been averted, and he is unexpectedly free tomorrow evening.

The problem is, it's the *Eurovision Song Contest*.

'I've already promised myself to Mum,' I said. 'We always watch *Eurovision* together in the pub.'

'I could always join you,' said Alex. 'I've never watched *Eurovision*. It will be an experience.'

'You want to sit and watch *Eurovision* in our pub?' I said, my voice a little high-pitched.

'Would that be a problem?' Alex asked.

'No,' I mumbled. But I was lying.

It would be a massive problem.

Alex has only ever had small doses of my family.

Coming to the pub on *Eurovision* night is like taking Duffy steroids.

Desperately trying to think of a way to un-invite him. Or stash Mum somewhere.

Saturday, 13th May

I couldn't think of a way to un-invite Alex, so he came to watch *Eurovision*.

The evening started OK.

Alex strolled into the pub in a spotless white polo shirt and pressed navy jeans, and helped me pin up Union Jack bunting.

Then the jukebox broke, and Mum started hitting it with a hammer, shouting, 'Play some fucking Bucks Fizz'.

'Mrs Duffy,' said Alex. 'I'd be careful. Your insurance is unlikely to cover hammering.'

'Insurance companies won't cover anything in this pub,' Mum replied. 'Not since Yorkie ripped the fireplace off the wall. How hard can you hit with a hammer?'

'It's not something I've ever measured,' said Alex, with a small smile. 'I've just been admiring your television. It's extremely large.'

Mum beamed with pride. 'It's literally the biggest one they sell,' she said, patting the screen like a proud parent. 'Brandi lent us it for *Eurovision*. You've got to have a big screen to appreciate all the outfits.'

'Outfits?' Alex asked. 'I thought it was a song contest.'

I explained that *Eurovision* wasn't really about singing, but laughing at other countries – what they wore, how they danced, etc.

Alex said, 'So the *Eurovision* song contest is something you routinely celebrate?'

'Most years,' I said.

'Where's your sister?' Alex asked.

'Out with her new boyfriend,' I told him.

'He's a cut above her usual type,' said Mum, strolling past with an armful of Union Jack paper plates. 'He has a job.'

Dad popped up from the cellar, wearing a Union Jack sunhat, and shouted, 'Would you lovebirds like a drink of something? I've put two new ales on.'

I wanted to be sophisticated and ask for a glass of white wine, but Dad had already poured my usual Guinness. He suggested Alex try this week's guest ale, Hoppy Endings, then began his usual speech about the declining standards of local breweries.

'I expect you find the same thing in your hotels,' Dad asked Alex.

'All these modern brewing methods ruin the taste. Do you go in much for real ales?'

'Not so much,' said Alex. 'But we have seventy different types of whisky from all over the world.'

Dad then began to rant about new whisky distillation processes.

Luckily Mum barked, '*Pour* the man a bloody whisky, Bob. No – not *that* one. The Scottish reserve. Oh, move out the way, let me.'

She poured Alex a double – which was really a quadruple. Mum measures the old-fashioned way, using her fingers. And she has really fat fingers.

'So, Alex,' said Dad, pouring himself a pint of Ginger Tosser. 'You've just got back from *Paris*, I hear?' He said it as if Alex had been to some mystical land.

'I was there earlier in the year, yes,' said Alex.

'You know, I hoped Juliette would learn French,' said Dad. 'But it wasn't meant to be. Laura picked it up in no time. She went on a French exchange and came back fluent.'

'We got that French exchange girl in return,' said Mum. 'She got confused about the toilet, didn't she Bob? And shat in the shower. Well – I'd better get the party food out.'

Mum fetched out plates of sausage rolls and the sweepstake tin.

'You're the guest,' said Mum, thrusting the Quality Street tin of paper slips under Alex's nose. 'So, you get first dibs.'

'On what?' Alex asked.

I explained about the *Eurovision* sweepstake – how we all picked countries to cheer on.

Alex drew Ireland, which was very good.

Mum got the United Kingdom.

'I've got no bloody chance,' she complained. 'Can't I drop it back in the tin and try for Sweden?'

I ended up with Hungary.

'My mother is from Hungary,' said Alex. 'I wonder how they'll do.'

The Hungarian song was performed by a fifteen-year-old boy, who sang about the rainforests dying out.

It didn't do very well.

Dad got Sweden, so, predictably, he won.

Alex and I sat together at the bar holding hands, and Alex said, 'Your family are a lot of fun, Juliette. Just like you. A *lot* of fun.'

'Exactly what every girl wants to be told,' I said. 'That she's fun.'

'It's a better compliment than "beautiful" or "accomplished",' said Alex. 'You're…yourself. There's no front. No PR spin. It's refreshing. The girls I'm used to mixing with… My world can be very serious. Very false, actually. People making acquaintances to further themselves. Women marrying for money. I *love* that you're yourself.'

'Does your mother think I'm after your money?' I asked.

Alex smiled. 'Of course she does. My mother is a social climber. She assumes all women think the way she does.'

'Well I'm definitely not a social climber,' I said. 'If anything, I'm slipping down the class system.'

Alex laughed. 'Stay exactly the way you are. Don't change.'

'If one of us doesn't change,' I said, 'how are we going to build a life together?'

'Maybe I'll change,' said Alex.

But…will he? If my experience with Nick has taught me anything, it's that men absolutely do *not* change. No matter how much you scream at them.

I didn't ask Alex to stay over, and he didn't suggest it.

There was no way it would have worked anyway, with Daisy in the travel cot and Mum roaming about in her Guinness dressing gown, accusing people of 'eating all the fucking bacon'.

Sunday, 14th May

Laura's birthday.

Big sis didn't want a fuss this year, so I just met her for coffee and gave her gifts from the family.

We chose a café in Bloomsbury because Laura's Maternity Health Advocate doesn't think she should travel on trains.

The café was extremely trendy and made partially of wood pallets. It wasn't really suitable for children because there were decorative cactuses everywhere.

Still, Daisy has learned a valuable lesson – nature can be cruel.

Laura will learn the same lesson when she goes into labour.

My big sister looked beautiful in crease-free maternity jeans and a billowing blouse. Her bump is showing a little, but she's still slim.

Over frothy cappuccinos in earthenware mugs, I handed Laura a bag of birthday presents.

I gave her a really pretty framed paper-cut picture. Mum bought her a bottle of Malibu.

Brandi actually remembered this year and gave Laura a giant bag of peanut M&Ms.

Asked Laura what Zach had given her.

Looking down at her decaf coffee, Laura said, 'He gave me this.'

She waved pale, slender fingers at me, and I caught a flash of a pretty antique diamond on her ring finger.

'Laura,' I said. 'Is that an *engagement* ring?'

'Oh, no,' Laura insisted. 'Just…this is a sort of promise type thing. To say we'll get married one day.'

'So, an engagement ring then.'

'Honestly,' Laura continued. 'It's nothing as official as that. Zach just asked me to marry him and popped the ring on. But we haven't set a date.'

'Laura,' I said. 'IT'S AN ENGAGEMENT RING.'

Trust my big sister to be so casual about getting engaged.

If Alex ever asks me to marry him, I'll be shouting about it from the rooftops.

But then again, I'm not sure I'll ever get married. Not after what happened with Nick. In fact, after the mediation sessions, I think I'm allergic to churches.

Phoned Alex to tell him that Laura and Zach are engaged.

He knew already.

I asked, jokingly, if he'd bought a hat for the wedding.

Alex took the question seriously and said he always wore the same headwear to weddings – a silk top hat from Savile Row.

Monday, 15th May

Should start thinking about packing stuff for the house move next month, but realistically I don't have much.

I can probably do it in a morning.

Tuesday, 16th May

Mediation session tomorrow.

Maybe it won't be too bad. Nick is acting quite normal these days. Almost reasonable. Like he's getting his act together.

Haven't told Alex about impending mediation.

He's jealous enough already.

Wednesday, 17th May

Mediation session with Nick.

Nick put forward ridiculous reasons why Daisy should live with him:

+ Daisy could have her own large bedroom at his new house,

complete with antique rocking horse and vintage collection of *Just Williams*.

♦ Daisy would have access to Netflix (Nick has just purchased a subscription), meaning she could watch unlimited *Peppa Pig* episodes.

♦ Nick has shaved his beard off, so Daisy is no longer afraid of him.

Fiona Skelton asked how I felt about *joint* custody as a compromise – a way to meet in the middle.

I said I *felt* it was fucking ridiculous.

'Nick isn't responsible,' I explained. 'He's living in La La Land, playing at happy families. But he can't manage one child for more than a few hours, let alone two. Daisy barely knows him. He abandoned her for six months last year and he STILL HASN'T PAID ANY BLOODY MAINTENANCE!'

Fiona asked if there was anything Nick and I were united about.

I said we were united in our disagreement.

'What about Nick's move to Great Oakley?' Fiona asked. 'Surely that's a positive step. That he wants to be near you and Daisy?'

I had to laugh about that.

'His mum bought him the house,' I said. 'If Nick had his way, he'd be in a Soho apartment.'

'All right, fair play,' said Nick. 'Mum did *buy* the house. But it's part of my long-term plan to get my family back.'

'You're not thinking about *Daisy*,' I said. 'What's best for her? And what about your *other* family? And Sadie? Does she know about this master plan? You two argue all the time. Is *that* good for Daisy?'

We talked about visitation, and once again Nick offered the very reasonable terms of once a month, 'while we sort out the legal shit'.

'That's fine with me,' I said. 'As long as they're supervised visits.

Daisy hardly knows you.'

'You'd be more than welcome to come with her,' said Nick, offering a hopeful smile.

Fiona drafted a visitation schedule, and I thought things were going well.

Then Nick said the schedule had to be checked over by his solicitor.

'Why?' I asked. 'We've just come to an agreement.'

'I don't want to do anything that could jeopardise the residency stuff,' Nick replied.

'You're not going to get residency,' I said, through gritted teeth.

With sad eyes, Fiona filled out the Child Arrangement Order papers for the next court hearing.

Thursday, 18th May

Callum is in trouble at school again.

He's been fighting with older boys.

'Did you win?' Brandi asked him.

'Yes,' said Callum. 'He started crying first.'

Brandi patted Callum on the head. 'Good boy.'

When Brandi left the room, I gave Callum the good aunty lecture.

'Listen,' I said. 'You can't go around hitting people. If kids say things, you have to just ignore it.'

'Even if they use really bad words and they're bigger than you?' Callum asked.

'Yes.'

'Can I use bad words back?' Callum wanted to know.

'No,' I said. 'You just have to walk away. Two wrongs don't make a right.'

Callum considered this. 'But I did *really* well in that fight,' he said. 'I hit a big boy who walks to school by himself. My girlfriend was really happy I stood up for her.'

'Hang on a minute,' I said. 'You have a girlfriend?'

Callum beamed with pride. 'I have now.'

Friday, 19th May

Went to Great Oakley Library with Althea today.

We didn't read any books because Daisy and Wolfgang spent the whole time fighting on the colourful rug.

Daisy started it by using Wolfgang as an unwilling walking frame.

Wolfgang kept shouting, 'Arg! Arg!' and trying to push her off. Then he snatched books from the big pile Daisy had built.

I have to say, Daisy's certainly learning to hold her own.

She looked murderous when she saw *Maisie's Nursery* in Wolfgang's beefy paw, and sunk her teeth right into his wrist.

Wolfgang had to beat her off with a hardback copy of *African Children's Tales*.

VERY excited about moving into Station Cottage now – less than a month to go!

Saturday, 20th May

John Boy wants to propose to Gwen. I suppose it's the next logical step – he's already had a rose tattooed on his arm for her.

'Don't you think it's a bit soon?' I said.

'But I love her,' John Boy replied.

'Do you think she'll say yes?' I asked.

'I doubt it,' said John Boy. 'But if you don't ask, you don't get.'

It's very brave he's willing to go headlong into heartbreak. But I suppose he's still young.

In a few years, he'll have had all the spirit beaten out of him, just like the rest of us.

Sunday, 21st May

Alex has invited Daisy and me to the grand opening of his flagship gym next week.

The gym is in London, just off Leicester Square.

'It had better be the best gym chain I've ever seen,' I told Alex. 'Good enough to have you leaving the country every five minutes.'

Alex promised me it certainly would be. And I'm sure he's right because I've only ever been to Fitness First.

Alex told me to pack swimming stuff because there are three different pools.

Monday, 22nd May

Work today.

Had to log all the charity collectors' wages, because I've finally convinced Cheryl, the accounts manager, that Lloyd can't count.

Hating work right now. Plus, I'm getting suspicious about how Hari runs things. A lot of these figures don't add up. I'm beginning to think Hari hired someone who couldn't count on purpose.

When I talked to Hari about numbers, he put an aftershave-fumed arm around my shoulder and said, 'Don't overcomplicate things. Life is simple. That's what all these people with degrees don't understand.'

'I have a degree,' I said.

'Good for you, Juliette,' said Hari. 'But don't let it go to your head.'

Tuesday, 23rd May

Nick's birthday today. He laid on a guilt trip at work, while I was body-slamming the vending machine, trying to dislodge a stuck packet of Hula Hoops.

'When can I see Daisy boo again?' Nick whined. 'I miss her so much. It's my *birthday*. At least let me see her on my birthday.'

'Are we going to do this again?' I said. 'How many times have I told you? THINK ABOUT YOUR BLOODY DAUGHTER, NOT YOURSELF. Give me the signed-off visitation schedule, and give Daisy some stability.'

Nick gave me big puppy-dog eyes. 'But my solicitor is still looking it over. Jules, I've been so low. Sadie kicks me in the balls over and over.'

I didn't know if he meant literally or figuratively.

'Can't you see I've changed?' Nick said. 'I'm in a nice place now. In Great Oakley. Just like you wanted.'

'Your mum bought you that house, Nick,' I said. 'To me, that's no change at all. A big change would be you paying maintenance. Actual money from your own pocket for your daughter. Without a court having to tell you to do it.'

'How about I pay you a few hundred quid this week,' said Nick. 'You know, to try and get things on the right track.'

'That would be a good start,' I agreed. 'You've got my bank details.'

But I'm not holding my breath.

Wednesday, 24th May

Hell just froze over.

Nick put two hundred pounds into my bank account.

I can't believe it.

Maybe his mum gave him birthday cash or something.

My nice side wants to think he's trying to be responsible.

My cynical side wonders what he's playing at.

Still – great to have a bit of extra cash before the house move. I'm sure there will be expenses I haven't thought of.

Another shock today – Gwen has accepted John Boy's marriage proposal.

She wants a long engagement, but even so, John Boy couldn't be happier.

He's already planning his wedding-ring tattoo and talking about hiring an Elvis suit for the big day.

Thursday, 25th May

Wow.

Alex's new gym was AMAZING.

Daisy LOVED the swimming pool.

Alex wasn't going to swim with us at first. But then I splashed him, so he grabbed a pair of £50 swimming trunks from the gift shop, paid the lifeguard to hold his Rolex and jumped in.

Then Alex and I played with Daisy, splashing her and pushing her through the water like a torpedo.

'TorPEEdo!' I shouted, as I jetted Daisy across the pool to Alex.

'Paedo! Paedo!' Daisy shouted happily.

A lot of men backed away from us.

After swimming, Alex showed us around the spa and the children's fitness area, then took us for lunch in the directors' lounge.

'Do you think Daisy enjoyed herself?' Alex wanted to know, over chunky tomato soup and chargrilled bread. 'It's OK for children here, don't you think?'

'She loved it,' I said. 'How could she not?'

'I'm pleased,' said Alex.

And it was sweet because you could tell he really was.

Friday, 26th May

Have agreed to let Nick see Daisy this weekend.

His visitation schedule still hasn't been 'checked over' by Penny Castle, but Fiona says we can 'informally' agree to a visit in the meantime.

I know Nick misses his daughter, and I don't want to keep her from him out of spite. Daisy needs a relationship with her dad.

Nick is going to meet us tomorrow at the pub, and we'll take it from there.

Saturday, 27th May

Nick arrived *on time* to see Daisy.

Couldn't believe it.

I totally wasn't expecting punctuality and hadn't even got Daisy dressed.

Nick had to wait in the pub for half an hour, while I stuffed Daisy into a pretty flowery dress.

And guess what?

Nick DIDN'T order himself a pint.

'Are you feeling OK?' I asked as I carried Daisy into the pub. 'It's gone noon. You're in a pub. And you're not drinking.'

'I don't drink much these days,' said Nick. 'You can't have a hangover when you've got kids to look after, can you? Daisy boo, Daisy boo!'

'You were hung-over loads of times after we had Daisy,' I pointed out.

Nick looked sad. 'I wasn't coping well back then. I'm not proud of myself, but I checked out. I let you be the adult. But now Horry's come along, I finally get it. It's time to grow up, isn't it?'

Nick growing up? Such a weird thought.

Sunday, 28th May

Alex phoned.

I told him Nick came by yesterday, and Alex went quiet. Then he said, 'Has the visitation schedule been finalised yet?'

'No,' I told him. 'But Nick paid me maintenance this month. Look, this isn't about what he *should* have done. I was doing it for Daisy.'

'He's treating you with no respect,' said Alex. 'Asking to see his daughter whenever he feels like it. No schedule. No warnings.'

'There's going to be a schedule,' I said. 'But this is an informal meeting. We both agreed to it.'

'This is marvellous, Juliette,' said Alex. 'You've gone from playing his mother to being a doormat.'

'I'm neither of those things,' I said.

'Oh? Agreeing to an *informal* visitation? Where is your power in that situation, Juliette? And what about Daisy? This is all very inconsistent for her.'

Which hit a nerve, because Alex is right.

'Daisy needs to see her father,' I said.

'And her father needs boundaries,' said Alex. 'You should have told him he couldn't see Daisy until the visitation schedule was finalised. Nick Spencer is totally spoiled, Juliette. His mother fawns over him. And he's playing you. He needs rules, and you need to start laying them down.'

'This isn't your business,' I said. 'I can make my own decisions about my daughter.'

'It *is* my business. Because Nick Spencer wants you back in his life. And he's using this situation to try and get what he wants. You'd have to be an idiot not to see it.'

I went quiet then.

'Look, I'll be travelling again soon,' said Alex. 'But I'd like to see you before I go. A lunch somewhere, perhaps? Near Great Oakley?'

'How long will you be away for?' I asked.

'A while. I have over 10,000 people working for me right now. They can be rather demanding.'

In the end, we arranged lunch on Tuesday, just before Alex jets off.

Another snatched date with a man who has 10,000 other people in his life.

Monday, 29th May
Spring Bank Holiday

Nick came to work wearing black-rimmed glasses and carrying a brown envelope.

'This is for you, Julesy,' he said, passing me the envelope. 'It's the visitation schedule. Everything's been looked over. We're good to go.'

I opened the envelope, expecting some outrageous demands to have been added to our original agreement.

But no.

Nick has asked to see Daisy on the last Saturday of the month, until the court makes a custody decision, just like we discussed.

Sadie will take Horatio to see her mother on that day, so it will just be Nick and Daisy. And I'm welcome to stay if I choose.

All very reasonable.

'This sounds fine,' I said. 'Do you want me to bring Daisy to you. Or ...'

'I can pick her up if you like,' said Nick. 'And drop her off. I got a new car last week. A Volvo.'

I was so shocked I dropped my armful of neon tabards. 'You have a Volvo? *You?*'

'I have new priorities now, Julesy. A Volvo is the safest car on the road.'

'What does Sadie think about that?'

Nick shrugged. 'She doesn't like any of my decisions right now. Things are…fragile.'

'Listen, you understand I'll accompany Daisy during the visits, don't you?' I said. 'At least at first. She might freak out, otherwise.'

'I was hoping you'd want to be there,' said Nick.

'Stop it, Nick,' I said. 'If you get flirty, I'm not signing anything.'

'Sorry,' Nick said, pushing up his glasses. 'Bad habit.'

Then he gathered his team together and had a serious chat about goal setting and positive thinking.

Afternoon

Alex's secretary just phoned.

She's made a lunch reservation somewhere called the Chimney House – a Michelin star restaurant just outside Great Oakley.

'Is there any sort of dress code?' I asked.

'It's a countryside setting,' she said. 'So…do you have any Laura Ashley?'

Looked through my wardrobe for suitable 'lunch with Alex' dresses.

Have decided on a nice green jumper (clean!), skinny jeans (clean!) and brown riding-type boots.

That's kind of a countryside look, right?

Tuesday, 30th May

Lunch with Alex.

The Chimney House was on the river, surrounded by willow trees.

It was quiet as a library and full of old people clinking wine glasses against false teeth.

Seemed an odd restaurant for Alex to have chosen, especially since the manager was so unhappy to see Daisy.

'We don't have the facilities for *such* a young child, madam,' he said, accosting me at the door. 'The child's age should have been given when making the booking.'

'It's OK,' I said. 'I can just tie her to a chair with my scarf. She won't fall off.'

The manager looked horrified. '*Tie* your child to a *chair?*'

'Look, I'll show you.' I attempted to attach a wiggling Daisy to an upholstered chair with my scarf.

The manager blinked quickly. 'You *cannot*…madam I *really* think… Wait, I'll try to find something more suitable.'

He reappeared with a solid-oak high chair.

While I was trying to get Daisy's legs through the holes, Alex arrived.

He was smart as always and unsmiling, casting his eyes around the restaurant.

'Juliette,' he said when he saw me. 'Why have they put you at this table? We're over there. Anya is here already.'

He pointed across the restaurant, and my smile froze. I then understood why he'd chosen such an old-lady place to eat.

Catrina Dalton sat at a window table, smiling at her reflection in the glass, white-blonde hair in a shiny French pleat.

She wore a black cocktail dress with shoulder pads and glittered with diamonds. It's true what they say about fashion – if you hold on long enough, it all comes around again.

'We're having lunch with your mother?' I said, hoping I didn't sound as horrified as I felt.

'Didn't my secretary tell you?' said Alex. 'I asked Anya to join us.'

I should have said, 'How delightful that your mother is here!' But all I could manage was a flat, 'Your secretary didn't tell me.'

'Anya's not been well recently, Juliette,' said Alex, pointedly. 'I know she can be difficult, but she's still my mother.'

Alex asked for the high chair to be moved, then led us to Catrina's table.

'Anya.' Alex stooped to kiss Catrina's taut, white cheek.

'Alex, *darling*.' Catrina tugged at his sleeve. 'Don't you look *handsome*.'

'How are you?' Alex asked.

'I am *sad* today darling. Carlos is being difficult. These young boys don't know how to be gentlemen.'

Catrina noticed me then, pinched nose twitching, brown-green eyes flitting between my face and outfit. 'Who is *zis*?'

'This is Juliette,' said Alex. 'You've met her before. And her daughter. At Westminster Cathedral. Remember? I've told you about Juliette many times.'

Catrina's eyes went far away, as if searching for a distant memory.

'Nice to see you again,' I said, pushing Daisy's high chair up to the table.

'Juliette is Laura Duffy's sister,' said Alex, pulling out my chair. 'And this is her daughter, Daisy. She reminds me of Jemima at that age. Don't you think?'

Catrina gave a passing waiter a dazzling smile. 'A Martini, Tony. VERY cold.'

'How are you?' I asked. 'Alex said you haven't been feeling well.'

Catrina gave me a film-star smile. '*Zank* you darling. I am love-sick more than anything else. My heart is *broken* when I am alone.'

'I didn't realise Carlos would be away,' said Alex. 'You should have told me.'

Catrina waved a dismissive hand. 'I'm too busy to call people. Alex, why do I bother with all this *charity*? Nobody appreciates it, and *nothing* is glamorous any more. Nobody dresses like they used to.' Then she put diamond-ringed fingers over mine and said, 'My son will never marry you, you know.'

I gave a shocked laugh.

'Anya.' Alex frowned.

'I'm only trying to help the girl,' said Catrina. 'What's her name…
Juliette? Didn't you say she wasn't marriage material?'

I turned to Alex. 'Did you say that?'

'I said some aspects of your life were…undesirable,' said Alex.
'Nick Spencer being the key undesirable.'

'You said I wasn't *marriage* material?'

'Men can be very insensitive when it comes to marriage,' said
Catrina. 'They don't understand what it means to a woman. But *I*
understand. You want the fairy tale, of course. But Alex will never
be your handsome prince.'

'*Anya.*' Alex's voice was thunderous. 'You're on dangerous
ground.'

Catrina squeezed my hand. 'My heart has broken a thousand
times. But still, I keep looking for love. No matter what, *keep
looking.*' She fixed me with earnest, sparkling eyes.

Then she sprang back and took a sip of the Martini that had
been placed by her elbow. '*Vell.* Tell me all the news, Alex. I want to
hear all about your father's latest acquisition. And I don't mean in
business. This new girlfriend of his…'

'Do you know what?' I said, dropping my napkin on the plate.
'I'd rather eat at home.'

'Juliette.' Alex looked at me meaningfully. 'Sit down. Please. My
mother is…this is my *mother.*'

'Isn't anyone going to ask me about my new necklace?' Catrina
asked. 'Carlos bought it.'

I stood up then, unthreading Daisy's chubby legs from the high
chair.

'I bloody well *am* marriage material,' I told Alex. 'And I would
never talk about you like that to my parents. Daisy. Say bye bye.'

'BYE BYE!' Daisy shouted, grabbing two crisp white rolls from
the breadbasket. She stuffed one roll into her mouth and threw the

other at an elderly female diner.

I manhandled Daisy out of the restaurant, as she shouted, 'Did POO Mummy. Did POO!'

She certainly picks her moments.

As I was changing Daisy's nappy on the car seat, I thought Alex might come out after me.

But he didn't.

Feel so hurt.

Marriage isn't the be-all-and-end-all to me, but that's not the point.

If Alex doesn't think I'm good enough to marry, then this is a waste of time.

I just have to eat lots of cake and get over it.

Wednesday, 31st May

I've been ignoring Alex's calls – ten of them since lunch yesterday.

We have nothing more to say to each other.

Laura had an antenatal visit today.

She didn't go to the doctors like I did. Instead, a private maternity specialist visited her in Bloomsbury, where she's now living with Zach.

Daisy wasn't *too* bad on the train up to London. Although a lot of travellers moved to the other carriage.

God – the big city feels so cutthroat when you have kids. I mean, people literally trample over you to get where they're going.

I had to form a barricade, threatening people with the chunky Maclaren wheels so Daisy could stumble up the underground steps by herself.

Part of me considered texting Nick to tell him Daisy and I were in London, but I decided against it. Daisy would be a nightmare around rattling buckets of money.

It's a whole new world to me – Nick and I being civil to each other.

Meeting Laura and Zach at their Bloomsbury townhouse was like visiting the pages of *Hello* magazine.

The couple stood on the doorstep to greet us – Zach, tall, blond and ruddy-cheeked; Laura with gleaming skin and shiny hair.

Zach gave Daisy a fluffy Steiff teddy bear with a giant silk bow, then welcomed us inside.

I bumped Daisy's pram up the stone steps, swearing when the Maclaren wheels caught under the overhangs (bloody Victorians – they *had* prams back then, surely, they knew to design better steps?), and smiling apologetically at the solicitors in the basement office below.

In the gleaming kitchen, Laura served homemade wheatgrass cookies. She apologised for the bitter aftertaste but, as she said, my insides will thank me.

Zach put a proud arm around Laura's shoulder and said, 'I hope you'll forgive this unplanned pregnancy. I would have liked to do things properly – marriage first and all that – but I have to tell you I feel like the luckiest man alive.'

Zach doesn't need to defend himself to me. Nick and I weren't even engaged when Daisy was born. At least Zach has been decent enough to shove a ring on Laura's finger.

Private healthcare is a world away from the NHS.

For a start, the maternity specialist turned up on time. She also sprayed the room with lavender oil and gave Laura a light head massage to relax her for the appointment.

After a detailed log of Laura's diet and daily activities, the specialist administered twenty different tests, including one for vitamin deficiency and blood platelet count. Then she gave Laura a sack of expensive organic vitamins to take and signed her up for a full-body pregnancy massage.

I remember my first NHS pre-natal visit.

The midwife asked if I was pregnant.

I said yes.

She said I should 'avoid cigarettes, alcohol and blue cheese if possible, or at least cut down'. Then she told me to drink a bottle of Lucozade before my next appointment for glucose-testing purposes.

And I had to buy my own Lucozade.

Was desperate to ask Zach about Alex, but resisted.

Not marriage material!

How *dare* he.

Thursday, 1st June

Brandi's birthday.

Don't have much disposable income right now due to impending house move, so bought Brandi a trio of nail polish in fluorescent shades and a box of Maltesers.

She was delighted – much more so than when I buy her those expensive pampering products.

At breakfast, she announced (while eating Maltesers) that she would be heading into London with some single-mum friends and would be back very late.

Nana Joan, who'd travelled over on her electric wheelchair to see the birthday girl, said, 'Well if Brandi's off out with her friends, will someone take me shopping?'

At Nana's time of life, her social life revolves around funerals, and she needed a new mourning dress.

Took Nana to Debenhams, and steered her towards conservative outfits, but she refused all of them, saying, 'Blondes should never wear black.'

In the end, Nana chose a peacock-blue prom dress with a lace panel over the cleavage, rainbow-feather fascinator and four-inch red heels. Then she popped into the hairdressers for 'a bit of a do before the big day'.

When I picked Nana up a few hours later, she had waist-length curly blonde hair extensions.

Nana loved her new look, throwing her hair extensions from one shoulder to the other.

'They've taken ten years off me, don't you think?' she asked.

I lied and said yes.

It would have been cruel to say she looked like Dog the Bounty Hunter.

Have just realised that sometime THIS month I will be the proud owner of Station Cottage.

Good news, after all this Alex stuff.

Onwards and upwards.

Friday, 2nd June

Weird day.

Got a phone call from Sadie, while playing hide and seek with Daisy.

It was a short game because Daisy thinks if she closes her eyes no one can see her.

When I saw Sadie's number flashing on the screen, I thought, *She's found out about Nick seeking residency. She's going to demand the truth, and frankly, I think she deserves to know – for Horatio's sake if anything.*

Foolishly picked up the phone.

Sadie was in hysterics. 'Jules! I can't cope anymore. I'm in old-person countryside hell. Nick's Mum is round *all* the time. If she brings another wooden duck ornament into our living room, I'm going to scream. I really need someone to talk to. *Please*, Jules. I'm so lonely.'

It was the phone call I deserved last year when Nick and Sadie moved in together. I should have felt tremendously smug. But all I could think about was poor Horatio.

'You need to find another friend,' I told Sadie. 'And try not to steal her boyfriend this time.'

'I can't make friends here,' Sadie sobbed. 'I tried the playgroup, but it smelt like old people. They didn't even serve real coffee. And some little kid filled my handbag with dried macaroni.'

'I can't help you, Sadie,' I told her. 'You broke all the rules of friendship. You're on your own.'

Hung up. Then had a bit of a moment, wondering if I should go round for Horatio's sake.

Sadie did sound on the edge.

In the end, I phoned Nick.

'Sadie needs you,' I told him. 'She's having a meltdown.'

Nick's response was casual. 'She's always having a meltdown.'

'I think this is pretty serious,' I insisted. 'She phoned me.'

Silence.

Then Nick said, 'Fucking hell, I'd better get round there. Hold the espresso mate.'

Saturday, 3rd June

Literally counting down the days now until the Station Cottage sale completes.

According to the solicitors, there are a few admin bits to do, but we're basically good to go. Everything is fine on the seller's side too.

Woo woo!

Sunday, 4th June

Laura's second scan tomorrow.

I remember seeing Daisy for the first time, via ultrasound.

It was a bit of a let-down – just a blurry white blob with a giant alien head.

Laura's scan is at the same private hospital where Madonna had baby Rocco.

Apparently, they have a wine list and resident chef.

Laura has already been emailed tomorrow's menu, which includes Cromer crab and samphire dumplings.

Monday, 5th June

Travelled into London for Laura's scan.

Zach was in tears before we'd even got into the ultrasound room.

'Our baby will be the size of a grape now,' he told Laura, reading the leather-bound literature.

It's ALWAYS fruit, isn't it?

Zach burst into tears when my blobby niece/nephew appeared on the ultrasound screen.

He kissed Laura's hand and said, 'Well done, darling,' over and over.

Nick and I had to wait an hour for our first ultrasound, in a litter-strewn waiting room by a sign that said:

'We would like to remind expectant parents that this is a medical procedure, NOT a celebration.

You may get bad news.

No extended family members or buffet food please.'

Once again, I resisted asking Zach about Alex.

Alex has called loads, but I don't answer.

If I'm not good enough to marry, what does he need to talk about anyway?

Tuesday, 6th June

Fucking hell.

Give a Damn has been closed down, pending an HMRC investigation.

Arrived at work this morning to find the building locked up and all the staff outside, staring forlornly at the electric-blue walls.

No one knows where Hari is.

I thought Nick would be f-ing and blinding, being a drama queen as usual. But he was comforting his team and rallying everyone for an emergency Starbucks meeting.

I asked Lloyd about pay cheques, and he snorted, 'Pigs might fly.'

Phoned the mortgage company on the way home to tentatively enquire about the employment documents, and how urgently they were needed.

The mortgage company told me *very* urgently, as the mortgage couldn't go through without them.

Asked what would happen if I changed my job.

The mortgage company said a change of job could cause the mortgage application to fail, especially if I took a job on an oil rig or as a bicycle courier.

'Can't you just hold off changing jobs until the application is finished?' the mortgage girl asked.

'Thanks for your time!' I said brightly and hung up.

Got back to the pub, cuddled Daisy, had a bit of a cry, then started applying for jobs.

Very worried about the mortgage. It all hinges on proof of income. So, if I don't have any income …

Wednesday, 7th June

Spent the day dragging Daisy from temp agency to temp agency, begging for employment. But no one was hiring.

Temp agencies are predominantly staffed by icy blonde twenty-somethings who look down their long, pointy noses at you, make you fill out twenty-page application forms, then tell you they don't have any jobs.

I think having a toddler with me wasn't a good move, especially when I had to pull paperclips out of Daisy's mouth. But Mum and Dad were both working, and Brandi was doing her course.

I did consider asking Nick for help, but a quick Facebook-spy told me he was out with Sadie, walking around the Tate Modern looking miserable and taking selfies.

Evening

Alex turned up at the pub, just after tea. 'Juliette. I heard the news.'

I burst into tears, right on the doorstep.

'Thanks for coming,' I blubbered.

Alex said, 'I can't say I'm surprised. That company was clearly on its last legs. At any rate, this is no time to overreact. You have a challenge ahead of you. Wallowing won't get you anywhere.'

Overreact! Wallowing!

I came to my senses then.

'What are you even doing here, Alex? After what you said to your mother...'

Alex thrust hands into his pockets. 'I didn't tell Anya you weren't marriage material. That was her...take on things. I said there were issues. There *are* issues.'

'A relationship is about being there for each other,' I said. 'You're never in the country more than five minutes, so what's the point?'

'Juliette, that's ridiculous.'

'No,' I said. 'What's ridiculous is pretending we have a relationship.'

'I'll talk to you another time,' said Alex. 'When you've calmed down.'

Calmed down. The words least likely to calm you down.

Alex left then, which I found even more infuriating.

Mum says I can work at the pub for a bit until I find something more suitable.

The wages aren't much, but at least I'll have money coming in.

Thursday, 8th June

The mortgage company just called. They need my employment documents URGENTLY, before releasing funds for the house purchase.

I'm terrible at lying, so ended up blurting out the truth.

'So, you're working in a pub now?' the mortgage woman asked. 'Does that mean you're on minimum wage?'

I had to admit that yes, it is a minimum-wage job. Although I will get free Guinness and crisps.

They are now 'reconsidering my application' because my current income doesn't match my former income.

Don't know what's going to happen, but have this sickly feeling in my stomach.

Hoped Alex would call today, but he hasn't. I suppose he's still waiting for me to calm down.

Patronising sod.

Brandi said, 'If *he* don't call YOU, find someone new.' Then she grinned like she'd just made an amazing scientific discovery, and posted the phrase on Instagram with a picture of a snowy mountain.

Friday, 9th June

Nick called round this morning, wearing faux glasses and his smartest leather jacket.

Daisy seemed pleased to see him, shouting, 'Baddy! Baddy!'

'I just wanted to see how you were doing,' said Nick. 'I know the Give a Damn thing must have come as a shock.'

'To all of us,' I said.

'Do you want me to take Daisy for a bit?' Nick asked. 'So, you can do some job-hunting?'

Was taken aback by his thoughtfulness, and said so.

'I'm getting there, Julesy,' said Nick, offering a hopeful smile.

Thanked Nick for the childminding offer, but still don't trust him alone with Daisy. He seems to be doing OK with Horatio, but I'm not sure he knows how to handle a child that moves around.

'Keep in touch,' said Nick, with a salute. 'Let me know how the job-hunting goes, yeah?'

Afternoon

Job applications have to be the most frustrating thing on the planet. Why do so many companies insist on handwritten forms?

Callum has learned to count up to three hundred now, meaning I keep writing my phone number wrong on job applications.

It doesn't look good.

Am using my old Canary Wharf address for correspondence, because Mum and Dad's pub raises too many questions.

Nick is going to forward post for me. He stays in Canary Wharf whenever he and Sadie have a row, so he's there quite a bit.

Saturday, 10th June

Althea came over to help me fill out more job applications.

'Why do they ask so many stupid questions?' she asked. 'Who

gives a shit what your hobbies are?'

I'm sure applications weren't this involved when I left university. Of course, back then I didn't have a baby trying to eat the paperwork.

'The best way to get jobs is through friends,' said Althea. 'Wolfy's Dad is a *shit* keyboard player, but his uncle knew Mick Jagger so…'

Althea and her ex-husband are having some problems because he hasn't seen Wolfgang in months.

Apparently, Wolfgang kicks his dad's shins whenever he visits.

'He needs to man up,' said Althea. 'If he can't handle Wolfgang now, what's going to happen when he's a teenager?'

God – that's a scary thought.

Sunday, 11th June

Nick just came by and handed me three rejection letters.

Feel like utter shit, and am having sleepless nights about my impending property purchase.

What's going to happen to Station Cottage if I don't get a job?

Monday, 12th June

Two more rejection letters, care of Nick.

Things are getting desperate.

Took Daisy for a walk this morning and passed Station Cottage.

Daisy said, 'House! Our house mummy!'

It was her most complete sentence to date.

'Yes, sweetheart,' I spluttered. 'Our house.'

Had a bit of a cry then, but didn't let Daisy see.

That's another hard part of being a mother.

The brave face.

Tuesday, 13th June

Got a letter from the mortgage company.

'On careful consideration, we are rejecting your mortgage application.'

Phoned up in a panic, begging them to reconsider.

But they wouldn't.

'What if I got a better paying job tomorrow?' I asked.

'You'd have to go through the application all over again,' said the call handler. 'I'm not sure your seller would want to wait that long.'

Wednesday, 14th June

Phone call from Belle Homes.

'The mortgage company won't release funds,' said Clarke. 'Are you still continuing with the purchase?'

I did a lot of fast talking, saying that everything was just on hold and that as soon as I got a new job, the mortgage would progress. But I could tell Clarke wasn't really listening – I could hear him typing on his keyboard.

'There's been a lot of interest in this property,' he said eventually. 'The buyer wants to complete sooner rather than later. We'll have to contact other interested parties.'

Thursday, 15th June

I'm still holding onto a dim hope that I can sort everything out with Station Cottage before we go back to court.

If I get another job in the city. If no one else buys Station Cottage in the meantime. If I reapply for a mortgage …

If, if, if …

With just under a month until the next court hearing, I need a miracle to happen.

Will start praying.

First shift in the pub tonight.

I haven't worked behind the bar since I was a teenager, so Mum wrote me a reminder list:

+ No vaping inside OR outside the premises. This is a pub, not a youth club. Smoke properly or don't smoke at all.

+ Polish Malik is forbidden from using the jukebox.

+ If Mick tells you he's having a heart attack, check his pork scratchings intake. The last time we called an ambulance, it turned out to be indigestion.

+ The 'last orders' baseball bat is located next to the pickled egg jar.

+Don't let Yorkie near the pickled eggs.

Friday, 16th June

Very tired this morning and did a bad-mum thing.

Plonked Daisy in front of *In the Night Garden* for two hours, while I filled in application forms.

Accidentally wrote 'Ninky Nonk' as a previous job title.

Saturday, 17th June

SOOO tired.

Worked in the bar until midnight last night.

Lucky John Boy was on shift too, because Yorkie was fighting-drunk.

Usually, Mum is the only one who can keep him in line, but John Boy did a good job – luring Yorkie outside with Scampi Fries, then locking the door and calling his mad girlfriend to take him home.

We ended up closing the pub late, by which time John Boy's

prosthetic leg was giving him grief.

John Boy took his sleeves and leg off, and his stump was red raw, with two huge, angry blisters.

'Bollocks,' said John Boy.

Apparently, the stump, once aggravated, takes a while to heal.

I asked John Boy if he could hop around, but he said phantom leg syndrome means he ends up falling over a lot – especially after drinking four pints of Stella, which he had done on shift. The NHS won't give him another wheelchair after he wrecked the last one in a downhill go-cart race.

I helped John Boy to the sofa upstairs and cleaned his stump, putting Savlon on the worst bits.

John Boy was very insistent that I *lay* his prosthetic leg *horizontal* on the carpet. Apparently, it startles him at night if stored in a standing position. He sometimes mistakes it for a knife-wielding Odd Job from James Bond and tries to wrestle it into a restraining hold.

More job applications, while Daisy watched TV.

Daisy said another sentence!

'Iggle Piggle, Iggle Onk.'

Texted everyone I knew, and put a picture of Iggle Piggle on Facebook.

Sunday, 18th June

Alex phoned asking if I'd 'calmed down yet'.

This provoked me to rage.

'You've got a bloody cheek,' I shouted. 'After what you said to your mum.'

'Have you been seeing Nick Spencer?' Alex asked.

'Yes, I bloody have,' I said. 'And you should have no opinion on it since I'm not marriage material.'

'I knew this would happen,' said Alex darkly. 'The minute my back is turned, you see him. I should have called sooner.'

'So why didn't you?' I asked.

Alex said he was giving me space.

Why do men think women want space?

WE WANT ATTENTION!

Monday, 19th June

Met Nick for coffee in Great Oakley today.

He had another pile of job rejections for me.

Weird him living nearby.

Nick asked about Alex.

'I don't really know what's happening,' I said.

'If he's so fantastic, how come you hardly ever see him?' Nick asked.

It was a fair question.

One I couldn't answer.

Poor John Boy still has blisters on his stump.

He had to sit on a bar stool during his afternoon shift and reach glasses with Callum's monster grabber claw.

Tuesday, 20th June

Someone else has offered on Station Cottage.

Feel totally and utterly gutted.

Mum found me blubbing in the kitchen, and made me her patented super-duper hot chocolate, made with instant hot chocolate, milk, single cream, double cream, Lyle's golden syrup and mashed-up bourbon biscuits, plus a shot of brandy. She topped it with whipped cream and broken up Aldi disco biscuits.

The drink was so sugary it made my teeth itch, and it didn't make me feel any better.

Althea texted me some photos – one of bombed-out houses in Syria, another of refugees camping in Calais.

'Count yourself lucky you have a roof over your head,' she wrote. 'These people have nothing.'

I told her Daisy's life could be ruined soon.

Althea wrote back, 'Live in the moment. It's not ruined now, is it?'

It's true that Daisy and I are warm, well fed and together at this moment in time.

But what if the courts decide Daisy should live with her irresponsible father and crazy girlfriend? Even if it were only joint residency, Daisy would still be so frightened and unsettled living at Nick's house without me.

Can't stop crying.

Wednesday, 21st June

Am throwing myself into work and job applications in the hope of demonstrating to the courts that I am a responsible mother.

If I get a good job and offer on another house before the court hearing, Jeremy Samuels says it will, 'carry some weight'.

Nick turned up at the pub last night, wearing a suit, faux glasses and red-laced brogues.

'I had to get out of the house,' he said, over a pint of soda water and orange juice. 'Sadie is just so fucking insane. I'm *literally* living in a mental house.'

'And this is the house you want Daisy to live in?' I said.

'Sadie won't be around for long,' said Nick dismissively. 'She packs her bags every other day.'

'Nick, you are a selfish, spoiled child stamping your feet to get what you want,' I shouted. 'Think of your daughter, for once in your life. Daisy needs a stable environment with a mother who loves her.'

'The courts will know what's best,' said Nick. 'Let's see what they say.'

Went quiet then. Nick doesn't know about Station Cottage yet.

Commented on Nick's smart appearance and non-alcoholic drink choice.

'Yeah,' he said, looking down at his suit. 'Henry's giving me a chance as factory manager. It's boring, but it pays well and it's only down the road. I'm off the booze for a bit too.'

Typical.

After a life of irresponsibility, Nick gets handed a management job on a plate, while I get nothing but job rejections.

Teachers tell you to pass exams, but that's bullshit.

No matter what qualifications you have, you can't compete with people like Nick, whose stepdad owns the company.

Thursday, 22nd June

Sports day at Callum's school.

We all went along to support him, including John Boy – who won the Fathers' race.

Even with his metal leg and blisters, John Boy was much fitter and stronger than the other racers, and ran backwards to 'make it fair'.

Mum made us 'Team Callum' T-shirts, and waved a big 'CALLUM NO.1' flag.

It was BOILING hot.

We were all right because visitors and schoolchildren got to sit in the shade, but the teachers were lobster red and kept losing their temper.

Very proud of Callum. He came second in the 10m sprint and first in the three-legged race (which he ran with his girlfriend).

Callum wasn't so good at the skipping race, but was very determined and kept going – even as a sweaty-faced teacher packed away the finish line and shouted at him to hurry up.

Friday, 23rd June

Took Daisy for a walk this evening to post more job applications.

Passed Station Cottage.

Daisy said, 'Our house, Mummy. Our house.'

'Not any more, sweetheart,' I told her. 'But I'll find us another house. Just as soon as I get a good job.'

'OK,' she said.

Just like that.

Althea's right about kids. They really do live in the moment. But maybe because they're too young to notice the shit storms gathering overhead…like this impending court hearing.

Posted all my job applications, then walked a different way home.

Evening

Alex called to say he's flying back to London on Tuesday.

I'm still furious with him, but have accepted an offer of dinner so we can 'talk'. Which in my case, could mean 'shout'.

Probably should walk away from Alex with my head held high, but fuck it.

I've lost my house and job.

What dignity do I have left?

Saturday, 24th June

Nick's first official visitation day.

Met him on the village green, after loading the Maclaren with picnic things.

As soon as I took Daisy out of the pram, it fell on its back like a drunken horse.

Nick was quite useful for a change, shouting, 'Fucking hell!' quick enough for me to prevent a squashed picnic bag.

It was a bit awkward at first – Nick and I having a picnic together. But I sidestepped all questions about 'moving house', and in the end, it wasn't so bad.

Nick didn't bring his usual six-pack of Peroni, which was a shock. And we had some nice chats about Daisy.

I want her to grow up happy, healthy and strong.

Nick wants her to be a musical theatre star.

Sunday, 25th June

Ugh.

Alex can't make it back to London after all. At least, not for a few weeks.

We did have quite a good chat on the phone, and he apologised again for all the stuff with his mother.

'Neither of us is perfect,' he said. 'You come with Nick Spencer.'

It was a fair point.

'Just don't talk to your mother about me,' I said.

'Agreed.'

Feel like maybe we're making progress, but still wish I could see Alex in person today.

Mum tried to cheer me up with a bacon sandwich and the offer of a shift in the pub.

'You can make some money while you're missing him,' she coaxed.

John Boy will be working too, so at least I'll have a laugh.

Very fond of my one-legged cousin. Underneath his tough exterior, he's soft as anything. He lets Daisy cover his prosthetic leg in Tinkerbell stickers, and Callum often plays drumsticks on his metal foot. Plus, John Boy mouths along to 'A Whole New World' whenever we put Disney's *Aladdin* on.

Monday, 26th June

Hung-over today and full of remorse.

It's John Boy's fault.

He gave out free out-of-date toffee vodka shots and dared me to drink the last two, so he could wash-up the tray.

After that, I lost all self-control and accepted John Boy's challenge of blindfold guessing the Aftershock flavours.

Then Nick turned up and ended up being my very inappropriate shoulder to cry on re Alex.

Admitted I'd been stood up. Then (arg!) sent drunken text messages to Alex accusing him of being an absent boyfriend and telling him that I spent more time with Nick than him.

Can't bear to re-read those messages this morning.

SO bloody embarrassing.

There should be some sort of app that measures your blood alcohol and shuts off all message functions if you're over the limit.

Afternoon

Have made an unfortunate discovery.

If I want to get Alex's attention, all I have to do is mention Nick.

Got a lunchtime call from Alex (7am New York Time), demanding to know what the hell I was doing, 'entertaining' Nick in the small hours.

Explained, rather sheepishly, that Nick had come to the pub.

There was an awkward silence, and then I said: 'How come you haven't called in so long?'

'Because of Nick Spencer.'

'You're being jealous.'

'Perhaps.'

'Well, maybe *you* need some space.'

And I meant it. With all this court stress and the possibility of Daisy living with Nick, I don't need this silly, childish jealousy drama.

Alex needs to grow up.

Maybe he's not so different from Nick after all.

Tuesday, 27th June

Got a job interview!

For a charity, somewhere near Victoria Station.

SO worried about court now, but if I get this job, Jeremy says it will be a 'tremendously positive step'.

Wednesday, 28th June

Bumped into Nick on his way to work this morning, pulling out of the driveway in his new Volvo.

He gave the horn a playful toot when he saw Daisy and me.

Daisy, who had been cuddling a lamppost, shouted, 'TOO NOISY Baddy. *Sakes*.'

When Daisy says *sakes*, she means 'For fuck's sake'.

It's a phrase I didn't know I used until my one-year-old parroted it back to me.

I genuinely didn't realise I swore that much, but children are horrible mirrors of truth.

Turns out I say, 'Oh buggering hell' (Buggers bell!) and 'Fuck beans' (Uck beans!) much more than I realise.

Thursday, 29th June

John Boy has bought Daisy a present. It's a soft toy called 'Lil Singing Sausage' that sings when you press its flashing heart-shaped tummy:

'I'm a friendly singing sausage, I'll teach you one, two, three. A sizzling, laughing, funny sausage. Hey – come and hug me!'

Over and over again.

There's no off switch.

VERY hard applying for jobs with that song repeatedly playing in the background.

Now I have 'I'm a friendly singing sausage' stuck in my head, like a feverish dream.

Predictably, Daisy loves the singing sausage and presses its heart-shaped tummy over and over again.

Mum suggested pulling the 'sodding batteries out before I hit that sausage with a hammer.'

But an intrusive investigation under the singing sausage's clothes has revealed no battery carriage.

Possibly, Lil Singing Sausage is powered by hugs.

Friday, 30th June

Bloody Lil Singing Sausage song stuck in my head all day.

Shut UP Lil Singing Sausage!

SHUT UP!

Dad doesn't like the sausage either because it runs on (we assume) batteries.

'In my day, everything was wind-up,' Dad reminisced. 'You had to work before you played.'

He then began a lecture about wasteful attitudes, which ended with Mum bellowing, 'BOB will you SHUT UP about the bloody 5p carrier-bag charge.'

Saturday, 1st July

John Boy has 'fixed' Lil Singing Sausage, using his army electrician training.

He's replaced the sausage's insides with Callum's 'record your own noises' toy.

Now the sausage sings, 'Bugger bugger, poo poo. Bugger bugger, poo,' continuously for three minutes.

John Boy and Callum think this is hilarious.

Have tried smashing Lil Singing Sausage to pieces on the beer-cellar floor, but his plastic shell is extremely sturdy. If anything, the sausage seems to like being hit. The more I smash it, the faster it sings, 'Buggerbuggerpoopoo, buggerbuggerpoo.'

Sunday, 2nd July

Have hidden Lil Singing Sausage in my handbag.

Daisy cried and cried when she couldn't find her 'light-up' cuddly sausage.

I'm pretending I don't know where it is.

Feel guilty for lying, but my sanity needs preserving.

I can't be a good mother if I've gone mad.

Monday, 3rd July

Job interview this morning.

People keep asking me how it went.

I wish they wouldn't.

Why didn't I clear out my handbag?

Got to London OK. The train was on time and a nice walk from the tube station.

My potential new employer's offices were in one of those shiny Ally McBeal buildings, which was exciting.

At the front desk, a well-groomed receptionist asked me for ID.

As I groped in my handbag, my fingers found Lil Singing Sausage.

He shouted, 'Bugger bugger poo poo, bugger bugger poo.'

'Is that your *phone?*' said the reception lady, looking horrified.

'Oh no,' I laughed. 'Just…uh, one of my daughter's toys.'

The receptionist stared at me like I was a maniac.

Before I could go into the difficulties of motherhood, a stern-looking lady appeared from a nearby conference room.

She had short, jet-black hair cut into lots of sharp edges, like a fashionable toilet brush, and go-getting chevron glasses that shouted: 'I mean business. And I mean it quickly.'

'Diana Fitz,' the woman announced, shaking my hand vigorously. 'Head of recruitment. You must be Ms Duffy. Here for the 11 o'clock interview?'

'Yes,' I said, clutching my handbag.

Mercifully, Lil Singing Sausage fell silent before Diana could discern Callum's fast-paced swearing.

Diana led me into an interview room, where two equally severe-looking women waited.

One had silver hair, like a frost-commanding supervillain, and the other a Mr-Sheen-shiny blonde bob.

'Let me introduce you to the other heads of HR,' said Diana. 'Malory Pipes and Karen Weaver. Miss Duffy, do you have your CV with you?'

'Yes of course,' I said, lowering my handbag carefully onto the table, and gingerly feeling inside for my CV folder. It was like a game of Operation, sliding the folder free without disturbing Lil

Singing Sausage.

The women watched me as I lifted the CV folder slowly, slowly from my handbag, then presented it with a flourish.

After some paper rustling, Diana, Malory and Karen took turns interrogating me about every detail of my CV – including my primary school maypole dancing club and the fact I once solved a Rubik's cube on a car journey to Scotland.

I went over all the great things I'd done at Give a Damn before Hari Khan took over, and I think they were impressed.

Then Diana looked me dead in the eye and said, 'I do have one concern, Miss Duffy. You have a one-year-old daughter.'

'Yes,' I said. 'Do you want to see a picture?'

Diana shook her head. 'We've noticed that people with children have a marked decrease in timekeeping and attendance. How can we be assured that you'll be as professional as someone without a family?'

'Do you have children?' I asked her.

'No,' said Diana.

'No,' said the two women either side of her.

'My career is my child,' the silver-haired woman added helpfully.

'I am a committed, hard-working employee,' I said. 'I give one hundred and ten percent. Having a child hasn't changed that.'

Diana nodded and made a note on her pad.

'Lovely, Miss Duffy,' said Karen. 'Well. Let me show you out.'

I shook hands with all three women, and made it to the door before Malory called out, 'Oh Miss Duffy! Your bag.'

I'd left my bloody handbag on the table.

Malory grasped the bag with firm fingers, at which point pastel-coloured lights flashed through soft leather, followed by, 'BUGGER BUGGER POO POO, BUGGER BUGGER POO!'

Malory blinked in alarm.

Diana and Karen exchanged surprised glances.

I took my bag and said the first thing that came into my head.

'Ha! Don't worry – it's just a little singing sausage.'

Then I slung the bag over my shoulder and walked out.

Tuesday, 4th July

According to my *Get That Job!* book, I'm supposed to ring after every interview and ask for feedback.

But realistically, I don't need feedback.

Just a little singing sausage…

Those recruiters must think I'm crazy.

Wednesday, 5th July

Didn't get the job.

Trying to tell myself it's for the best.

I didn't like those women, anyway. They weren't the sort to understand that chewed-up food on clothing is part of life, post-children.

Am now petrified about the court hearing.

Thursday, 6th July

Broke down today over losing the house and not getting the job.

Dad found me in the kitchen, crying into a tub of banana Nesquik.

He put his arm around my shoulder and said, 'There's more than one house in the world, love.'

'But what's going to happen in court now?' I sobbed.

'I'm sure they'll understand. You'll get a job soon. *And* find a nice house.'

'But I wanted *that* house. It had a wood-burning stove.'

Which was a silly thing to say, because Dad began a lecture about 'excessive heating in this day and age', and how his childhood was heated by one daily lump of coal.

'That house just felt meant to be,' I told Dad.

'Sometimes shiny baubles break,' said Dad. 'Keep looking. You'll find somewhere.'

'But not in time for court,' I said. 'What if they make Daisy live with Nick and *Sadie*?'

'Oh, I'm sure they won't.'

I wonder…is Alex a shiny bauble? Or the real thing?

Put on the best smile I could manage.

'Good girl,' said Dad. 'We're not quitters, are we?'

Mum, who was watching *Catchphrase* on Challenge TV, shouted, 'That's my girl, Julesy. Keep pressing, keep guessing.'

Friday, 7th July

Another shift in the pub last night.

The regulars were very sympathetic about the job interview and the house falling through.

Scottish George tapped one of his few remaining teeth and said, 'In the words of Doris Day, what will be will be.'

Yorkie offered me his camper van as temporary accommodation.

'I'm not homeless,' I explained. 'Daisy and I are staying at the pub.'

Dad popped his head up from the cellar and said, 'I love a bit of camping, Yorkie. Cooking in the open air. Games of an evening. Sleeping under the stars. Do you remember those camping trips with your Scottish Grandma, Juliette? The ones your mum refused to come on?'

As if I could forget summer holiday trips to Grandma Duffy's.

A ten-hour drive to rainy Scotland – the highlight of which

would be a Tunnock's teacake and plastic-tasting tea from Dad's tartan flask, enjoyed in drizzly rain.

After stopping at various scenes of 'spectacular natural beauty', we'd reach Scotland and camp in Grandma Duffy's thistle-covered garden.

On the positive side, Dad's saggy army tent was always warmer than Grandma Duffy's stone cottage.

'What kind of camper van do you have, Yorkie?' Dad wanted to know. 'A two-berth? Four-berth?'

Yorkie said his camper van was a one-berth.

'I've never heard of a one-berth before,' said Dad.

Yorkie explained the camper was a transit van with a mattress and bucket in the back, parked on wasteland by the sewage works.

Saturday, 8th July

More bad news.

Got my bill from Badger Partridge solicitors today, for legal work on a house I didn't buy.

£1,800.

Additionally, the mortgage company is charging me £500 for a survey they booked in but never carried out.

Will need a small loan to pay everything off – the repayments for which will lower my already-low income. This means I can't afford to rent *anywhere*, not even a bedsit, and am eligible for the teeniest mortgage ever.

I suppose house stuff doesn't matter right now, anyway. I'm hardly going to find a shiny new home between now and Monday.

The courts will have to make a decision based on me living at the pub.

Shitting myself.

Sunday, 9th July

Court tomorrow.

Went to the village church today. I'm one of those pretend Christians who only believe in God when they want something.

Our anger-management-issues vicar got extremely cross when Daisy chewed on the prayer cushions – f-ing and blinding, talking about the fiery pits of hell.

But he did some deep-breathing exercises in the vestry, then gave Daisy pink wafers left over from Sunday School, so everyone was happy.

Please, God, I said. *Please, please God, don't let Nick get residency. He can see Daisy whenever he wants, but don't make her live with him and Sadie. She'd just be so sad...*

Monday, 10th July

Court hearing.

Anxiety woke me up at 5 am.

Typically, Daisy slept in until 8 am.

She certainly picks her moments.

Got to the courthouse an hour early.

Lots of separated couples were in the waiting area, sitting on beige chairs and glaring at each other.

I sat on my own beige chair, hands shaking, and watched the clock tick round.

After half an hour, I decided to risk the 1980s coffee machine.

It delivered me a cup of coffee granules and powdered milk, but no hot water.

As I was hitting the machine, I heard a voice behind me.

'Juliette.'

It was Alex, dressed more appropriately for court than anyone in the room.

He carried two deli takeaway coffees in a cardboard beverage holder.

Did a stupid thing then.

Cried.

'What are you doing here?' I sobbed.

It meant so much. Not least because he'd brought good coffee.

'You needed me.'

'I don't want to drag you into my mess.'

'Juliette, why *wouldn't* you want to drag me into your mess?'

We sat on beige chairs and waited, Alex holding my shaking hand.

Soon, Jeremy arrived with a briefcase and a bagged croissant.

He shook our hands vigorously, then had a long chat with the usher about the local golf course.

Nick turned up after that, with Penny Castle and Helen.

Alex glared at Nick, squeezing my hand extra tight.

'What's fancy pants doing here?' Nick muttered as he walked past me.

'The same as your mother,' I fired back.

An hour later, we still hadn't been seen.

Alex barked at the usher about 'atrocious time-scheduling', and when no satisfactory answers were provided, he demanded other people were fetched to be shouted at.

After the shouting, we were next up and went into a proper courtroom this time – not the 'informal' one.

I suppose we did sort of push in. But there was no reason for that dad to throw powdered coffee at us.

The courtroom wasn't what I expected.

No benches or gavels.

Just a big table, at which sat a shrivelled-up man, with a black dicky bow around his wrinkly neck.

The shrivelled man turned out to be our new judge. The previous one died last week.

We sat around the table, and the judge asked Jeremy and Penny the same questions as last time:

+ Where is Daisy Duffy living at present?
+ Why is a change in residence being requested?

And so on.

'Mr Spencer feels the child's needs are better met at his home,' said Penny Castle, 'because Miss Duffy's home is unsuitable. She also has anger management issues.'

Penny handed over pictures of our pub, with detailed notes about the adults currently living there.

The judge's watery eyes swam with confusion, and he took a settling suck from his asthma inhaler.

The judge asked Jeremy, 'So this is Miss Duffy's residence? It says in my notes she is looking for her own home.'

Jeremy said, 'Miss Duffy *is* currently looking for her own house.'

'Well she's had plenty of time,' said the judge. 'Why hasn't she found somewhere?'

'The house sale fell through,' said Jeremy.

'Because she lost her job,' Penny piped up.

'So *where* is Miss Duffy living at present?' asked the judge.

Jeremy confirmed I was still living at Mum and Dad's pub.

'There are four other adults and two children at Miss Duffy's residence,' said Penny, when she was allowed to speak, 'If I may, your worship, I'd like to present a diary log of Miss Duffy's aggressive behaviour towards Mr Spencer and Mrs Jolly-Piggott.'

She read out a list of text messages I'd sent Nick and gave diary accounts, written by Helen, about me shouting outside her house, calling her a dragon by the church and telling her to 'fuck off back to her Land Rover' at the play park.

'Actually, that wasn't me,' I said. 'It was my friend who told her to fuck off back to her Land Rover.'

'Miss Duffy,' said the judge. 'You need to keep your emotions in check. I think it sensible that you and Mr Spencer attend a few more mediation sessions. If you still can't come to an agreement, I'll make a residency decision at the next hearing. And Miss Duffy – if you don't have somewhere more suitable to live by then, I will strongly consider the Cafcass recommendation of joint residency, followed by a later consideration of full residency in favour of Mr Spencer.'

Jeremy said, 'May we request some additional time before the next hearing, to give Miss Duffy chance to find another property?'

Penny said, 'A lengthy wait would be *deeply* distressing for my client. I must request that the hearing—'

'You can have until the end of the year, Miss Duffy,' said the judge, shuffling papers. 'Assuming you can't reach an agreement in mediation, the next hearing will be in December. The court will send a letter confirming the exact date. Miss Duffy, that should give you ample time to find a property. And Mr Spencer, we'll have everything sewn up for you before Christmas.'

The judge told Johnny Jiggens to arrange a 'pre-court living assessment' with me a few weeks before the final hearing.

Then he strapped on an oxygen mask, signifying the end of the session.

So, there is going to be another court hearing.

Don't know whether to laugh or cry.

'What am I going to do?' I asked Jeremy. 'I can't afford a decent house right now.'

'Had you considered buying at auction?' Jeremy suggested. 'It could be a way of getting something on a low budget.'

It's worth looking into I suppose. Desperate times and all of that.

Alex was waiting for me outside the courtroom.

'Juliette,' he said. 'I'll drive you home.'

Tuesday, 11th July

Have phoned dozens of estate agents, telling them I'm willing to consider anything within my tiny budget.

They've consequently clocked me as a desperate buyer, and are booking me in to see any old shit they can't sell.

Wednesday, 12th July

House viewings today.

Have looked at damp flats and a one-up, one-down house made entirely of timber.

The timber house didn't seem all that bad if you ignored the woodworm.

But when I asked the estate agent why it hadn't sold, he said, 'Too much of a fire risk. Cash buyers only.'

So that was that.

Thursday, 13th July

Took Jeremy's advice and looked into property auctions today.

Found a repossessed house for sale in Great Oakley – a dilapidated squat hidden behind a wall of overgrown brambles.

'You could get it dead cheap,' the estate agent told me. 'You won't find another three-bed detached house for this price. Not anywhere near here.'

'Really?' I brightened. 'It's a three-bed detached house?'

'Before the fire got to it.'

I suppose the house could have nice views because it's down the old farm track.

'There's a kitchen too,' the estate agent boasted. 'Well – part of one. At least that's what the bank says. I haven't seen the house myself because the brambles are too overgrown.'

He says I can have a viewing tomorrow, once he's tracked down a pair of garden shears.

Friday, 14th July

Went to see the bramble house today.

Mum and Dad came with me, although Mum moaned about the five-minute walk, claiming her ankle had swollen up.

The estate agent waited for us on the farm path, shears in hand.

'Watch the broken glass,' he said, as he snipped the undergrowth. 'Hold this bramble, would you?'

Twenty minutes later, he'd cleared a small path.

Mum manoeuvred herself through the thorns, swearing and shouting.

She returned a minute later, scratched from head to toe. Tufts of bleached-blonde hair waved on thorns.

'It's a bloody state,' Mum informed me. 'I would have taken a few pictures, but there's no point. I can describe it in two words. Shit hole.'

I pushed my way through the brambles and saw a burned-out chimney, boarded-up windows, graffiti, drug paraphernalia and faded litter.

It was the exact opposite of a family home.

'Nice views, aren't there?' said the estate agent.

'The roof is nothing but burned timber,' Mum barked, from the other side of the hedge. 'You should be paying *her* to take it off your hands. I wouldn't even go *inside* that place Jules – you might get hepatitis.'

'Do you want to see inside?' the estate agent asked.

Decided I may as well take a look.

The heavy-duty repossession security door swung back with an eerie creak, releasing smells of rancid cider and damp.

'It's a good size,' said the estate agent, gesturing to the burnt-out fireplace and bright-red seventies carpet. 'Plenty of potential.'

Then he showed me the kitchen.

'Those green, psychedelic tiles saved this room from the worst of the fire,' he clarified. 'So, some bits still function. Once you've cleared out the rats.'

We couldn't go upstairs because the staircase had collapsed.

'This place was really cutting-edge in its day,' said the estate agent, gesturing to the bright-yellow downstairs toilet with black water in the bowl. He turned taps at the sink. 'Look! Running water. And from what I'm told, the old heating system could still work. Although it could just as easily blow the place up – check with a gas engineer.'

Was a relief to get outside, away from the gloomy interior.

'Look at that view,' said the estate agent, gesturing over the fields.

Had to admit, the view *was* lovely when the house wasn't in it.

I was quiet all the way home. So quiet, that Mum asked if I had indigestion.

'You're not thinking about buying that place, are you?' said Mum. 'It looks like somewhere Yorkie would live.'

Even Dad, who grew up without running water, said, 'I wouldn't touch it with a barge pole, love.'

But it's within my budget. Which means I'm considering it.

Saturday, 15th July

Grilled the estate agents about the bramble house today, asking who was selling it, how long it had been on for, etc.

They gave me all the gossip.

Officially, the house is called 'Hillcrest House', and was part of Hillcrest Farm.

It was left to rot in the 1980s after a nasty divorce when the owner ran off to the Costa del Sol with a local hairdresser (whose bubble perms were renowned for turning green in the swimming pool). The owner died in debt last year, so the bank repossessed the house.

The roof and west wall at Hillcrest House are listed, so the house can't be knocked down – hence the very low price.

This means any new owner would have to contact the council before repairing the roof, but this is just a formality as there are only charred timbers left.

The bad news is Hillcrest House is being sold in two weeks by the auction team. This means I have two weeks to work out how property auctions work, and whether I could actually renovate within budget.

'You could get it at a great price,' the estate agent enthused. 'After all – who else would want to bid on it?'

He told me the recommended auction price was £75,000.

Wow.

'Surely it won't go for such a low amount,' I said. 'It's a three-bedroom detached *house* in a sought-after village.'

'It could do,' said the estate agent. 'It could even go for less. But then again, it could go for twice as much.'

On my pub salary and with my child tax credits, Alex's broker says I can get a mortgage of £90,000.

If I *did* get Hillcrest House for £75,000, that would give me £15,000 for renovation works.

Surely a roof, stairs and kitchen can't cost *that* much?

Sunday, 16th July

Phoned Alex today.

'Juliette,' he said. 'To what do I owe the pleasure?'

'I need help,' I said. 'Do you know about property auctions?'

'Yes,' he said. 'I wouldn't recommend them in your case. They can be risky with a mortgage. You can lose a lot of money.'

'Will you go to an auction with me in a few weeks?'

'A few weeks?' said Alex. 'Why the rush?'

'I think I've found something with potential.'

'Don't get pulled into fast auctions,' Alex told me. 'Especially with a mortgage. Properties are about patience. Wait until something good comes on the market and buy the usual way.'

'I can't wait,' I said. 'I have another court case looming, and an OCD Dad constantly tidying away my job applications. Daisy and I need our own place.'

'I'll help you,' said Alex. 'But not until I've seen the property.'

He's coming this afternoon to take a look, which I appreciate.

Afternoon

Drove to Hillcrest House in Alex's shiny silver MG.

It was awkwardly quiet in the car, so I asked Alex if he had any music.

'Try the glove box,' he said. 'I think there's some Dire Straits in there.'

Laughed. Then realised he wasn't joking.

'I suppose my musical experiences have been rather limited,' Alex admitted. 'We weren't allowed music at boarding school.'

Alex's glove box was extremely messy, which was a surprise since everything else in his life is in straight lines.

'What's the story here?' I said, pulling a crinkled chamois leather from an old paper coffee cup. 'I thought you were tidy.'

'A car is different. I'm more anarchic in my car.'

When we reached the house, I showed Alex through the tunnel of brambles, and we stood together, looking over the squalid building.

If anything, it looked worse on second viewing.

'It needs condemning,' Alex said simply.

'Don't you think it has potential?' I asked.

'There's a *lot* of work here, Juliette. You're almost talking about building a new house. Do you have the budget for that?'

'Depends how much it goes for at auction.'

'It shouldn't go for too much,' said Alex, shielding his eyes from the sun. 'No developer would touch this plot. And those overhead lines place huge limitations. But you never know. It all depends on who shows up on the day.'

'Will you help me bid?' I asked.

'You definitely want to bid on this place? This is a huge undertaking.'

'Alex, if I don't get a home for Daisy, she could end up living with Nick.'

'It's a *lot* of work.'

'I think I'm going to go for it.'

Alex turned to me then, and said, 'You know, I didn't realise you were this brave. I commend you.'

'You could call it bravery,' I said. 'Or you could call it having no choice.'

Monday, 17th July

Spent all day costing out building work, kitchens, roofs etc. using online DIY forums.

If I get Hillcrest House for the right price, I really think I can do this.

Have drawn up a downstairs plan with rough kitchen layout, and ideas for removing a wall so the kitchen/dining room area will be open (for entertaining!), and there'll be a cosy living room (for relaxed, fireside chats!).

Alex's broker has confirmed that the mortgage company will

lend £92,000 on the property (amusingly, it's considered 'habitable' because it has a kitchen). This will cover mortgage fees, and the mortgage company has some sort of deal right now to cover my legal costs.

I think I should go for it.

Or to put it another way, what choice do I have *but* go for it?

Tuesday, 18th July

Two official letters today, one from family court, one from MIAM.

Nick and I have been booked in for mediation next week.

The next court hearing date has also been decided: 5th December.

That gives me four and a half months to buy and renovate Hillcrest House.

Maybe I can ask Santa for help.

On the negative side, Christmas could be ruined.

Then Santa will have a lot to answer for.

Wednesday, 19th July

Last minute calculations before the auction.

Want to make sure I've *definitely* done my sums right but so hard getting anything done with Daisy around.

How does anyone have two kids? The moment I do anything that isn't direct interaction, Daisy is round my ankles, lifting her little arms up.

'Mummy, mummy. Cuddle. *Cuddle.*'

Althea says I should count myself lucky. 'At least Daisy follows you around. Wolfgang makes a run for it the minute my back is turned.'

She'd lost him in the vegetarian supermarket that morning apparently, while studying a Quorn bacon slices packet.

Wolfgang had made it all the way to the car park and ripped the tyres off a child's Tinkerbell bicycle.

My costings so far, based on DIY forum:

+ Roof – £3,000
+ Staircase – £1,000
+ Kitchen – £5,000
+ Taking out and repairing walls – £3,000
+ Downstairs toilet, tiling and fitting – £500
+ Upstairs bath, shower and toilet – £2,000
+ Flooring – £2,000
+ Boiler etc. – £1,000

Total: £16,500

My renovation budget: £15,000

Dad says that when it comes to housing renovation, you should take your initial budget and double it. But since I don't have enough to cover the initial costings, I'm going to ignore this advice.

These are all rough estimates, and if I economise here and there, I think I can do this.

If the worst comes to the worst, I'll live without a bath for a while and Daisy, and I can shower at the pub.

Come on Juliette. COME ON!

Thursday, 20th July

Auction tomorrow.

It's on a Friday.

Good things happen on Friday, right?

Have to admit, I'm scared shitless. But feel the fear and do it anyway, and all of that.

I have no experience of building or house renovation. But I had no experience of babies until Daisy came along. And things turned out OK.

Sort of.

Need to stay calm.

If I get this house for the right price, my mortgage repayments will be £550 per month.

With my pub salary, child tax credits and working tax credits, this is manageable.

The jumbo fly in the ointment is the major renovation project I'll be taking on.

But I've watched *loads* of episodes of *Grand Designs* and *Property Ladder*.

Come on Juliette, *come on*!

Friday, 21st July

I did it.

I just bought myself a house that 'should be condemned'.

Can't believe this is really happening.

Feel absolutely terrified.

Alex was brilliant at the auction.

He knew the auction house owner, Bobby Swindell (they both use the same private jet from time to time) and got us great seats at the front.

We were both given paddles, but Alex confiscated mine because I kept playing nervous tunes on my leg.

Then the auction began.

I thought Alex would bid as soon as Hillcrest House came up, but he looked completely disinterested, giving the auctioneer a cursory shake of his head.

The price was lowered once, then twice. On the third occasion, Alex nonchalantly raised his paddle.

There was one other interested party – a nervous-looking couple, who kept glancing at Alex and whispering.

They dropped out of the bidding when Alex glared at them.

We got the property for £73,500 – just under budget.

Couldn't believe it.

Laughed hysterically when the hammer fell.

'Congratulations, Juliette,' said Alex. 'You've just bought yourself a three-bedroom house. The very best of British luck.'

Alex is helping with completion stuff because when you buy at auction you have to close the sale *really* quickly.

Can't help thinking I may have made a big mistake.

Mum said, 'Well, you do one stupid thing every year, Juliette. Last year was the marathon. The year before, you got pregnant by Nick. And it all worked out in the end.'

Saturday, 22nd July

Took Daisy and Callum to see Hillcrest House this morning.

Feels so weird to think I'm now committed to buying this place.

Held Daisy over the brambles so she could see the crumbling walls and rotten roof.

'Look, Daisy boo,' I told her. 'Our new home.'

She whimpered and said, 'Want cuddle.'

'What do you think, Callum?' I asked.

'It looks like it's from a horror film,' Callum said.

Brandi really should stop him watching those.

'I'm going to make a lot of changes,' I enthused.

'Is the first change knocking it down?' Callum asked.

'No one can knock it down,' I said. 'The roof and west wall are listed.'

'In what?' Callum snorted. 'The haunted house directory?'

Sunday, 23rd July

After a long pub shift last night, I spent the morning drawing up plans for Hillcrest House.

On paper, it looks great. It's only when I look at the house itself that I feel terrified and overwhelmed.

Have pencilled a lovely open-plan downstairs area, with sliding doors leading off the kitchen into the garden.

I plan to demolish most of the hallway, so the front door will pretty much lead right into the big kitchen/dining area.

And there'll be a snug-type room, plus a downstairs toilet. AND a bathroom upstairs.

TWO toilets. Luxury.

There's only one family bathroom at the pub, and it's almost always occupied these days.

John Boy takes AGES gelling his hair, and Brandi puts on a full set of false eyelashes every morning, top and bottom.

This causes problems, as my bladder isn't what it was, pre-Daisy. Holding in wee is tricky, and sometimes impossible.

The downstairs saloon-bar toilets are locked in the morning, and I don't fancy using Nana Joan's Tena Lady incontinence pads, so I've had to resort to emergency measures when I really need a wee.

A Pyrex jug in the beer cellar.

Monday, 24th July

Ugh.

Mediation with Nick.

Fiona is still under the delusion that we can avoid going back to court. She doesn't understand that we're never going to agree.

Tried to talk about my new house, but Fiona said I was going off-topic.

She decided to 'wrap up' the session by touching on our extended family – i.e. Helen.

Fiona thought it important we 'get everything out', so put her hand up whenever Nick tried to defend his mother, saying, 'No, this is Juliette's point of view.'

After half an hour, I felt purged. Although I noticed Fiona kept checking her watch.

'Let's talk about building bridges now,' said Fiona. 'Juliette – it would be really wonderful if you and Nick's mother could get along again.'

'Again?' I said. 'We never got along.'

'A meal is often a good way to build a relationship,' Fiona continued. 'How about you and your family have lunch with Nick and his family?'

I gave a horrified laugh.

Nick zipped up his leather jacket in alarm.

'I want you both to be open-minded,' said Fiona. 'That's how we move forward.'

Nick and I told Fiona that we didn't think a family lunch was a good idea.

But she explained, sadly and sympathetically, that we were here by court order and must do as we were told.

'So, let's talk about venues,' said Fiona. 'Where would be a good place to meet?'

'My parent's pub?' I offered.

Expected Nick to argue, but he was surprisingly agreeable, saying, 'It's going to be horrible wherever we have it.'

Tuesday, 25th July

House sale moving forward.

The solicitors have 'fast-tracked' the searches (Mum says this probably means using first-class stamps), and the mortgage funds are nearly 'ready to be released'.

The mortgage company needed an employment reference, so Mum wrote me one. She's confirmed I've never stolen from the till or got staggering drunk on shift.

Afternoon

Just told Mum and Dad about the court-ordered family lunch.

They were suitably appalled.

'What kind of mediator sets up a great big row?' Mum asked.

'What am I going to cook for this lunch from hell?' I said.

'The pub kitchen will do you a meal,' said Mum. 'Might be a bit low on gravy though. I still can't find the three-litre Pyrex jug.'

Which reminds me.

MUST EMPTY THE PYREX JUG.

Wednesday, 26th July

Visited Nana Joan today.

Told her about the mediation lunch, and she scanned her 1970s cookbooks for menu ideas.

I'd forgotten about Stork margarine.

After flicking through pictures of wobbly, grey-looking meat in watery sauces, I politely told Nana that the pub kitchen would do something more up-to-date.

Then I made the mistake of talking about Waitrose recipe cards.

'Waitrose?' Nana shrieked. 'Why on earth would you shop there? Just chuck twenty quid out your purse right now, why don't you. They charge *70p* for Heinz baked beans.'

After we'd argued about the price of beans, I helped Nana do some online clothes shopping.

She's into Superdry right now, because the name makes her chuckle.

'Here I am, an incontinence sufferer, with the words "Superdry" printed over my arse!'

Mortgage funds will be released this afternoon.

Woo, woo!

House sale could complete this week, according to Alex.

VERY excited.

Thursday, 27th July

Phoned solicitors for an update.

They're 'poised' for completion tomorrow.

Mum snorted at that. '"Poised" is legal speak for "won't happen",' she said.

During my pub shift, I asked Dad if he knew any good builders.

He said, 'The good ones are booked up months in advance. You should have got onto this in May, Juliette.'

But I hadn't even viewed Hillcrest House in May.

Dad said, 'Well most building jobs you can do yourself, with the right instruction manual and attention to detail.'

But I don't trust myself to do practical stuff.

I've set fire to a toasted sandwich before. My home economics teacher was really annoyed because the Belling oven had been with the school since 1971.

Mum told me to try Uncle Danny.

'He used to be in the building trade,' she said. 'He's bound to know somebody.'

Friday, 28th July

Sale didn't complete today.

It will be Monday at the earliest now because solicitors don't work weekends.

Mum snorted and said, 'I could have told you that. When have you ever known solicitors keep their word?'

Skyped Uncle Danny.

I asked if he knew any local builders from his contractor days.

'I wouldn't do that to you, Julesy,' he said, looking alarmed. 'You're family. Why do you need a builder, anyway?'

Told him I'd just bought the property by Hillcrest Farm.

'Not that old squat down the farm tracks?' he asked. 'I thought they'd knocked that down.'

Ah…home sweet home!

Saturday, 29th July

Nick's visitation day.

We took Daisy to the zoo because I can never go there with Althea. She calls it 'animal prison' and encourages Wolfgang to free animals from cages.

Thought Nick was hung-over at first, because he was so quiet. But it turns out he was thinking about the mediation lunch.

'It's going to be fucking awful,' he said.

For once, we were in agreement.

Evening

Alex just called while I was working behind the bar.

I told him about the mediation lunch.

There was a long silence.

Then he said, 'Good lord.'

'I know.'

'But your family will be there too?' he asked.

'Yes. We're supposed to be building bridges.'

Alex laughed and said, 'I think to build bridges, there has to be firm soil underfoot. What if I came along too? To support you.'

'I'd love that,' I said.

'Then I'll come.'

It's so confusing with Alex.

One minute, I think things are never going to work. The next I feel like…maybe.

He *is* always there when I really need him.

And that counts for a lot.

Sunday, 30th July

Emailed Fiona Skelton to ask if extended, extended family members were OK (meaning Alex) at the lunch from hell, and she said it was fine, as long as everyone brought their best listening ears to the table.

I didn't tell her my family don't possess listening ears, best or otherwise.

Certainly, our best shouting mouths will come along.

Just want to get the lunch over with now.

Daisy seems to sense there is emotional trauma in the air because she's being a nightmare – clinging to me and crying about ridiculous things like wanting the apple she already has in her hand.

Monday, 31st July

House sale still not complete.

The solicitors are now saying it won't happen until Wednesday, meaning I'll have to endure the dreaded mediation lunch tomorrow before everything is signed and sealed.

Yorkie asked if I wanted him to 'beat anyone up' to speed things along, but I politely declined.

Just realised I STILL haven't emptied the Pyrex jug of wee in the beer cellar.

It's been there over a week now.

Aside from the disgustingness of week-old wee, it's good to keep the jug empty for emergencies. John Boy's girlfriend is staying over tonight, which means yet another person in the bathroom

Tuesday, 1st August

Mediation lunch.

Really appreciated Alex arriving early. Although I wish I'd been doing something more glamorous than sweeping up cigarette butts when he strolled into the back garden.

Also, why did I kiss him, continental-style, on both cheeks?

I think that confused both of us.

'Nick Spencer hasn't arrived yet, I see,' said Alex, scanning the garden.

Mum bounded outside, bellowing, 'Let's get you a drink, Alex. What do you fancy? Beer?'

Alex held up the bottle of red he was carrying, and said, 'Wine will be fine for me.'

But Mum shouted to Dad in the open cellar, 'Bob. BOB!'

'What IS it, Shirley?' Dad shouted back.

'Alex is here. He needs a drink. You can finish the wine order tomorrow.'

'SHIRLEY, I AM RIGHT IN THE MIDDLE OF SOMETHING.'

Mum turned to Alex, and in her best voice said, 'Excuse me a moment, would you?'

Then she stormed down the cellar steps. 'FOR CHRIST SAKE

BOB, WE HAVE A SODDING GUEST. LET JOHN BOY DO THE WINE ORDER.'

'JOHN BOY CAN'T COUNT PAST FIFTY, SHIRLEY! THERE ARE AT LEAST SIXTY BOTTLES HERE.'

'Um…so, how are you?' I asked Alex.

'I'm fine,' said Alex, with an amused smile. 'Where's Daisy?'

'Sleeping,' I said. 'Do you want to sit down?'

I showed him to a garden table, where Nana Joan was perched under a Heineken umbrella, gin and tonic in hand.

'This is my nana,' I said.

Alex shook Nana's hand and said, 'A pleasure to meet you.'

'Well you're certainly a strapping young man,' said Nana approvingly. 'I'll bet your mum gave you plenty of Mars Bars growing up.'

'Not so many actually,' said Alex, with a smile.

Mum came up from the cellar then. 'Bob's just getting you a beer, Alex,' she said, in her best hostess voice.

'Actually, wine will do for me,' said Alex, holding up his bottle again. 'So, you needn't—'

'Wine?' Mum queried. 'BOB! *BOB*! Take TWO bottles off your list – and bring them to the table.'

Dad shouted up from the cellar, 'FOR HEAVEN'S SAKES, SHIRLEY, I'VE JUST ADDED EVERYTHING UP!'

'WELL, YOU'LL HAVE TO UN-ADD IT THEN.' Mum shouted back.

She turned to Alex. 'Was it red you wanted?'

'Yes, but I already have a bottle here—'

Mum narrowed her eyes appraisingly. 'Bob. BOB! We need RED wine.'

Dad appeared from the cellar.

He had a bottle of red in one hand and, to my horror, the emergency Pyrex jug in the other.

It was full of what looked like white wine. But of course, the last time I'd seen that jug, it was half-full of my wee.

'Good news, Shirley,' he announced. 'I've found your Pyrex jug.'

'Why did you put white wine in it?' Mum asked. 'It's not a serving jug, Bob. You'll make the table look like a home economics class.'

'There was already wine *in* the jug, Shirley,' said Dad, putting it on the table. 'John Boy must have broken a bottle. I think it was a bit on the turn, but it'll be fine mixed with the fresh stuff.'

I just stood there, frozen in horror, staring at the wee and wine mixture.

Dad has never had a good sense of smell. He can't tell the difference between pork and tuna.

'Bloody hell, Bob, just get a fresh bottle,' said Mum. 'Let's try and look a bit civilised.'

'That would be a waste, Shirley,' said Dad. 'I'm not throwing away perfectly good wine when there are people starving in the world.'

'Dad we should throw it away!' I said, my voice shrill.

Then we heard voices outside: Helen, telling Henry off for not tucking his shirt in, and Nick talking to baby Horatio about his big sister, Daisy.

'Not *sister*, Nick,' I heard Helen correct. '*Half*-sister.'

The back gate opened, and the Jolly-Piggott family were upon us, tight-lipped and tense.

Helen was dressed in weekend 'casual' gear – a crisp, white blouse tucked into ironed jeans.

Henry wore a tweed cap and swung a polished walking stick.

Nick pushed the pram and looked henpecked.

Alex glared at Nick.

Nick glared at Alex.

'Nice to see you all,' I said, glancing at the Pyrex jug. 'What a pleasure.'

'Juliette.' Helen gave me an appraising nod. 'You look tired.'

Mum folded her arms and bellowed, 'No amount of sleep will fix *your* haggard old face, Helen.'

Helen coloured. 'Can we at least be *civil* today, Shirley?'

Mum snorted.

Nick bumped Horatio's pram over the lawn and pulled Peroni bottles from the net shopping compartment. 'Can I crack these open?' he said. 'Where's Daisy boo?'

'Daisy's sleeping,' I said. 'Do you have any white wine? We really need *white* wine.'

'Did someone want white wine?' said Dad, holding up the Pyrex jug. 'Joan?'

'NANA-YOU-SHOULD-TRY-THE-RED-WINE!' I said, grabbing Alex's wine bottle.

Nana squinted. 'Is it a Madeira? I like a Madeira.'

'Similar,' I lied. While I was filling Nana's glass, Dad said: 'Helen, what can I get you to drink?'

'White wine,' said Helen, putting her sunglasses on the table. 'But only if it's cold.'

'This has been in the cellar,' said Dad, holding up the Pyrex jug, then filling Helen's glass.

Helen eyed the jug disdainfully, but a sideways glance at Mum kept her quiet. She took a sip from her wineglass, then winced.

'Is this the house white?' she asked, blinking her nasty bird eyes. 'It's *very* sharp.'

'Glad I had the red, then,' said Nana Joan. 'I don't like sharp. Like I say, I'm more of a Madeira girl.'

In the end, it was only Helen who drank white wine.

Alex, Nana, Henry and I drank red, Nick had Peroni, Dad drank cider and Mum had pints of Guinness.

The pub kitchen served us lasagne and salad.

To think I was worried lunch would be awful.

It was the best meal I've had in ages.

Wednesday, 2nd August

The house sale is complete!

Got a phone call from the solicitors today, congratulating me on my purchase.

Can't believe it.

I have a house.

A shitty, falling-down house.

Alex phoned to congratulate me, and also to say he's off to Dubai this afternoon.

That pretty much sums up our relationship.

Nice lunch.

Supportive conversation.

Alex leaves the country.

Thursday, 3rd August

Dad and I have just been at Hillcrest House, clearing rubbish.

We delighted in the faded, vintage litter, oohing and aahing over Wham Bar, Hubba Bubba and Highland Toffee wrappers, and faded Corona fizzy pop bottles.

Mum popped back and forth with Daisy on her hip, throwing Cadbury's Heroes at us and telling us she could have done the work in half the time.

Friday, 4th August

Have just ordered a skip for Hillcrest House, so I can start clearing big items like the rotten old carpet.

Was so tired working at the pub last night that I poured Yorkie a shot of Baileys instead of his usual Bell's.

How we laughed.

Saturday, 5th August

Dad's birthday.

No surprise party for him this year, because Mick the Hat is getting married (again) and having his wedding reception at the pub.

Instead, we had a nice breakfast and gave Dad his presents.

Dad is easy to buy for because he likes practical gifts, like new batteries for his bike lights.

Bought him some fishing line (he's nearly run out), which he was delighted by. Also, took a risk and bought him a non-practical gift – a special edition hardback copy of *Lord of the Rings*.

I shouldn't have bothered because it only confused him.

'But I already *have* all three *Lord of the Rings* books,' he said.

'Yes, but you have the 1970s paperback versions,' I pointed out. 'This is a new hardback limited edition.'

'My old versions are in mint condition,' said Dad. 'Why do I need new ones? I take care of my things. Unlike your mother.'

This started an argument about Mum's 'disposable attitude', and how her £7 so-called 'reusable' flask mug from Starbucks *still* hasn't been washed.

After Dad's special birthday breakfast (Sainsbury's Taste the Difference muesli with crème fraîche), I headed up to Hillcrest House for more rubbish clearing, while Mum babysat.

Felt pretty tired after my shift in the pub last night, but the skip had arrived so had to get on with it.

Filled the skip with rotten old 1970s carpet, then started on the brambles.

Those bloody brambles!

The next few months are going to be hard work.

I'll be working in the pub at night, then doing what I can to the house in the day.

Mum and Dad say they'll help with Daisy as much as possible.
Really appreciate that.
Don't know what I'd do without my family.

Sunday, 6th August

Getting a bit panicked about STILL not having a builder. I have
four months until the next court hearing, in which time I need a
functioning staircase, roof, heating system, kitchen, bathroom and
toilet.

There's a LOT to do.

Am stressed just thinking about it.

Have got a list together.

Essentials

Roof

Kitchen

At least one new toilet

Bath

Staircase

Furniture

Structural repairs to fire-damaged parts

Carpet

Kitchen flooring

Double glazing

Would be nice, but unlikely to afford for a few years

Fridge with ice dispenser

Fake antler coat stand

Princess wallpaper for Daisy's room

Monday, 7th August

Have spent the morning calling roofing contractors, builders, etc.

Everyone is on holiday in Spain, Egypt or the Caribbean.

Dad gave me the number of an 'all-round builder' called Alf Leake who has 'two new hips and all his own tools'.

Alf retired years ago, but sometimes takes on projects if they're not too far from home.

Tried Alf's number.

A crackly voice came on the line and shouted, 'What do you want? I was just dozing off.'

'I'm Juliette Duffy,' I explained. 'My dad gave me your number.'

'For building work?' Alf snapped.

'Yes,' I said. 'Building and roofing. Near Hillcrest Farm.'

The line went quiet then, and I heard a cigarette being lit and inhaled. Then an explosion of coughing.

'That the bottom of the village?' said Alf gruffly.

I told him it was.

'I'd rather not,' Alf barked and hung up.

Tuesday, 8th August

Really went to town on the brambles today.

My conclusion is – brambles are evil.

The garden shears I borrowed from Mum and Dad broke within half an hour, and my new 'ultra-tough' garden gloves instantly ripped to shreds.

Thank god for Althea with her welding mask and petrol-powered chainsaw.

It took four hours to fill seven garden bags and take them to the tip.

I'd estimate there are another hundred garden bags to go.

Wednesday, 9th August

Spent another morning ringing builders. Have tried every local person, and am now ringing anyone this side of London.

I'm trying to sound professional – like a proper project manager. But it's hard, with Daisy grabbing at the phone and shouting, 'Mummy STINKY old dingo.'

I wish Callum wouldn't teach her all these new insults.

I know they're not technically swearing, but the sentiment is still hurtful.

Althea has offered to help with Hillcrest House.

She loves a DIY project.

'Wolfgang can learn to use a sledgehammer,' she enthused. 'He saw one on CBeebies and hasn't shut up about it. Big hammer, big hammer.'

God.

The thought of Wolfgang with tools is scary.

Pub shift now. Need to down a can of Red Bull.

Thursday, 10th August

So sick of sodding brambles.

Althea is a good motivator because whenever I say I need a break, she shouts at me.

I can't believe we've still got so much to do. If I think about it too much, I want to cry. But I can't back out now.

Onwards and upwards.

Friday, 11th August

Oh god, I'm so tired.

I HATE FUCKING BRAMBLES!

Have to work at the pub again tonight, which I'm not looking forward to. Will just have to push on through with the aid of Red Bull.

Was so tired this afternoon that I dozed off on the sofa while filling in a job application form.

Fortunately, Daisy head-butted me awake, then climbed on top of me and pulled my eyes open.

Saturday, 12th August

Broke down in the pub last night when someone ordered a pint of Cloudy Bramble cider.

It's too much!

I can't work and renovate a house and look after a baby.

John Boy was very nice. He sat me on a bar stool, shooed the drunks away and poured us both a quadruple vodka.

'Drink that and go to bed,' he said. 'I'll sort this lot out. Everything will look better in the morning.'

Things do look a little better this morning.

Although the brambles are still impossibly huge.

Sunday, 13th August

John Boy told Mum and Dad about my hysterical outburst, and the whole family, plus Althea, helped clear brambles today.

Was extremely grateful.

I think John Boy enjoyed himself, bare-chested and swinging the giant machete he'd borrowed from Yorkie.

Mum was supposed to be looking after Wolfgang and Daisy, but soon got annoyed with Dad's 'half-hearted' bramble-chopping and threw herself headlong into cutting and clearing.

Dad was a little hurt, but on Mum's suggestion took himself off to investigate the old heating system. He was cheered to discover my boiler is the same model he and Mum had back in the 1970s.

'A Firefly HDII,' he told me, admiringly. 'Top of the range in its day, heating a bath load of water in under four hours. These old boilers are built to last. I wouldn't be surprised if it still works.'

But I don't share Dad's love of the past.

I'm from the disposable generation. We like things new and shiny.

Monday, 14th August

Thank GOD.

We've cleared the brambles.

Now I can see the wreck of a house I've bought.

It's not pretty, but at least my lacerated skin will have a chance to heal.

Tuesday, 15th August

Alex phoned from Dubai.

'Juliette,' he said, 'How's the house renovating going?'

'Hard,' I said. 'I didn't realise it would be so hard.'

He laughed and said, 'It's only one house. Do you know how many hotels I'm renovating right now?'

Which I didn't think was very sympathetic, and told him so.

'Well, what needs doing?' Alex asked.

'Everything,' I said. 'Roof. Stairs. Walls. Furniture – and possibly an antler coat stand for the hall.'

He laughed and said, 'The last one sounds easy enough. Unless you want real antlers.'

'Of course not,' I said. 'That would be barbaric. Bambi won't lose another parent on my account.'

'You eat meat, don't you?' said Alex. 'Wear leather shoes?'

'Please don't tell me you go hunting,' I said.

'Certainly not,' he said curtly. 'My father always wanted me to go, but I point-blank refused.'

Which I thought was sort of nice.

Wednesday, 16th August

I'm getting increasingly frantic now re finding a builder.

I've made so many phone calls that my ear is suffering from heat rash.

Have abandoned feeding Daisy healthy food, and gave her fish fingers with a Dairylea dip for lunch and tea today.

Again.

'What are you fussing about?' said Mum, when I told her I was feeling guilty. 'You and your sisters had breaded stuff every day. And you turned out just fine.'

Thursday, 17th August

Just told Mum about the builder situation, and she said, 'Haven't you tried Alf Leake yet? I thought your dad gave you his number.'

I told her Alf had refused the job.

'Give me your phone,' said Mum, hefting her boobs up.

She dialled Alf's number and shouted, 'Alf, you old bugger. It's Shirley Duffy. If you want to drink in my pub again, you'll do this job for my little girl.' Then she covered the phone and said, 'He wants to know when you'd like him to start.'

Friday, 18th August

Met Alf at Hillcrest House today.

He was a tiny, wizened figure with crew-cut white hair and paint-splattered overalls, and arrived on a rattling old pushbike, pulling a trailer of rusty tools.

I have to say, Alf moved well for someone with two new hips.

'It's a bleddy mess,' Alf told me, looking over the house. 'I'd better get cracking.'

And off he went.

I've never seen such a tiny person carry heavy loads like that.

It was like watching an ant dragging a tree.

Offered Alf tea and sandwiches from the pub, but he refused, saying he had condensed milk and four cans of pilchards in his trailer.

Alf is cracking on with structural repairs but says he needs written planning permission before he can do the roof.

'I thought all I'd have to do was phone the council,' I said. 'The estate agent said the planning stuff was a formality.'

'When have you known the council to do anything by phone?' Alf barked. 'It's always by letter.'

'How long will it take?' I asked.

'It's the council,' said Alf. 'How long's a piece of string?'

Saturday, 19th August

Mum and Callum's birthday today.

They both wanted to go go-karting.

It was fun, but Mum was a very bad loser, moaning about 'unfair' cornering and 'why can't you all let me win on my bloody birthday?'

She calmed down when we got to Pizza Hut, after the first round of cheesy garlic bread.

Callum is now six and the oldest in his class. He could have started school aged four and ended up the youngest, but August children are allowed to start late these days.

Brandi was against it at first. She wanted an extra year of free childcare. But the headmistress persuaded her, explaining about all the extra reading Brandi would have to do if Callum got behind.

Sunday, 20th August

Have downloaded LOTS of paperwork, and am struggling to interpret the council's planning website.

Was hard doing all the official stuff with Daisy around.

She kept bashing the computer keyboard and making weird symbols appear like °©†^ø.

May have accidentally symbol-sworn on my planning application.

Monday, 21st August

Planning application done.

Now I just have to wait, and periodically nag the council with phone calls.

Right.

Time to don my barmaid's apron and drink a super-strong coffee.

Tuesday, 22nd August

Stress!

Work at Hillcrest House has come to a standstill because there's no running water.

I offered to bring Alf cups of tea from the pub while the problem was sorted, but apparently, he needs water to mix cement and so forth.

Alf says the water board must have cut off the water – probably because I've failed to pay a bill.

'You'll have to get in touch with them quick,' Alf said. 'Send your letter first-class, if I were you.'

'It'll probably be quicker to phone,' I replied.

Alf scratched his bristly head and said, 'The water board use phone lines these days? That's a new one.'

Wednesday, 23rd August

Phoned my local water company, Amigo Water.

They confirmed the water has been cut off and said I'd have to make a full application before they'll re-supply Hillcrest House.

This means tracing the pipes and working out where water should come in, then sending diagrams.

Have enlisted Dad for help with this.

He has an engineering background and likes nothing better than strapping on his head torch and exploring dark spaces.

Thursday, 24th August

Big problem.

Not only does Hillcrest House not have running water, but it has also been blocked off from the sewage outlet.

Dad found the problem while we were arguing over the 1970s bile-yellow bathroom suite. ('*Look* at the quality of that ceramic. You just don't get scalloping like that these days. Why in heaven's name would you want to replace it?')

Dad pulled the fish-shaped flush handle to demonstrate the longevity of 1970s craftsmanship, and we discovered a worrying truth.

The flush worked. But the black toilet water didn't go anywhere.

'Everything was plumbed-in before,' I said. 'The estate agent tried one of the taps.'

After a quick trip home for his waterproof overalls, Dad strapped on his head torch and climbed into the nearest drain.

He discovered the waste pipe had been blocked off.

'It'll be to do with privatisation,' said Mum, when we got back to the pub. 'Life was much better when everything was state-owned. You went to the dentist, they fixed your teeth. You shat in the toilet, they took it away.'

Have made lots of panicked calls to Amigo Water, but keep being transferred to different departments and promised call-backs that don't happen. No one wants to take responsibility.

Tried to phone Alex, but I think he was flying because the call wouldn't connect.

DESPERATE for advice re sewage.

Not very romantic, but this is my life right now.

Maybe I can ask the pub regulars for sewage advice during my shit…I mean *shift* tonight.

Very tired.

Friday, 25th August

Have spent the day phoning various officials, literally talking shit.

Of course, I used polite terms like 'waste material' and 'sewage'.

But we all know what I meant.

Got passed around to twenty different people, and left messages with several others.

Am really panicking about this.

My life so far has been one of privilege.

I've always had access to toilets and running water (except one time at the Reading festival, when drunk people were pushing the portaloos over, and I was too scared to go).

Phoned Althea for advice, and she shouted at me for 'overthinking' and 'mental female worrying'.

'What are you stressing about?' she said. 'Just live off-grid.'

Apparently, a friend of hers shits on a compost heap and pisses directly on his vegetables.

Told the pub regulars about this, and Yorkie said he did the same thing when his toilet was broken. Except he doesn't grow vegetables or have a compost heap. And he doesn't have a back garden. So he pretty much just shat on the weeds in his front garden.

Saturday, 26th August

In all the house stress, I forgot to take Daisy round Nick's today.

It was like a weird role reversal, having Nick phone and ask what was happening.

Rushed Daisy to our agreed meeting spot at the local library, and found Nick waiting anxiously with a load of art and craft materials.

Told Nick about the sewage disaster, and he was very sympathetic, hugging me and telling me it would all be all right.

Was nice.

Wish he'd been more like that when we were together.

Nick asked if he could see Daisy again, mid-September, to make up for the 'half visit'.

Agreed.

We'll meet at Nick's house then, which I'm not all that happy about. I think mainly out of jealousy, because I know he'll have at least two flushing toilets, and maybe even an en-suite.

Sunday, 27th August

Have been Googling, 'How to make your own cesspit'.

There are some biological toilet options that don't seem too bad.

Yes – I would have to shovel shit at some point. But there are worse things.

Monday, 28th August
Summer Bank Holiday

Did a shift in the pub yesterday, and chatted to Polish Malik about relationships.

According to Malik, Alex is a good man, but we have a 'lifestyle conflict'.

I can't cut Nick out of my life, and I don't think Alex can stop being jealous. Which leaves us nowhere.

Along with relationship advice, Malik gave me some good news re Hillcrest House.

Apparently, I don't need a specialist kitchen fitter.

'I will save you some money here, Juliette,' he said. 'Because you can fit your own kitchen very easily. When you think about it, it's only hanging cupboards.'

This cheered me up, as the kitchen fitter Mum recommended is on a Royal Caribbean cruise.

Sent Alex a text just before closing time:

'*Can you really see us working? Juliette. xx*'

Alex replied immediately:

'*If I didn't see us working, I wouldn't be trying.*'

I texted back: '*I don't see you trying all that hard, Alex.*'

Then he replied: '*If that's what you think, then perhaps we're too different after all.*'

No kisses or anything.

Texted back: '*You think we're different?*'

He replied: '*Certainly we're different. Our journey won't be easy.*'

I wrote back: '*I don't want challenges right now, Alex. I want a proper relationship, where we see each other every day, and you don't* go all cold and angry because I've seen Daisy's father.'

Alex texted: 'You're asking for more than I can give.'

I texted back: 'I'm not going to ask for less. If you can't give more, then we're over.'

He replied: 'If that's what you want.'

Feel really, really sad, but what can I do?

I'm sick of Alex going all distant whenever I see Nick. Maybe he'll change. But I'm not going to wait around.

That road only leads to pain.

Tuesday, 29th August

Amigo Water STILL hasn't responded to my complaint, even though I ring them every day.

They talk about 'in the queue' and 'received on the system', but apparently, they have a backlog. Which doesn't sound good, coming from a company that handles raw sewage.

Afternoon

Letter from Amigo Water.

Apparently, they disconnected Hillcrest House from the water supply when the bank sold the 'unoccupied' property to an 'occupier'. At the same time, the sewage pipes were blocked off.

This was done because maintaining that level of pipework for one house isn't cost-effective.

So, they aren't going to reconnect me.

Major crisis.

Mum suggested carrying shit up the road and dumping it in the pub toilet, adding, 'I've got shed-loads of Londis carrier bags – take as many as you need.'

But the thought of swinging a Londis bag of poo up the lane every day is unappealing.

Made repeated phone calls to Amigo Water, but am still being given the runaround.

Have lodged another official complaint.

Wednesday, 30th August

Met Laura at her Bloomsbury house for coffee today. We talked, while Daisy played with Zach's solid-gold cufflink collection.

Laura's life is an interesting contrast to mine right now, in that she is a fairy princess, and I am a shit-covered servant girl.

Big sis is 'a little tired' of pregnancy because the doctor says she should only run five miles a day and can't eat sashimi.

While I was detailing my sewage issues, there was a knock at the door.

Laura thought it was the laundry company, coming to take clothes to be washed, dried and wrapped in lavender-scented paper.

But it was Alex. With an envelope of documents.

I stared at him. 'I thought we were over.'

'This is a business call,' he said. 'Zach said you were here. Read these.' Then he left.

Spread out the documents on Zach's solid-wood dining table and tried my very best to make sense of them.

Couldn't.

Laura interpreted for me, a frown on her lovely, pale forehead.

'It's to do with your sewage problem,' she said. 'Alex has found a loophole. Look here – you see where he's used five different-coloured highlighter pens.'

'But Hillcrest House was uninhabited in the 1990s,' I said. 'It was a squat.'

'Exactly,' said Laura. 'People lived in it.'

Thursday, 31st August

Phoned Amigo Water first thing, and read out the highlights on Alex's documents.

Was immediately transferred out of call-centre hell to the big boss: Jeff Cakebread, Raw Sewage Manager.

Jeff was a jolly old soul, accepting a toffee from his secretary during our conversation.

'Fax your documents over,' he said, between appraising sucks. 'We'll see what we can do.'

Friday, 1st September

Hallelujah!

Just had a call from Jeff Cakebread himself, apologising for the 'erroneous disconnection' and saying I'll be connected 'as a matter of urgency'.

WOO WOO!

Was so happy, I momentarily forgot about problems with Alex and phoned him.

He didn't answer. Got an automated text from his number: 'I can't talk right now.'

Remembered our problems. Decided not to call again.

But still grateful, nonetheless.

Saturday, 2nd September

Mediation with Nick.

We talked about assets and finance, which I suppose is a timely topic since my renovation budget is dwindling fast.

Fiona asked us to write down shared 'assets and liabilities' – i.e. cars, houses etc.

Our only shared property was Daisy's original pram system, which cost £700.

'As much as a second-hand car,' Fiona pointed out.

For the first time in my life, I felt grateful that Nick and I didn't own a house together. At least on the financial front, we have very little to unpick.

We talked about maintenance, and I was given a full ten minutes to rant about Nick's untaxed income and little-prince payments from Helen.

Fiona asked Nick, 'How do you feel about that?'

Nick rested his elbows on his knees and said, 'I just feel like, as soon as I start paying maintenance we're really over. And I'm not ready to lose my family yet. I still think we have a chance.'

He even managed to squeeze out a few tears.

Fiona said, 'But can you understand, Nick, no matter how you're feeling, your daughter needs support?'

Nick nodded. 'I'll sort it,' he sniffed. 'I will.'

He agreed to pay £200 each month and signed a document to that effect.

Couldn't believe it.

'Is that legally binding?' I asked Fiona.

Fiona nodded sadly. 'Yes. If you get sole residency, the court will sign it off.'

I did something a little inappropriate then.

Shouted 'YES!' and punched the air.

Sunday, 3rd September

John Boy has had tattoos done for Daisy and Callum: Ariel the Little Mermaid on his right thigh, Optimus Prime on his left.

Callum is 'well chuffed' with the huge, red-and-blue transformer tattoo, and continually demands John Boy pull up his cargo trousers.

Daisy strokes the wonky-eyed Princess Ariel and says, 'Piss-cess.'

Her Disney princess allegiance changes on a weekly basis, but I won't tell John Boy that.

Very sweet gesture.

Monday, 4th September

The water people came first thing to hack great big holes in the floor.

There is now rubble everywhere, but I couldn't care less.

I'm getting WATER and pipes to take my shit away.

Cha cha cha, cha cha cha!

'Bloody hell,' said Mum, when she saw the smashed-up concrete. 'Even an estate agent would have trouble describing this place now.'

I've decided to keep the bile-yellow 1970s toilet because it feels like a lucky mascot.

Will call the colour 'sunset' yellow, and work out a retro design around it.

Have spent the morning flushing the toilet and clapping with delight.

Sent Alex a 'thank you' message and a video of the flushing toilet.

Alf will be back on site tomorrow. He's planning on a long day, saying he'll bring cement mix and eight tins of pilchards.

Tuesday, 5th September

Alf is really cracking on.

Offered my services as his labourer, but he just blinked and said, 'S'all right. I can open my own pilchards.'

So am taking a backseat to spend precious time with Daisy, work in the pub and nag the council re the roof planning application. The council are still, as expected, elusive about timescales.

Will keep nagging.

The squeaky wheel gets the grease.

Wednesday, 6th September

My nagging phone calls have yielded results!

A council planning inspector called Brian Bush is coming out tomorrow to sign off the listed roof.

Mum can't believe the council has responded so quickly, saying, 'They must have brought in a new load of pigeons to fly the post around.'

Thursday, 7th September

Visit from council planning officer, Brian Bush, today.

Dad and I met him at Hillcrest House, under the small section of roof that still keeps the rain off.

Brian took an instant liking to Dad, shaking his hand and complimenting him on his practical helmet and clipboard arrangement.

'So, tell us the news, Brian,' said Dad. 'How long will Juliette have to wait for this thing to be signed off?'

'Signed off?' said Brian, straightening his tie. 'This roof needs to be restored to its historic glory.'

My heart dropped to my feet. 'But the estate agent said this was a "rubber stamp" sort of thing. Just a formality. They said no sensible planning officer would consider restoring a burned-down roof.'

'Well they haven't met planning officer *Bush* before,' said Brian, tapping his clipboard. 'I stick to the rules. ALL the rules. Call me petty, but if you let the little things go, you end up with a five-storey car park on Windsor Castle. It's a slippery slope.'

'What exactly does restoring burned timbers involve?' I asked.

'There'll be specialist firms who can help you,' said Brian. 'It'll cost a fair bit.'

'I don't have a "fair bit",' I said.

'As I say, rules are rules,' said Brian, slipping his pen into his clipboard case. 'No matter how silly they are, we still have to follow them.'

Friday, 8th September

Brian just phoned.

He's written his report stating that the burnt timbers can't be removed, and must be painstakingly restored by a listed-building expert.

Wish I could go back to last month when I only had raw sewage to worry about.

'You can always appeal,' said Brian. 'But we never change our minds.'

Phoned a local roofing specialist to get an approximate quote.

As predicted, the cost of restoring burned roof timbers is likely to run into tens of thousands.

Lodged an appeal with the council.

Now all I can do is wait.

Saturday, 9th September

Couldn't sleep for worrying last night.

A roof is one of those living essentials you can't really do without.

Had red-rimmed eyes this morning, and the whole family watched me anxiously over breakfast.

Callum very kindly offered me some of his Coco Pops and said, 'Don't worry, Aunty Julesy. You'll fix things. My teacher says anything is possible.'

I wanted to tell him his teacher lived in childish La La Land and had probably never dealt with the local council.

But obviously, you can't say that.

Apparently, there's going to be rain all week.

This pretty much fits my mood.

Daisy's not old enough to do craft stuff or knitting or anything, so it's a nightmare keeping her inside.

VERY worried about the roof.

Checked on the status of my planning appeal, but apparently, it's in the non-urgent pile.

Which means it could take months to be processed.

Without a home, I could lose my little girl.

Weather warnings on TV.

The world is ending.

Sunday, 10th September

11.30 pm

Just finished a shift in the pub.

Terrible storm.

Daisy is sleeping through it, but Callum is wide awake, watching thunder and lightning through his bedroom window and shouting, 'WOW!' every five minutes.

Monday, 11th September.

More weather warnings.

A bad storm predicted tonight.

The Co-op couldn't get its deliveries today or yesterday, and people are panic-buying bottled water and cupboard goods.

The only sensible things left on the shelves are baked beans and sliced white bread.

Mum is always happy for an excuse to stay indoors, but very annoyed that the Co-op has run out of coconut sponge cake and Cadbury's chocolate trifles.

Baked beans on toast for tea.

Tuesday, 12th September

Bad weather has FINALLY cleared.

Blue skies this morning.

Mum was in the kitchen first thing, fully dressed.

'Where's your dressing gown, Nana?' Callum asked.

'I've been out stretching my legs,' said Mum. 'It's been raining all bloody week.'

'You left the house already?' said Dad, blinking at her.

'You never get dressed before nine,' I added.

'I think all that NHS stuff must be getting to me,' said Mum.

Pleased Mum is finally starting to think of her health, but also a little suspicious.

Mum rarely walks anywhere, unless there's some kind of sugary treat at the end of it.

Took Daisy to play in the garden as soon as she was dressed.

Noticed the sledgehammer had been left outside Mum and Dad's shed.

Don't know what Mum's been smashing up this time, but lucky I was around to put the sledgehammer away. Who knows what damage Callum could have done with a tool that size.

Wednesday, 13th September

Something astonishing has happened.

The roof frame at Hillcrest House has totally collapsed.

All the timbers have fallen in – I suppose due to the storm.

'Someone up there must like you,' said Dad. 'The council can't make you restore it now.'

'*Really?*' I said.

'Of course,' said Dad. 'The frame has gone. There's nothing left.'

Cried happy tears.

Promised Dad I will definitely start going to church.

Thursday, 14th September

Dad has got all religious, talking about God and the 'miracle storm'.

Went to church this morning, and the vicar (after a brief four-letter rant about the bell ringers dropping litter) said a special prayer of gratitude for 'Juliette's broken roof'.

Friday, 15th September

Spoke to Brian Bush first thing, and he agreed to an emergency site visit.

After kicking around charred timbers, he admitted restoration was *probably* impossible.

'Although you might want to ring a few specialists,' he said. 'Just to be sure.'

Lost my temper then.

'The whole frame has collapsed,' I said. 'The specialist would have to be trained at Hogwarts.'

Brian looked a bit frightened and agreed to go back to the council offices to think things over.

Saturday, 16th September

Nick's visitation day.

Took Daisy to his new house, the Gables.

I have to admit, it's lovely.

As I yanked the old-fashioned doorbell pull, I gazed enviously at honeysuckle climbing sunset-red bricks.

Nick met us at the door, wearing oversized black glasses and a grey hipster suit with black lapels.

'You're looking smart,' I said.

Nick gave a casual laugh. 'This is my look these days. You can't manage a factory looking like a student. How is my Daisy boo?'

He knelt down to help Daisy out of the Maclaren.

'This is a lovely house,' I said, as Daisy stamped her neon Nikes on the herringbone bricks and stroked the fragrant lavender bush.

'Sadie hates it. She says its old.' Nick led us inside, along the parquet-floored hallway, and into a large, farmhouse-style kitchen with a butler sink and views over a tree-filled garden.

Daisy stroked the warm, bright-red Aga and said, 'Baddy cook. Baddy cook.'

Nick told us casually that he'd bought pizza dough, and would Daisy like to make her own Margherita?

Had an unexpectedly nice time, helping Daisy roll out dough on the oak countertops and scatter cheese all over the floor.

It didn't quite work out how Nick planned because Daisy's pizza was basically a pile of sweetcorn.

'The pizza should look like this picture,' Nick fretted.

He held up *Kidaround Magazine*, which showed smiley face pizzas and adorable children waving tomato-sauce-covered fingers.

Reassured Nick that Daisy didn't know or care what her pizza looked like and that she was enjoying her sweetcorn bread creation.

Nick said, 'Yeah, I know you're right. I just wanted today to be perfect.'

How much he still has to learn.

With kids, nothing ever goes to plan.

Nick asked if Daisy could spend the night. He had a room made up with a pink cot and a giant Peppa Pig stuffed toy, apparently.

I told him one thing at a time.

'Oh, come on, Julesy,' said Nick. 'Daisy could be living with me soon. She has to get used to the place.'

If it had been earlier in the year, I would have gone into a huge rant about Nick never getting residency.

But right now, I can't be sure of anything.

Sunday, 17th September

Extremely tired today, but have a shift in the pub tonight.

Feel like Anneka Rice, but a really stressed, tired version in need of a root touch-up.

Monday, 18th September

Brian Bush was too scared to take my call today, but a lady on his team spoke to me instead.

'Good news,' she said. 'You can put a brand-new roof on. Brian is drafting a permission order as we speak. You got lucky with that storm, didn't you?'

'Yes,' I told her. 'Very lucky.'

Told Mum and Dad the good news.

'You see, Shirley?' said Dad. 'God really does perform miracles.'

Mum winked at me and said, 'Sometimes we make our own miracles.'

Tuesday, 19th September

Whoop whoop!

Work has started again on Hillcrest House.

Alf wants me 'out the bleedin' way', which suits me just fine right now.

Am sick of all the renovation stress and want to forget all about it.

Wednesday, 20th September

Laura's doing hypnobirthing classes.

Apparently, they're so relaxing that she and Zach often fall asleep.

'So, birth should be no trouble!' Laura laughed.

Ha!

I shouldn't laugh, though.

What she's about to go through isn't funny.

Thursday, 21st September

Alf keeps telling me off for bothering him onsite, so Laura suggested I accompany her to the giant Mothercare at Lakeside today.

She wanted some 'pretty maternity bras', among other things.

All the bra packets showed beautiful blonde models with lovely vein-free breasts.

'You're better off with cheap, stretchy sports bras,' I told Laura. 'Post pregnancy, your boobs turn into big, milk-filled udders. You won't want to draw attention to them.'

I made sure she stocked up on post-pregnancy essentials: Lanolin nipple cream, ibuprofen, big pants, a few oversized sweatshirts and some dummies.

'I don't want to give my baby a dummy,' said Laura.

'When your baby cries, all your morality goes out the window,' I explained. 'You'll stuff anything in its mouth to shut it up.'

Laura went a bit white when she saw how many painkillers I'd thrown in the trolley for early labour.

'The hypnobirthing book says I can just breathe the baby out,' she said.

I smiled inwardly and kindly at her naivety.

Was quite fun, maternity shopping.

The calm before the storm.

I remember when Nick and I did the pre-Daisy Mothercare trip.

Nick put me in a pram and pushed me around the shop.

Then he put on a maternity bra, stuck out his lips and did a Mick Jagger impression.

They threw us out after that.

We *did* have fun.

Before nature came crashing down on our heads.

Friday, 22nd September

Dad inspected Hillcrest House this morning, and declared it 'fit for a king.'

'Do you need help moving your things in?' he asked.

'We're not moving in yet,' I told him. 'There's no roof or kitchen. I have to show the Cafcass officer that Daisy lives in a nice, modern home.'

'You'll make Daisy spoiled if you're not careful,' said Dad. 'A bit of tarpaulin will see you right while Alf puts your roof on. And we had none of this fitted-kitchen nonsense in my day. Your Grandma Duffy did all her cooking in one cauldron over a coal fire. And we counted ourselves lucky if we had a newspaper to eat our dinner off.'

Bit worried about the kitchen because there's so little money left.

Am scouring DIY forums for budget tips. The general advice is to fit your own Ikea kitchen, although there's an equal amount of posts from people saying they'd never fit an Ikea kitchen ever again.

Saturday, 23rd September

Althea says she'll help fit the kitchen.

I'm pleased about this because there's no limit to Althea's ambition. She believes she can build anything, given enough MDF and spray paint, and all mistakes can be fixed with Gorilla Glue.

Sunday, 24th September

Laura says she doesn't want a baby shower, but Mum and I have decided to do her one anyway.

We've ordered a huge cake shaped like a nappy.

Could have chosen a chocolate filling, but that seemed borderline disgusting. Decided on coconut sponge in the end.

Have planned lots of fun games to prepare Laura for motherhood. Brandi has even ordered one of those 'authentic' baby dolls they use for sex education classes. The ones that cry until you rock them for ten minutes.

Mum is doing a funny quiz about what to do when the baby throws up, wheezes, grunts, etc.

So, should be fun.

Monday, 25th September

Have spent HOURS trying to figure out Ikea's kitchen planner app.

Althea and I huddled over her laptop this morning, while Daisy and Wolfgang pulled at our legs and cried for attention.

Eventually, Althea had the genius idea of hiding toys around her house for them both to find. But we ended that game when Wolfgang found Althea's blowtorch.

Althea got angry with the kitchen app before I did.

But I wanted to punch the laptop too.

We're driving to Ikea this weekend, so a real person can help us.

Tuesday, 26th September

Laura's baby shower didn't go well.

Brandi should NEVER have ordered that realistic, crying baby doll.

And then there was Mum's quiz:

+ 'What should you do when you need the toilet, but your baby wants to be constantly held?'

+ 'What should you do when your baby cries for two hours straight, and nothing will soothe it?'

+ 'What should you do when your baby keeps throwing up milk, and you're worried it will die of dehydration?'

Soon Laura was mumbling, 'I'm not sure I can do this. I may have changed my mind.'

I made Laura camomile tea, while Mum bashed the crying baby about to shut it up. Unfortunately, the baby had some sort of abuse sensor, and the crying turned to heart-felt screeching.

Dad had the bright idea of driving it around in Laura's new baby car seat.

He returned half an hour later, chuckling, 'Just like a real baby! A few laps in the car and she nodded right off.'

Laura had calmed down by then and was apologising.

'All that crying sent me over the edge,' she explained. 'But I've got things in perspective now. I mean, a real baby can't cry for that long.'

We were too kind to correct her.

Wednesday, 27th September

Good news.

Alf has nearly finished the roof.

He's got a few friends helping him now – one with chronic arthritis and another with very bad cataracts.

They divide up the jobs sensibly, so the cataract friend never has to climb a ladder.

Alf says the roof will be finished tomorrow.

Then he just needs to do the staircase, windows, plastering and structural works.

Alf's original solution to the broken patio doors was to brick them over, but I persuaded him that glazed doors aren't draughty these days and there's just about enough in the budget for them.

I think Alf is a bit perplexed by my 'modern' ideas – especially the open-plan living area, heated by radiators instead of coal fires.

Thursday, 28th September

The house is really coming along.

I have a ROOF, which is probably the best news I've had all year.

When I was with Nick, I never thought I'd own my own home – let alone a three-bedroom detached house.

Yet, here I am.

OK – so I don't have a kitchen yet, or a bathroom, and there is graffiti upstairs.

But we're getting there.

Friday, 29th September

Headed up to Hillcrest House with a broom and various cleaning products, while Dad babysat Daisy.

Swept up rubble, scrubbed graffiti and washed everything I could.

Then Alf turned up and told me the wall I'd just spent an hour scrubbing clean of 'Chelsea is a Slag' would be plastered today. So, I've just wasted a lot of time and two spray bottles of Mr Muscle.

Saturday, 30th September

Arranged to meet Nick on the waterfront today for his visitation.

He was pushing Horatio back and forth over the decked promenade when we arrived, and his face lit up when he saw us.

Daisy shouted, 'Baddy. Baddy.'

Had a fairly mature chat about the impending court hearing, and Nick said, 'I just want us all to be together.'

Then he started crying.

I let him blub on my shoulder, while Daisy ran up and down the promenade shouting, 'Baddy cry! Baddy cry!'

'It's not going to happen, Nick,' I said. 'Look – why don't you just drop the court case? Save us all the stress. I'm killing myself trying to get this house ready in time. You know I respect you as Daisy's father. I'd never stop you seeing her.'

Nick sniffed, 'I know, I know. But it's too late to turn back now.'

Sunday, 1st October

Ikea trip with Althea.

Wolfgang had to go in the front seat because he's a violent chair-kicker. Somehow, he managed to change the sat nav to 'avoid all motorways', so our one-hour drive took three.

By the time we'd reached Ikea, Wolfgang had ripped the glove box to pieces.

Daisy was snivelling, 'Hate car, Mummy. Shut up car.'

Althea and I both felt we deserved a slice of Swedish Daim bar cake and a plate of meatballs (Althea is currently taking yet another 'chill out' from vegetarianism), so we set Daisy and Wolfgang loose in the restaurant's futuristic kiddie play circle.

Wolfgang actually *broke* one of the unbreakable spinning Perspex things.

Althea tried to take it off him, while 'nurturing his inquisitive spirit'.

'Well done, Wolfgang,' she said. 'Now give Mummy the magic wheel.'

Wolfgang bared his single, large tooth and scampered into the Ikea showroom maze, whirling the Perspex disc around his head like a battle-axe.

By the time we found him, he'd ripped off a kitchen-cupboard door, put his fist through a wall canvas and smashed a display jar of pasta.

Two yellow-t-shirted Ikea assistants circled Wolfgang, like RSPCA officers around a hissing swan.

One offered a lollypop. The other held a geometric-patterned cushion like a shield.

Althea was furious when she saw Wolfgang had destroyed the wall canvas.

'Wolfgang!' she shouted. 'That's *art*. You don't destroy art! Somewhere, a fairy has just fallen down dead.'

She grabbed him, howling, by the scruff of the neck and shoved him into a trolley, saying, 'I've had enough now, Wolfy. You're going to baby prison.'

Then she took him to the complimentary soft-play area.

Felt very sorry for the soft-play people. You could tell they didn't want to let Wolfgang in, but there was no queue, so they had to.

God knows what damage Wolfgang did in there, but frankly, I was happy to have him out of the way.

Daisy was sad when Wolfgang got banged up.

'Where Wiffy?' she kept asking.

I explained that Wolfgang had been naughty and was doing time.

Managed to order the kitchen without too much fuss.

It's due to be delivered in a few weeks.

The Ikea lady assured us that the kitchen *really is* simple enough for anyone to fit.

'If a builder can do it, you can too, right?' she enthused.

Althea got angry then. She hates job stereotyping and educational prejudice.

'Are you saying builders are thick?' she barked.

The lady mumbled something about builders not needing GCSEs, which sent Althea into a long rant about education, judgement and subjectivity.

Maybe she had a point. But she didn't need to make someone cry so early in the morning.

Monday, 2nd October

Alf has got the boiler working at Hillcrest House, by hitting various pipes with a hammer.

He fancied warming his pilchards in hot water, so he thought he might as well 'have a bash'.

A Corgi-registered plumber friend checked everything over, and amazingly the boiler passed as gas-safe. Even the radiators work.

We've now nicknamed the boiler 'Old Beryl', after Alf's late wife.

The hot water takes a while to get going, but I'm not going to complain.

I think the plumber was more surprised than anyone – especially since he found an old bird's nest in the flue.

Dad was very impressed that the boiler still works.

'You see, Shirley?' he told Mum. 'We should have held onto our old system. Things were built to last, pre-Margaret Thatcher.'

Mum insisted on a new boiler in the late Eighties, because she was 'sick of playing sodding Russian roulette' every time she needed a hot bath. She also wanted an extra cupboard for her towels.

They've replaced the boiler five times since then.

So, I suppose Dad has a point.

Tuesday, 3rd October

Daisy's birthday.

Two years old! I can't believe it.

Where did the time go?

Bought Daisy a Tiny Bike, which she went whizzing around on, and some new shoes, which she ignored in favour of her neon trainers.

Wednesday, 4th October

Bit of an incident in the pub last night.

Yorkie set fire to his moustache doing a flaming Sambuca shot.

Fortunately, Dad is St John's Ambulance-trained.

He talked in an authoritative, calm voice, then wrapped Yorkie in one of the three fire blankets he keeps in strategic places around the pub.

Novelty flammable spirits are now banned from the Oakley Arms.

This goes on a long list of banned items, including Cards Against Humanity and Pokémon Go.

Thursday, 5th October

Realise I need furniture for the house.

Lots of furniture.

Our Canary Wharf flat was furnished by Helen, primarily in white leather, so at the grand age of thirty-one, I don't even possess my own bed.

The trouble is, I didn't budget for furniture. I saw it as a minor cost, but in fact, it runs into thousands.

Althea offered to make some bespoke pieces, but her furniture is always impractical. Her last sofa was made from reclaimed cheese graters.

Laura suggested I bring a van up to Bloomsbury and drive around the streets looking for things people have thrown out.

'I'm always seeing amazing furniture left on the curb up here,' Laura told me. 'Everyone is so rich; they think Marks & Spencer is where you get cheap stuff.'

Yorkie has offered his van, and John Boy says he can drive it, so the two of us are heading to London tomorrow.

Let's see what we can find.

Friday, 6th October

Went to London in Yorkie's van.

Meant to leave first thing, but John Boy and I had to give the van a good scrub first and clear out all the Tennent's Super cans.

I should never have trusted John Boy's assertion that he could drive a van, but that's a side issue.

For future reference, a metal foot and an accelerator pedal equal two near collisions, a squashed traffic cone and several outraged pedestrians.

Anyway.

Laura was totally right.

We found some great furniture in Bloomsbury, including a double bed, wardrobe and loads of lounge stuff.

Our first find was a beautiful cream sofa suite left out on the pavement by a three-storey townhouse. There was nothing wrong with it, except for a tiny stain on one sofa arm.

'They can't be throwing that out, can they?' said John Boy.

We knocked on the door to check.

A raven-haired, Botoxed housewife greeted us, with full assurances that the suite was ours for the taking.

'Oh yes, have it, have it!' she insisted, before adding apologetically, 'It's only from M&S.'

A few roads later, we found a solid-wood coffee table and some chairs and tables. And then a solid-wood dresser in someone's front garden.

The dresser was especially beautiful – an antique, we thought, and lovingly crafted. It was a bit sticky, but after the state of Yorkie's van, John Boy and I didn't mind getting our hands dirty.

When we got it back to Great Oakley, John Boy said, 'Something smells of paint.'

He was right.

There was definitely a painty smell coming from the van.

We realised it was the dresser, which was not dirty after all, but tacky with a fresh coat of varnish.

'Why would you varnish something, then throw it out?' I asked.

'Maybe they varnished it, then put it out to dry,' John Boy suggested.

We looked at each other.

'Shit,' said John Boy. 'Better put it back.'

We drove around Bloomsbury with Daisy howling in the front seat, but neither of us could remember which house we'd taken the dresser from.

I knocked on a few doors but just got odd looks.

'What are we going to do?' I asked John Boy.

'You'll just have to keep it,' he said.

The dresser is currently in my living room, displaying three mismatched wine glasses and a Kilner jar of multi-coloured pasta.

Saturday, 7th October

The house is…well, it's *beginning* to look like a *house*.

Fire-damaged parts have been repaired and plastered over. The staircase is in.

The double-glazed sliding doors are going in today, which means we'll have a lovely view from the kitchen over the fields, without having to wear our coats.

Technically we could *live* there now. Although I doubt Johnny Jiggens would call it a 'suitable family home' just yet.

But we've come a long way.

Heating. Water. Roof.

It's all going on!

Sunday, 8th October

Laura is already getting 'twinges'.

She's really excited because she has absolutely no idea what's in store for her.

Sex education classes should definitely include a few scenes from *One Born Every Minute*.

Laura and Zach are going for a moonlit walk around Bloomsbury to try and 'get things moving'.

I remember doing the same thing when I was pregnant.

Silly.

I should have enjoyed my freedom while it lasted.

Monday, 9th October

Laura's twinges have slowed down.

She's feeling a bit disappointed.

Zach has gone to buy organic pineapple slices, which are supposed to hurry things along.

Asked Laura what the rush was.

Expected her to say, 'So fucking sick of strangers rubbing my belly' or 'Desperate to sit still for half an hour without needing a wee.'

But she said, 'I just can't wait to meet my baby.'

Tuesday, 10th October

Laura's private birthing consultation today.

She wanted me to come along because, as someone who's given birth, Laura sees me as an expert.

If only she knew.

There is hardly anything about labour I can actually remember – and the few bits I can, I wish I could forget.

Truth be told, I'm terrified of ever giving birth again. Those giant barbeque tongs haunt my dreams.

Laura and Zach have decided on a homebirth.

Knowing Laura, it will be perfect and spiritual and pain-free.

But probably not.

Still – I can't tell Laura the potentially awful truth. It goes against everything she's learning in her hypno-birthing classes.

Laura's perfect pregnancy is ongoing. No throwing up, no tiredness.

How did she sidestep all the bad stuff?

When I was pregnant with Daisy, I went to bed at 7pm every night.

And my morning sickness lasted *months*.

The midwife always said:

'Eat some dry crackers first thing in the morning.'

It never worked. And even now, Jacob's Cream Crackers turn my stomach.

Wednesday, 11th October

The Ikea kitchen arrived at 7am.

Althea and I tried to install it, while Mum looked after Wolfgang and Daisy. Mum is one of the few adults who actually likes Wolfgang, calling him a 'tough little sod'.

The kitchen definitely was NOT like hanging cupboards.

Within an hour, Althea and I were both in tears. And Althea never cries.

'I can't do all this measuring shit,' Althea moaned. 'I'm too much of a free thinker. And where can all these fucking screws go?'

At midday, Dad came over with ham sandwiches and crisps.

He found Althea and I clutching each other and sobbing.

'What's all this then?' Dad asked, setting down his tartan flask and picking up the kitchen plans. 'It looks dead simple to me.'

The word 'simple' set Althea off again, and she began to wail loudly.

'Let's have some lunch, and I'll take a look at it,' said Dad.

After sandwiches, Dad fetched his tool belt, three tape measures, tinted eye protectors and a hardhat.

'Who will run the pub?' I asked.

'John Boy can manage,' said Dad. 'My little girl needs me.'

He sorted screws into twenty different piles and made neat little pencil marks all over the kitchen.

By teatime, Dad had fitted the lower cupboards and half the countertop.

'I'll be back tomorrow to fit the rest,' he assured us, tucking his pencil behind his ear. 'They're right about Ikea kitchens, aren't they? They're a doddle.'

Thursday, 12th October

Dad fitted the rest of the kitchen today, so I took his shift in the pub, while Mum looked after Daisy.

It's a different world, dealing with daytime drinkers.

Amazing how intellectual some of the regulars are before they reach the drunkenness of early evening.

Yorkie made some excellent observations about electoral reform and the refugee crisis.

Am so excited to have a kitchen.

Have ordered more Kilner jars and multi-coloured pasta, ready for the grand finale.

Court hearing in six weeks.

I think I can do this, you know. I think I can get the house ready in time.

The only problem is not having enough money left to fit a bathroom.

My current solution is simply not to let Johnny Jiggens upstairs when he visits for his pre-court living assessment.

Friday, 13th October

I have a kitchen! And on a supposedly unlucky day of the year, which just goes to show how stupid superstition is.

Dad has done an amazing job – the kitchen looks just like the Ikea website.

He's even managed to get the cupboards straight against the wonky west wall.

Have spent the morning twirling around the lovely, rot-free kitchen cupboards with Daisy in my arms.

I am SO grateful it is ridiculous.

It's like Mum says about Mr Lao's Chinese.

You only know stuff is good because you've had it bad.

Saturday, 14th October

Laura's in labour!

It's definitely real labour because she's stopped saying please and thank you.

Mum and I are going up to London in a minute, and Dad will stay with Daisy.

I'll drive because Mum can't be trusted in an emergency. She's erratic at the best of times – often treating traffic lights and zebra crossings as suggestions.

Have phoned Alex to tell him the news.

It seemed like the right thing to do, even though we haven't spoken for a while.

We had a formal sort of phone call, during which Alex told me he couldn't come to Zach's house because women often take their clothes off during labour.

'Zachary will message when my nephew arrives,' said Alex.

'How do you know it's a boy?' I asked.

'Tradition,' said Alex. 'In our family, we always have boys first. When Zach is ready, and the dust has settled, he'll book me in for a visit.'

Typical Daltons.

So bloody formal.

I'm well rid of all that.

It may work for Laura, but not for me.

Sunday, 15th October

Still at hospital, waiting for Laura to give birth.

Pity Laura's homebirth plans fell through, but I suppose it wasn't meant to be.

When we arrived in Bloomsbury yesterday, Laura had turned Zach's wooden-floored living room into a magical birthing cave.

There was an aroma lamp blowing out clouds of lavender steam, and twinkling candles on every surface.

Laura's contractions had slowed down when we arrived, so everything felt very calm.

We were welcomed, between contractions. Laura even offered us herbal tea.

Zach looked at her fondly and said, 'I'll make the tea, darling. You're doing all the hard work.'

Mum pulled out a Bell's whisky bottle and said, 'Anyone fancy a splash of this?'

I gave Mum a long lecture about pregnancy and alcohol.

'What about Bailey's then?' said Mum, rummaging in her shopping bag.

'Laura can't have *any* alcohol,' I said. 'She's pregnant.'

'You're all being so bloody precious,' Mum argued. 'I'm telling you. We'll be glad of this when things kick off.'

'Kick off?' said Laura, looking confused. 'But things have already kicked off.'

Mum and I exchanged glances.

'It's going to get worse, love,' said Mum, matter-of-factly. 'This is just the start. Pace yourself. You could still be going tomorrow. Or even the day after, if you're really unlucky.'

I realised that my niece or nephew could be born on my birthday. How exciting!

'The baby will be here *today*,' Laura insisted. 'Things are really full on. You probably don't realise, because I'm doing hypnobirthing exercises.'

Mum and I exchanged more glances.

'Maybe we should get the birthing pool ready,' Zach suggested.

An hour later, he was still blowing air into the giant, inflatable pool.

'Darling,' said Laura. 'Is it nearly ready? I'm getting quite uncomfortable.'

Zach said, 'Apologies. I should have thought about a pump.'

'Why didn't you think to blow it up earlier?' Laura snapped. 'It's taking *blimmin* hours.'

Mum and I both gasped in shock.

Laura *nearly swearing*.

'Give it here, let me have a try,' said Mum, grabbing the valve. She huffed and puffed and delivered great lungfuls of air, but after another half-hour, the birthing pool still looked like a sad, week-old party balloon.

I had a go but did little better.

'I *think* it's getting bigger,' said Zach.

'Just fill it with water!' Laura shouted.

'That could take rather a while too,' Zach admitted.

'How long?' asked Laura, through gritted teeth.

Zach scanned the birthing pool instructions and said, 'Half an hour. Or more.'

'It HURTS,' Laura sobbed, rocking back and forth on her birthing ball. 'It really, really HURTS. *PLEASE*. Just get me some warm water to sit in.'

Zach ran a hose from the sink, and a tiny stream of water began trickling into the pool.

Laura threw off her clothes.

'Darling,' said Zach. 'It's not full yet.'

'I don't care,' said Laura, kneeling in the ankle-deep water. 'More water. MORE WATER.'

Zach ran back and forth with kettle loads of boiling water.

He had to forgo a partial kettle load though because Mum had made herself a cup of tea.

For the next two hours, we watched a naked Laura in the pool, moaning and wailing, while we added more water.

'Would you like a Jaffa Cake, love?' Mum suggested. 'They're from Aldi, but they taste just like the real ones.'

With screwed-shut eyes, Laura shook her head.

'Anyone else?' asked Mum, offering the packet.

Suddenly, there was an ominous groaning, creaking sound.

Mum leapt towards Laura, clutching faux Jaffa Cakes to her chest. 'The bloody pool is sinking,' she shouted. 'Look.'

She was right.

A big, soft dip had appeared in the pool, behind a moaning, wailing Laura.

Mum hauled Laura out of the water, but the dip was still growing and widening.

By the time we got Laura to the sofa, the whole birthing pool had sagged right into the floor. Then, with a slow and determined creak, it crashed down into the solicitor's office below.

Three suited, soaking-wet solicitors stared up at us, one mid-bite of a now-soggy caramel shortbread slice.

There was an outraged cry about original land registry documents, and a recently restored ceiling rose.

Then one solicitor pointed right at me and said, 'It's *her*, Jonathan. The woman who *stole* my antique dresser!'

I gave an awkward wave.

'Would anyone like some whisky?' Mum bellowed. 'Or I've got Bailey's if you're driving home?'

Monday, 16th October

Poor Laura.

I'd forgotten labour could be so *long*.

We're STILL in the hospital, with Laura dozing fitfully on Zach's shoulder.

Laura was in too much pain to dress at Zach's house, so we had to wrap her in towels and carry her down to the ambulance.

The solicitors glared at us through their office window.

'What are you bloody looking at?' Mum snapped, as we carried a semi-naked Laura down the townhouse steps. 'Pull a mop and bucket out and get on with it. And what do you expect if you leave a dresser out on the street?'

By the time we got to hospital, Laura was so far dilated she couldn't walk.

Zach and an especially strong hospital orderly had to carry her up to the maternity ward.

Our family has now consumed a bottle and a half of Bell's whisky, a bottle of Bailey's, a triple pack of Aldi-own Jaffa Cakes, several foot-long Italian Subway Sandwiches, three packets of Kettle chips and a large Indian takeaway with papadums and naan.

The midwife told us off for having takeaway food delivered to the labour ward but turned a blind eye when Mum gave her a shot of Bailey's in a specimen cup.

Praying the baby will be here soon.

Poor Laura.

Tuesday, 17th October

Just realised it's my birthday tomorrow.

Laura STILL in labour.

Managed a brief trip home to see Daisy, but was soon back at the hospital because the midwives told Mum the baby would arrive any minute.

By the time I returned, Laura was accusing the midwives of lying and selling false promises. Then she screeched about never, ever wanting another baby.

'I hate seeing her suffer,' said Zach, taking a fretful sip of whisky. 'But I'd rather hoped we'd have three children.'

'Oh, she won't remember any of this,' Mum reassured him. 'Juliette was moaning like a cow and asking for Crunchy Nut Cornflakes at 10cm dilated. And you don't remember a thing, do you love?'

I nodded in agreement.

Wednesday, 18th October
1 am

Have just realised it's my birthday RIGHT NOW.

Seems a bit inappropriate to get everyone singing Happy Birthday, so will just write it down.

Happy birthday to me, happy birthday to me ...

Afternoon

Very weird birthday so far, spent in the labour ward by my screaming sister.

Poor Laura!

Brandi turned up at lunchtime with supplies from the pub (whisky and vodka), wanting to know why Laura couldn't have an epidural.

'It wasn't part of our birthing plan,' Zach admitted. 'And now it's too late. We didn't know. We didn't *know*.'

Laura moaned and swore about 'bloody hypno-birthing'.

Then a new midwife came on shift.

Laura screeched, 'Give me an epidural! That other bitch said no.

You have to help me!'

'Oh, it's far too late for that,' said the new midwife. 'Baby will be along in a minute. I can get you a couple of aspirin if you like.'

A cacophony of swearing followed.

'I think she needs something stronger,' I said. 'She's been in labour for days.'

'I've seen labours last two weeks before,' said the midwife. 'The human body is designed to suffer. She'll be just fine.'

I suppose midwives have to be a bit oblivious to pain, or they wouldn't be able to do their job. Mind you, I can also see why some people call them 'madwives'.

'Laura, love,' Mum whispered. 'Do you want some more whisky?'

Evening

HAPPY BIRTHDAY TO ME!

I have another nephew. A beautiful, scrunchy-faced blond nephew.

And we share the same birthday.

What a day. And night. And then another day and night. And a day.

Am exhausted, but happy.

Laura is even more exhausted and even happier.

She's calling the baby 'Bear' after Bear Grylls – a surprisingly unusual name for her, but she's spent days without proper sleep.

Zach likes the name, saying the baby must be very strong and determined to give Laura such a hard labour.

Nice he's looking at things that way. Other people might think of their child as cursed or a bringer of disaster.

Phoned Alex again.

He asked me if I'd been home yet.

'Only briefly,' I said. 'Laura wanted me with her. She's been in labour for days.'

'There's a birthday present waiting for you,' he said.

'You didn't have to do that,' I said. 'We're not even together.'

'We're still friends aren't we, Juliette? That hasn't changed.'

Agreed with that. We *are* still friends.

Alex seemed happy about his nephew, but was critical of Zach and Laura's 'outlandish' name choice, saying it would 'severely affect the boy's career options'.

'What are you talking about?' I said. 'It's just a name.'

'How many high-court judges do you know called Bear?' Alex replied.

Late Evening

Got home to find Alex's present – an antler coat stand.

It was made of resin, which was a relief. He hadn't shot any deer.

Good choice of gift, I think. Not romantic. But thoughtful. The sort of thing a friend might buy another friend.

Thanked Alex for the present, and let myself miss him for a moment. Then I put a billion photos of baby Bear on Facebook.

Couldn't be prouder.

Daisy was still awake, bright-eyed and bushy-tailed, wanting stories of baby Bear and the hospital.

She'd had a good time with Dad, helping to squirt Mr Sheen and sort nuts and bolts into containers.

I think she was glad to see me home again, even though I was exhausted.

Told Daisy that a magical prince had been born, then fell asleep on the sofa.

Woke up to hear Daisy and Callum giggling like maniacs.

They'd scribbled permanent marker on my eyebrows and written 'stinky' on my cheek.

Dad said, 'You'll want to get that off before your pub shift, love.'

ARRRRRG!

Thursday, 19th October

The permanent marker *still* won't come off.

I can't work in the pub like this.

I look like an evil vampire princess. A stinky one.

Friday, 20th October

The pub regulars all teased me about the permanent marker last night.

Felt annoyed about their insensitivity and said so.

Have managed to remove most of the word 'stinky' from my cheek, but my eyebrows are still black and pointed. To scrub at them too persistently would mean losing eyebrow hair, so it's a tough call.

Evil vampire princess or sickly heroin user?

Saturday, 21st October

Promised Laura I'd see baby Bear today, so Mum offered to take Daisy to Nick's for visitation.

Mum said there were packed suitcases in Nick's hall because Sadie is threatening to move out again.

Typical Nick and Sadie drama.

'How was Nick?' I asked Mum. 'Is he nervous about court?'

'He just went on and on about wanting you back, love,' Mum told me. 'I was so bored in the end, I had to bash open the Terry's chocolate orange I'd bought for the Halloween raffle.'

When I shouted at her about diabetes, Mum looked hurt and said, 'I only had eight segments, Julesy. That's progress, don't you think?'

Sunday, 22nd October

Have decided Daisy and I should move into Hillcrest House.

The property still looks like a concrete squat and has no bathing facilities, but I'll get lots more done if I'm actually living there.

Time is running out.

There's no way Johnny Jiggens will assess it as a 'nice family home' right now, and there's no budget to pay decorators. I need to be onsite all the time, doing whatever I can.

Hope I'm not fucking Daisy up for life, moving her into a concrete-floored house, but she must understand ... this is for *her*. For HER.

Daisy 'helped' with packing by putting the TV remote and old toast crusts into the net compartment of my suitcase.

This resulted in Mum going ballistic because she couldn't turn the TV on and missed *The Apprentice*.

Monday, 23rd October

Packed all our boxes into Mum and Dad's Honda Civic Shuttle.

Would have used my car, but couldn't remove Daisy's child seat to tip the back seats forward.

Carved several deep gouges into my hand trying to pull the seatbelt free from the spiky plastic internals, then gave up.

Mum drove the two minutes down the country lane and managed to get a speeding warning from an off-duty police officer out on a nature ramble.

Tuesday, 24th October

Unpacked boxes this morning, while Daisy ran around the house, all excited.

One month to turn this place into a nice family home with carpets, painted walls and adequate washing facilities.

We've climbed many mountains, but there's still a few more to go.

Mum brought over some 'cupboard fillers', raided from the pub catering kitchen:

+ 5 kilograms smoked back bacon
+ 1 catering-size Heinz tomato ketchup (too big to stand up in any cupboard)
+ 5 loaves Chef Essentials sliced bread.
+ 1-kilogram tub of Chef Essentials butter
+ 50 luxury mini apple pies
+ A box of 20 McVitie's chocolate digestive packets, totalling 360 biscuits
+ A five-litre bottle of cooking sherry

Very grateful.

Had bacon sandwiches for lunch and tea, with apple pie for afters.

When Daisy fell asleep, I treated myself to a chocolate digestive for every wall I painted with undercoat.

Wednesday, 25th October
Woke up this morning to birdsong.

It's very quiet and peaceful here.

Daisy slept brilliantly.

I didn't sleep so well, worrying about court in a month, unpainted walls etc.

It turns out that living in a very unfinished house is quite stressful.

When I was at the pub, I could forget about everything that

needed doing.

But not here.

Ended up painting walls like a mad woman at 3am last night.

When the sun came up, everything looked streaky.

But soldiered on after a bacon sandwich, and finished the upstairs before Daisy woke up.

Will do more painting when Daisy is in bed because she's a bugger when the tins are out.

'Paint, paint!' she cries, trying to jam her pudgy little fingers into chemical emulsion.

VERY tired today, but couldn't rest my eyes as I had to make sure Daisy didn't touch any walls.

Thursday, 26th October

LOTS of painting.

Nearly finished the WHOLE downstairs, but ran out of paint at 10 pm.

B&Q had already closed, so put in an emergency call to Dad.

He keeps a library of half-used paint tins in his garage, neatly arranged by shade and date.

Within ten minutes, he was at the house with just the shade I needed.

He would have been quicker, but Mum had mis-shelved a tin of Dulux Natural Hessian and thrown out his system, causing a row.

Between the two of us, Dad and I finished the painting by midnight and had a bottle of Guinness each to celebrate.

What a difference paint makes!

Just the cement and bare-board floors now, plus installing washing facilities upstairs.

Have no idea how I'll do that last, fairly urgent, one – there just isn't enough money.

Friday, 27th October

This morning, the boiler shuddered to a start, made a popping sound, then stopped.

Every radiator has now gone cold.

I only have myself to blame.

Should never have listened to Dad's assertions about 1970s boilers.

Wanted to burst into tears.

I must admit, right now Daisy doesn't seem to mind the cold. She must have inherited Dad's Scottish blood.

When I take her out in cold weather, she often (rather randomly) removes a single shoe and sock from her left foot, and doesn't mind her toes going blue.

I always get tutting grannies telling me to wrap her up better, or alerting me in panicked voices, 'EXCUSE ME! Your daughter has LOST A SHOE!'

Mum said she'd lend me money for a plumber, but all the local ones are on urgent jobs, or in Florida, or the Bahamas and can't fit us in until mid-December.

If I'd realised tradespeople went abroad so much, I would have seriously reconsidered my post-college training.

Saturday, 28th October

Pub shift last night.

Returned home with Daisy this morning to a VERY cold house.

Daisy seems positively enlivened by the freezing temperature.

She took off all her clothes and played for hours in a washing-up tub of icy-cold water.

Have asked everyone I know for emergency plumber recommendations, but no one is free.

Phoned Dad, but he refused to help with the boiler because he's not Corgi-registered.

Asked Mum if she had any bright ideas, and she offered to watch a YouTube video on boiler maintenance.

'You don't know the first thing about plumbing,' I said.

'Bollocks,' Mum replied. 'Plumbing is just hitting things in the right places, then charging eighty quid.'

I have to admit, that's pretty much what Alf did – although he didn't charge me.

Mum says she'll be here tomorrow morning.

Hopefully, I'll have found a plumber by then.

Sunday, 29th October

Mum turned up at 11am with a Chef's Kitchen catering-sized apple strudel, a three-pint carton of cream (elevenses!) and a large hammer.

She's of the 'bang it until it works' persuasion. To be fair, she has a 50% success rate. But it didn't work this time.

Sambuca followed Mum from the pub, and is still here, preening himself and leaving cat hair on my bed.

Daisy loves Sambuca, so I don't have the heart to throw him out yet.

I'm sure Daisy will change her mind when he scratches her.

Monday, 30th October

Had a nightmare last night about Daisy drowning under blankets.

Not sure what to do for the best.

Are six too many? Or not enough?

Phoned Althea and told her about my anxieties.

'Just go with your mother's instinct,' she said.

But mother's instinct, anxiety and paranoia all feel exactly the same.

I remember when Daisy threw up her milk as a new-born.

I was convinced that:

A: She was seriously ill

B: She would starve to death

C: Members of the medical profession were irresponsible and uncaring and not to be trusted

But Mum was right.

Daisy *was* just fine.

Although a quick Google of cot death proves, it *has* happened since the 1980s. Quite a bit, actually.

Sambuca still hasn't returned to the pub, so I've bought him some cat food. Hopefully, this will stop him knocking our bin over and tearing through the bag for scraps.

On the positive side, he hasn't scratched Daisy yet, even though she keeps dragging him around by his tail.

Tuesday, 31st October
Halloween

Sadie called round this evening, as Daisy and I were heading to the pub for my evening shift.

She was dressed in a sexy witch costume. Baby Horatio was in the pram, wearing a fluffy, blue monster baby-gro.

In my confusion, I nearly offered Sadie a choice of milk-chocolate skull lollipop or pumpkin-shaped all-butter shortbread.

Withdrew the treat bucket when I realised who she was.

'What the fuck do you want?' I asked.

Sadie gave a tentative, 'Trick or treat!', and took a small pink pot plant from the pram's beverage holder.

'What's that?' I asked.

'Look, I know something's going on with you and Nick,' said Sadie, presenting me with the plant. 'He's been sneaking around for months. I thought – I'd bring this and we could talk. I mean, it's only from the Co-op. But it's a peace offering.'

'You don't need to worry about Nick and me getting back together,' I said. 'You're welcome to him.'

Sadie gave a gay little laugh, eyes slightly manic and said, 'But what if I don't want him any more?'

I just said, 'Um…look, talk to your boyfriend. I can't help you.'

Sadie placed the pot plant cautiously on the doorstep, then left.

Later, Sambuca dug the plant out of its pot.

I gave Sambuca apple strudel and a few spoons of cream to say thank you.

Wednesday, 1st November

Alex phoned this afternoon, while I was bathing Daisy in the sink.

As usual, Daisy was oblivious to the cold. In fact, she was thoroughly enjoying sink bath time, splashing me with freezing water and doing her Sid James laugh when I screamed in shock.

I wasn't looking forward to washing after her. One of the taps had ice around it.

I asked Alex why he was calling, and he said he wanted to see how I was.

'So, you're calling as a friend?' I asked.

'As a friend who cares about you a lot.'

Told Alex about the broken heating.

He was sympathetic, but I don't think he could get his head around the temperature because he was on Bondi Beach, where they'd just had a severe heat warning.

Back to the pub now for a long shift tonight.

Time to pack up Daisy's things and get going.

It's tiring going back and forth, but not half as tiring as renovating a house.

SO many things still to do.

And even if I get the renovation stuff done, what's Johnny Jiggens going to think if the heating doesn't work?

Thursday, 2nd November

Went to bed at 8 pm yesterday, wearing all my clothes under three duvets.

Unconsciousness was a blessed relief from the cold.

Sambuca slept on the bed with me, which was actually quite nice – like a little hot water bottle. He's in no hurry to return home. I suppose, like Daisy, he doesn't mind the cold.

On the positive side, we're having carpets fitted after the weekend. This will go some way to insulating the house and keeping us warm.

The local carpet company, 'All For Floors', can fit me in early next week because one of their customers died yesterday, and no longer needs a cream Berber on her hall and landing.

They've offered me a heavy discount on her brand-new cream Berber carpet roll, but Sambuca's still here, and I don't trust him near a chunky weave. He's already clawed my pyjamas to pieces and attacks the free newspapers and junk mail with frantic yowling noises.

Friday, 3rd November

A huge bundle of ski-gear arrived today, special delivery from Alex.

It was a lovely gesture, but deep down I still want ALEX to keep me warm.

Silly, I know.

We tried. It didn't work. Time to move on.

I really enjoyed the ski-gear and stayed up late watching *Apprentice* episodes on my phone.

You could tell a man had designed the thermal all-in-one suit though because a woman would have added an escape hatch.

It wasn't easy stripping off the whole suit to use the toilet. But on the positive side, it has cut down my late-night Guinness consumption.

Saturday, 4th November

Was so sick of the heating not working that I took a hammer to it myself, and guess what? It spluttered to life!

The pipes make a weird, groaning noise every so often – sort of like a cow giving birth. But the house is warm! WARM!

Cha cha cha, da da da, cha cha cha!

Mum was over the moon when I told her how I fixed the boiler.

'See, Bob!' she crowed. 'I told you all those counter-balancing, measure wrench things of yours are a waste of time. It WAS a hammer that fixed it.'

The flooring delivery man arrived to find Daisy and me running around the house, arms outstretched, singing, 'Feeling Hot Hot Hot'.

We now have two huge rolls of carpet and one roll of underlay spanning the open-plan dining area, plus boxes of solid-wood flooring – all ready for fitting on Monday.

Can't walk on the kitchen floor right now, because it's covered in latex floor leveller.

Alex's birthday tomorrow. This poses a few dilemmas:

A: Should I get him a present, given the current state of affairs, or would that be a humiliating act?

B: If I did get him a present, what on earth would I buy him?

C: He said his family aren't big on birthdays anyway, so maybe he just wants to forget about it. I mean, I would. If I'd nearly burned to death on my birthday.

Considering all of the above, I won't get Alex anything.

It's just too much of a minefield.

Sunday, 5th November
Bonfire night

Had a mini bonfire party before my pub shift, because the kids can throw whatever they like on the floors today.

New carpets and wooden flooring tomorrow!

Poor little Daisy deserves some fun – I've been like a zombie these last few months.

Althea and Brandi came over with their kids, and we drank mulled wine and held sparklers in the overgrown garden, while Callum, Wolfgang and Daisy ran around the house shrieking.

We threw some hotdogs in a pan and let the kids eat outside, while we set off a few Tesco fireworks.

'I've always been pro the European Union,' said Althea, as we watched the pathetic fireworks fizzle and die in seconds. 'But I have to say, all these EU safety requirements have ruined fireworks night.'

Sambuca didn't like the fireworks and ran back to Mum and Dad's house.

Mum was pleased to have him home.

She texted to say her 'little boy' was back, and that she'd given him two cans of Whiskas and a toffee apple.

She's since texted to say Sambuca has vomited on her bed and attacked Brandi's big television.

Texted Alex, 'Happy Birthday'.
He didn't reply.

Monday, 6th November

The carpets and flooring have been fitted, and the house looks so much better. Four men came at 7 am, and had everything done before lunch.

NO MORE CONCRETE.

The wooden kitchen floor looks especially beautiful, and I love the sophisticated grey-beige carpet everywhere else. Feel like I'm living in a hotel. And a good one – like a Dalton hotel. Not a purple-carpeted Premier Inn.

It's made such a difference to my mood, running up and downstairs with soft carpet beneath my feet, and sweeping up Daisy's discarded lunch from real wood.

Ah…home!

After paying the carpet people, I have now completely run out of money.

This has led to an uncomfortable realisation.

I won't be able to fit the bathroom before the court hearing.

On the positive side, the heating still works. The boiler needs a daily whack with a hammer to get it going, but the house is warm.

WARM!

Will just have to hope that Johnny Jiggens sees all the work I've done, and overlooks the lack of washing facilities.

Tuesday, 7th November

Yesterday was such an amazing day. But now…

Life.

Why isn't it ever simple?

After the new carpets were fitted yesterday morning, Mum came over with a load of leftovers from the pub Sunday roast, and we ate cold beef and talked about Laura's baby.

Made scones during Daisy's afternoon nap, and had a fun afternoon tea on the kitchen floor when she woke up, watching the cows in the field through the sliding doors.

Poor cows.

They must be so cold.

Put Daisy to bed at seven, and made spaghetti bolognaise for my own tea.

Had some red wine left over from Bonfire Night, so threw a splash in the pan, then took a medicinal swig from the bottle.

Just as I was doing that, Alex walked in.

He had a potted rose bush under one arm, and a brown-paper deli bag under the other.

'Bad day?' he asked, a half-smile on his face.

I put the wine guiltily back on the counter.

Was tempted to say, 'I don't usually drink out of the bottle.' But that would have been a lie, provable by dozens of Facebook photos.

'What are you doing here?' I asked, feeling a huge smile light up my face.

'Visiting my good friend Juliette.' Alex gestured to the painted walls. 'This place is coming along. I can't believe how good it looks, actually.'

'Nearly there,' I said, still smiling. 'And then I'll need to think about Christmas trees and all of that.'

'Ah yes. The yearly race towards Christmas Day.'

'Has your tree gone up yet?'

'It's November, Juliette. I very much doubt it.'

'You don't know?'

'I haven't been home in a while. And the housekeeper sorts out the Christmas decoration schedule.'

'Don't you decorate your own Christmas tree?'

'No. I'd make a pig's ear of it. I leave that sort of thing to people who know what they're doing. Where's Daisy?'

'In her cot,' I said. 'She's wiped out.'

'Shame,' said Alex. 'I brought you a house-warming present.' He passed me the rose bush. 'You said you wanted a cottage with roses around the door. So...I thought this could be a good start.'

'I would offer you a drink,' I said. 'But I've just downed the last of it.'

'Lucky I brought some then.' Alex clunked the brown-paper deli bag on the breakfast bar. 'There's a paella in there too. For supper. I didn't expect you to be eating so early.'

'It's not early,' I said. 'It's nearly six o'clock.'

'Six is early.'

'What time do you usually eat then?'

'Eight. Nine.' Alex pulled Champagne, wrapped in an ice sleeve, out of the deli bag. 'May we toast to your new home?'

I didn't have any clean wine glasses, so Alex poured us Champagne into the housewarming mugs Mum bought me.

The mugs weren't really appropriate, since one said, 'Home is where the Fart is' and the other was shaped like a pair of boobs. But Alex didn't seem to mind.

We sat at the breakfast bar, drinking Champagne and watching the darkening sky and twinkling stars.

There's a lovely view over the fields at night.

Alex filled up my mug and said, 'You know Juliette, I never planned anything when it came to you. Maybe that was my mistake.'

'You can't plan other people,' I said. 'That's not how relationships work.'

'You're right – people do have a wretched amount of free will.' Alex raised an eyebrow. 'Maybe that's why I like business better. Employees do what you tell them. They're so much more predictable. But New Year's Eve was incredible. Wasn't it?'

I nodded. 'Before reality came along.'

'Moments,' said Alex. 'That's all life is, when all is said and done. I'll say this, though. There'll never be anyone else like you.'

I looked at Alex.

He looked at me.

And we both knew this moment was special.

Alex pulled me onto his lap, his gaze intense and unwavering.

Then he kissed me.

A whole year of missed time faded away.

Alex scooped me up into his arms and kissed me with an intensity that left me breathless.

I pulled back and said, 'This isn't sensible.'

'Yes, it is,' said Alex.

He carried me upstairs and lay me on the bed. Then he put his watch, wallet and phone on the bedside table and undressed.

I watched his chest move in the moonlight.

Naked, Alex climbed onto the bed beside me and lifted my jumper over my head.

'You're cold,' he said, rubbing my fingers and pulling the duvet over me.

'Actually, not that cold at all,' I said, looking up at him.

He kissed me again, holding my face in his hands, running fingers through my hair.

I'd almost forgotten being with him could make me feel this way – so safe and warm and adored.

Alex is so *intense*.

He didn't take his eyes off mine, and his gaze was impossible to turn away from.

'You still do this to me,' he said, eyes soft but serious. 'You still make me lose control.'

'What's wrong with losing control?' I asked.

'Everything.'

When I woke this morning, Alex was gone.

The bathroom towels had been folded into neat squares, the soap was parallel to the sink, and the lid was screwed back on the toothpaste.

There was a message by the bed, scrawled on a Moleskine notebook page:

'Thank you for the moment. Love A.'

Wednesday, 8th November

SO furious with myself.

Yes, it was a good moment. But I've also just thrown my dignity away.

How could Alex just *leave* like that?

I *knew* I was right to end things on my terms. Now I've made everything muddy.

Bloody alcohol.

Althea says it sounds like typical alpha-male behaviour.

'All sex and no closeness,' she said. 'He's probably got a fear of intimacy. And a tiny penis.'

'No,' I said. 'It's not tiny.'

'Listen, Jules. Is this really who you want in your life?'

'I *want* Alex in my life,' I said. 'But there are so many issues.'

'You're telling me.'

Shift in the pub tonight.

Am hoping Polish Malik can shed some wisdom on my relationship drama.

Thursday, 9th November

Mum gave me money for a TV today, saying it would be an early Christmas present for Daisy and a living essential for me.

'What kind of social life can you have if you don't know who's won *The Apprentice?*' she said.

She handed over a wodge of cash from the pub till and directed me to Currys in the out-of-town shopping complex.

Was extremely grateful.

Will now be able to see Alan Sugar firing people on the big screen.

As soon as the automatic doors opened at Currys, an aftershave-soaked teenager sprinted towards us.

He led us around the store, explaining the various different TV models.

Daisy got bored within a minute and started wrecking the shop.

The teenage salesman didn't seem to mind, and actively encouraged Daisy by handing her an iPad from the tablet display.

'I just want a normal telly,' I said.

'We don't have one of those,' said the teenager, apologetically.

Ended up with a super-duper voice-recognition TV, on special offer because the voice recognition didn't really work, and old people couldn't read the remote-control buttons.

Felt I'd got a real bargain until the teenage salesman tried to add a £50 'mounting charge' at the till.

'What's that extra charge for?' I asked.

'That TV weighs nearly seventy-five pounds madam,' he said. 'You should have someone mount it for you.'

'Take that charge off right now,' I said. 'My dad has an engineering degree and will be happy to mount it for me.'

Fifty quid for mounting a telly!

Jog on.

Will ask Dad tonight when I do my shift at the pub.

Friday, 10th November

Dad refused to mount the TV!

It was my own fault – I let him read the instructions, which advised the TV should only be mounted by a Currys professional.

'But that's just a suggestion,' I said. 'Look – there are mounting instructions on page six.'

Dad went on about invalidated guarantees and 'risking the ship for a ha'p'orth of tar'.

Mum won't help either, saying, 'Brandi made me spend all bloody afternoon holding that telly of hers, while she fiddled around, dropping teeny screws under the bed. The NHS is forcing me to exercise once a week. There's no bloody way I'm doing more of it in my spare time.'

John Boy offered to have a go, but I don't really trust his patience or attention to detail.

He never lets the Guinness settle for long enough before topping it up, and his foam shamrocks look like swastikas.

Saturday, 11th November

Have mounted the TV with Brandi's help.

She's surprisingly strong for someone who spends her time painting fingernails, but then I suppose she has to pin Callum down from time to time.

The TV didn't fit the mounting kit I'd bought, so I had to use some of Callum's Meccano to fit all the screws in the right places, but everything was surprisingly solid in the end.

Brandi and I both hung off the telly for a few minutes to test the mount. Just to be sure.

We didn't let Mum do that though. It would have been asking for trouble.

Sunday, 12th November

Remembrance Sunday

Sad day watching the village remembrance parade and wearing my poppy to honour my dead granddad.

Had planned on fish and chips for Daisy's tea, but the good chip shop was closed for the parade, so took Daisy to Stu's Plaice.

When we arrived, Stu was pinning his new hygiene certificate to the wall.

He's got two stars this year, which is an improvement.

Requested two portions of chips.

Stu asked if I wanted cod.

'No thanks, Stu,' I said brightly. 'I don't fancy food poisoning.'

We both laughed. But I wasn't joking.

Feel a bit bad giving Daisy rubbish food now we have our own kitchen, but going back and forth to the pub, staying overnight with Daisy, ALWAYS forgetting my toothbrush (although infuriatingly, I ALWAYS remember Daisy's) there's little time for shopping.

SO tired.

Monday, 13th November

Johnny Jiggens phoned.

He's going to visit in ten days' time for the pre-court living assessment.

Worried of course, but what else can I do now? I have no money for a shower or bath or curtains or a dining table. I've done what I can. Surely, he'll see the miracles I've performed.

I have a flushing toilet for crying out loud!

God, I just can't wait for this Cafcass assessment to be over now. And the court hearing.

Truth be told, I'm terrified.

Tuesday, 14th November

I've ordered a local, organic veg bag to be delivered so that I can cook Daisy lovely seasonal meals.

Apparently, healthy food lowers stress. Which is something I desperately need to do right now.

Wednesday, 15th November

Jeremy Samuels phoned this morning to 'get up to speed', prior to court and Johnny Jiggens's visit.

'How's the house?' he asked.

I told him the house was coming along, but that we still needed a bathroom.

'A bathroom?' said Jeremy. 'You definitely need one of those. Cafcass take a dim view of poorly washed children.'

'There's nothing I can do,' I said. 'I've run out of money. We shower at the pub – Johnny Jiggens must see that I'm doing my best.'

SO anxious about court.

Would ideally like someone with me for moral support, but taking Mum is a bad idea. She has no respect for authority.

Ditto, Althea.

Brandi is obviously completely out of the question.

Laura has just had a baby.

And Dad is too emotional. It's embarrassing seeing a grown man cry in public.

Alex and I...well, don't even go there.

Thursday, 16th November

Organic veg bag arrived today. It came in a delightful wooden box lined with hessian.

There were rosy apples with little wormholes, mud-covered potatoes, misshapen carrots and some enormous green beans.

Gave Daisy an apple, and cooked a jacket potato for tea.

Will have to get creative with the other stuff.

Asked Althea for recipe advice, and she said, 'Chuck it all into a soup. That's what everyone does.'

I said, 'But it's supposed to last the week.'

Althea said, 'You're being swept along by the novelty. By next week, you'll be sick of preparing veg. And then you'll bung it into a soup just before the next bag is delivered. Like everyone else does.'

Althea gets three different organic veg bags from various local farms.

She didn't mean to sign up for so many, but she's a magnet for hippy salespeople.

Friday, 17th November

Alex phoned.

Nearly didn't take his call – I was so furious with him for walking out on me after our night of passion.

But I answered because I needed to vent.

'Are you quite finished?' Alex asked, after ten minutes of shouting.

'I'm not sure,' I said. 'It depends what you say next.'

'Listen, Juliette,' said Alex. 'I'm not handling things well. I haven't handled things well all year.'

'Oh, so this is about *you?*' I said. 'Silly me. I thought it was me who'd been made to feel like shit.'

'I don't want it to be like this,' said Alex. 'It's hard for me too. I adore you. But I just can't come to terms with Nick Spencer.'

Saturday, 18th November

Another tiring shift at the pub last night. Am battling through. Whenever I feel sorry for myself, I think of John Boy's backache and stump rash and phantom leg pain, and the fact he never says a word about it. Then I count myself bloody lucky and get on with it.

Sunday, 19th November

Asked Dad to pray for me at church this morning re Johnny Jiggens' visit.

Like Tesco says, every little helps.

John Boy overhead our religious chat, and said, 'I'm gonna marry Gwen in the church. It's the proper way to do things, innit?'

He got permission to marry at the local church when the vicar came into the pub for his post-service Jack Daniels and Coke.

Apparently, the vicar will orchestrate the wedding, as long as John Boy promises to 'wear a fucking shirt, for the love of God' on the big day.

Monday, 20th November

Yorkie offered me a second-hand toilet and bath for Hillcrest House last night.

He found them at the tip, while scavenging for a new bed.

Polish Malik says he'll fit them as a 'friendly favour'.

VERY excited. If everything goes to plan, I could have a bathroom by the end of today.

Malik works full-time but says he can do the job this evening.

'Won't you be tired?' I asked him.

Malik assured me he works a very short day right now – 6 am until 6 pm.

Tuesday, 21st November

Polish Malik has fitted my upstairs toilet and bath. Even better, he had a spare power shower from an old job and has fitted that too.

The toilet leans a little to the side, but that's because the wall is wonky.

'The flush mechanism will be fine, Juliette,' Malik assured me. 'Water always flows down. One of the few constants in life.'

Was very impressed by Malik's workmanship.

All his tools were neatly organised, and he lifted the toilet and bath effortlessly up the stairs.

Everything was fitted by midnight.

I tried to give Malik the pathetic amount of cash in my purse as a thank you, but he waved my money away, saying, 'What is one late night for a friend?'

'But you've already worked a full day,' I said.

Malik laughed. 'Juliette, all I've done is wake at 6 am and lift a few steel girders. Your mother gave me a bar tab when I first came to the UK and was alone in a strange country. That sort of kindness has no price.'

Wednesday, 22nd November

A bathroom! At last!

And it's been installed before my living assessment tomorrow.

Talk about cutting it fine.

Of course, we still don't have any curtains, and the old, broken toilet is in the back garden with 'If you want sex call Cindi Bailey' written on the porcelain in permanent marker.

But life isn't perfect.

Surely Johnny Jiggens must realise that.

Thursday, 23rd November

Johnny Jiggens arrived at 11 am today.

I was ready for him with a selection of teas and three different kinds of biscuits.

Johnny gave me a limp handshake, then looked over the newly painted walls.

'You know, this place was a squat before,' I enthused. 'And now we have a roof. And a bath with a shower. And *two* flushing toilets.'

'All the essentials then,' said Johnny.

The boiler gave a long, loud moan at that moment.

Johnny looked embarrassed, clearly thinking I'd farted.

'That wasn't me,' I said. 'It was the boiler.'

'Maybe you should have it checked over.'

'At the moment I'm hitting it with a hammer,' I said. 'I mean…ha ha ha! What I mean is, I'll have a new boiler fitted at some point.'

Not exactly a lie, as 'at some point' could mean 'in three years'.

Am praying Old Beryl survives the winter.

'A new boiler?' Johnny asked. 'What – you've still got the one that came with the house?'

'Yes,' I conceded. 'But 1970s boilers were built to last.'

'You don't want to take any chances with gas,' said Johnny, peering into the downstairs toilet and staring at the bile-yellow porcelain. 'I see there's still a fair bit to do here.'

'I like that toilet,' I said. 'It still flushes. Do you want to see? And we have an open fire in the living room.'

After a poke around downstairs, Johnny asked if he could see Daisy's bedroom.

'It's not finished,' I said. 'We're going to put up princess wallpaper and curtains at some point.'

'Ah, right,' said Johnny. 'I'll just take a quick look.'

He disappeared upstairs and reappeared making notes.

Then he stuck his head into the back garden and noted the broken toilet – possibly scribbling down the number for a sexual experience with Cindi Bailey.

'Do you want a cup of tea or anything?' I asked. 'I've got five different kinds—'

'It's all right,' said Johnny. 'Just a flying visit today.'

And off he went.

Friday, 24th November
Black Friday

In a bid to forget about the court hearing, I drove into town with Brandi, Callum and Daisy today, and elbowed past shoppers, looking for bargains.

'This is all crap,' Brandi decided, a few shops in. 'They're just discounting stuff no one wants.'

Agreed.

Went to Poundland, which is cheap all year round, and bought a trolley load of Christmas decorations, mince pies and discontinued apple-flavoured hot chocolate.

Also picked up a white tinsel tree, which I thought was an absolute bargain. It looks horrible – really cheap and tacky.

But it was a pound!

Saturday, 25th November

Ten days until the court hearing.

Feeling VERY bloated and booby and hormonal, and keep

bursting into tears – I imagine because of stress.

In a feat of spectacularly bad timing, it's Nick's visitation day.

Dad has taken Daisy, which I hugely appreciate.

The world is turning Christmassy around me, but I'm too anxious to care.

Sunday, 26th November

Watched YouTube videos about family court today.

It's illegal to film real court cases, so have watched lots of actors pretending to argue over children.

Some of them are very convincing, resorting to actual physical violence.

I wonder if the scenes are based on real events.

Monday, 27th November

Alex phoned to 'check up' on me, prior to the final court hearing.

Told him I was unbelievably stressed and anxious.

'I want to be there for you at the court hearing,' he said. 'As a friend.'

'Friend seems best,' I said.

'I hope you can forgive my behaviour,' said Alex. 'Relationships don't come easily to me. Growing up the way I did. Would it help if I told you I've been closer to you than I have anyone my whole life?'

'Yes,' I said. 'It does help. But we both know it's not going to work. I need more than a few crumbs of attention before you get jealous and run out the door.'

Tuesday, 28th November

Woke up last night worrying.

You'd think, after everything that happened last year, I would be immune to anxiety.

Surely, I've sapped the worry pool dry?

But I'm really scared.

Althea keeps telling me to live in the moment. But I don't want to live in the moment. I want to live in a shiny, glittery future where my ex-partner has lost the residency battle, and my little girl is safe at home with her mum.

Wednesday, 29th November

Boobs still massive and stomach bloated. I had a paranoid moment and did a pregnancy test. Of course it came back negative – Alex was the careful and responsible gentleman you'd expect and used what I imagine he'd call 'precautions'.

It's easy to get paranoid about pregnancy, though – especially when you're under stress. Someone always has a story about a teenage friend of a friend who got pregnant by shaking a boy's hand and ended up giving birth in the school toilets on prom night.

Thursday, 30th November

Court five days away.

Am distracting myself by hanging tinsel, eating Poundland mince pies and listening to Christmas tunes on Radio Two.

Brandi and Callum came over, and Callum taught Daisy a new game: 'Stinky Father Christmas.'

Brandi and I had a minor argument over tinsel swags (she favours an obscenely low hang), but other than that, it was a lovely afternoon.

Made cheese on toast for tea, and got the fire going.

Brandi and I had a few Christmas sherries while the kids watched *Home Alone* on TV.

Callum loves that movie because of all the violence.

Daisy seemed to be getting bad ideas from the movie though, and kept asking me, 'Mummy leave home, please? Mummy go away, Callum Daisy have FUN!'

Friday, 1st December

Nick called round this evening with sherry, mince pies and a large sprig of mistletoe.

'I'm here to make peace before court,' he said. 'Season of goodwill and all that.'

I suppose it's brave of him. Although he also mentioned something about 'getting away from Sadie'.

'I thought we could have a drink,' said Nick. 'Maybe talk about Christmas plans.'

In some ways, things were better when Nick was absent.

Now he's trying to get involved, it means potentially sharing Daisy at major Christian festivals.

'You'd better come in,' I said. 'We'll both need a drink for that discussion.'

'I see you've done your usual Poundland Christmas shop,' said Nick, hanging his jacket on the tinsel-covered antler coat stand.

I poured us both a large measure of cooking sherry.

'If you wanted to have Daisy at Christmas, you should have said before,' I told him. 'We've already made plans.'

'Yeah, yeah, I know,' said Nick. 'It's just I thought…Christmas Day, maybe I could pop over? While you're at your Mum and Dad's? Just to say hello.'

From her cot upstairs, Daisy called out, 'Baddy?'

'Daisy boo!' said Nick, sounding choked up.

I let Nick go up and give Daisy a quick kiss and cuddle.

It is Christmas time, after all.

'So,' said Nick, when he came back down. 'Court on Tuesday. How are you feeling?'

'Terrified,' I said. 'And hating you for putting us through this.'

Nick said, 'Try and see it from my point of view, Jules. I've lost everything.'

Saturday, 2nd December

Jeremy says that Nick could win joint residency.

It's a 'possibility', even though I've now got a house.

'The courts are looking for stability,' said Jeremy. 'If you still haven't got a fully functioning boiler…well let's not dwell on that, it's too late now.'

The thought of my little girl living half her life in a madhouse with two rowing, irresponsible, selfish actors… Oh god.

Asked Daisy how she felt about living with Baddy sometimes.

'Baddy house,' she said.

I tried to explain again.

'Daisy,' I said. 'Would you like to live at Baddy's house sometimes?'

'Yes, Baddy house,' she said.

I rephrased the question.

'Daisy, do you want to live at Mummy's house *all* the time?'

'Yes, Mummy house,' she replied.

'No Baddy house?' I asked.

'No Baddy house!' she replied.

I ended the questions there.

This is what Johnny Jiggens, even with the help of emoji cushions, didn't understand. Two-year-olds don't make much sense and have no idea what's best for them. If I asked Daisy to call the shots, she'd wear swimwear in winter and eat cake for breakfast.

Sunday, 3rd December

Althea came round this morning while I was touching up the paintwork.

She was appalled I was covering up Daisy's biro vandalism.

'The last thing the world needs is another bland, white house where kids aren't allowed to be creative,' she said. 'I've got a box of spray paints in the car. Why not let the kids express themselves?'

Told her no way.

Actually, I may have screeched a little bit, because Althea said, 'All right, all right. I get it. You've spent hours painting your sodding house.'

Told Althea how worried I am about court.

'They're not going to let Nick have residency, joint or otherwise,' she said. 'He's been an absent father.'

'He's not absent now,' I said. 'And his solicitor told the judge I kept Daisy from him. Plus, he's got a nice house with a bee hotel in the garden.'

'You have a nice house too,' said Althea. 'It just needs brightening up a bit.'

Monday, 4th December

Court tomorrow.

Sick with worry.

Can't stop cuddling Daisy.

Tuesday, 5th December

Final court hearing.

Woke up three times last night, fretting and chewing my nails.

Went through the usual routine of giving Daisy porridge, then muesli, then relenting and giving her Coco Pops when she rejected the nutritious options.

Felt too sick to eat myself.

Dad came over at 8am for babysitting duties.

He'd already had a gentle stroll around the frosty village lanes and was full of the joys of nature.

'I've got a grand day planned for this little one,' he told me, dusting frost from his bobble hat. 'We're going on a winter nature ramble, and then we'll make some wholemeal bread and eat fresh winter radishes from the garden.'

Felt a bit sorry for Daisy then.

Luckily Mum will be at the pub, so she'll probably give Daisy Warburton's thick-sliced bread with Billy Bear ham slices.

The drive to court was a blur, although I recall someone tooting me on the giant quadruple roundabout. But you *have* to be a bit pushy there, or you end up veering onto the pansy display.

I was nervous when I arrived but felt better when I saw Alex and Jeremy in the waiting area.

Jeremy has that reassuring loud voice and Alex…well, he always makes me feel safe. Maybe it's the suit.

I was so glad Alex was there, regardless of our messy year. His friendship means a lot.

Nick was at the far end of the waiting area, with Penny Castle and Helen. He was smartly dressed in a suit and faux glasses, balancing a Starbucks on his jittery knee. He gave me a tired smile and half salute.

The hearing ended up being delayed because the judge had some kind of medical emergency.

It didn't take place until gone lunchtime.

My stomach was growling by then, and even Penny Castle had cracked open some parmesan and herb straws from her briefcase.

Finally, the decrepit judge wheeled past us, oxygen tank strapped to his chair, and we were allowed to enter the courtroom.

Alex and Helen waited outside.

In the courtroom, the judge coughed, sucked from his asthma inhalers, made honking noises and turned pages of court documents.

Then he said: 'Has any agreement been reached in mediation?'

Both solicitors confirmed no agreement had been made.

'Well then,' said the judge. 'It'll be down to me to make a residency ruling today.'

He asked questions about my new living arrangements and listened to Johnny Jiggens's report about Hillcrest House.

As expected, Johnny talked about potentially unsafe gas appliances, combined with an open fire, but also mentioned a large garden with 'potential for meeting early learning requirements'.

The judge must have been watching the *X-Factor* or similar, because he kept us on tenterhooks, waiting for his decision.

He began with a long preamble about how terrible separation was for children, and how he liked the Saudi Arabian model, where couples were shamed into staying together and imprisoned for divorce.

Then he rattled on about the lost art of letter writing.

Eventually, he tapped papers meaningfully on the desk and told us his ruling.

'I believe children should primarily be with their mother,' he announced. 'Therefore, I am awarding sole custody to Ms Duffy. Mr Spencer will be allowed unsupervised visitation one weekend every fortnight. And let me sign off that maintenance agreement.'

There were more orders noting the specifics of Nick's visitations, but I didn't really hear them.

I was too busy crying happy tears.

Jeremy shook my hand and put an arm around my shoulder.

'Well done,' he said.

Penny Castle was whispering to Nick about an appeal, but he muttered, 'Yeah. Can we just get out of here now?'

Outside the court, Helen took one look at Nick's crestfallen face and said, 'Oh, *Nick*.' Then she glared at me. 'For the judge not to see the *truth*.'

'The judge did see the truth, Helen,' I said. 'Happy fucking Christmas.'

A bit childish, but sometimes maturity is overrated.

Alex took my arm, and we went outside.

Mum, Dad and Daisy were waiting for us on a metal bench.

I grabbed Daisy and squeezed the life out of her.

'They've given me sole residency,' I told Mum and Dad. 'And Nick has to pay maintenance every month. Everything's going to be all right.'

Then I started crying again.

'Oh, *love*,' said Dad.

'That hearing took bloody forever,' Mum complained. 'We ended up eating your packed lunch.'

'Don't blame *me*, Shirley,' said Dad, incensed. 'All *I* had was one buffet sausage roll and half a ham sandwich.'

'Oh, don't lie, Bob,' said Mum. 'You had those ready-salted Walkers too.'

While Mum and Dad were rowing, Jeremy Samuels strolled towards us.

'A fair result, I think,' he declared, shaking everyone's hand. 'Well done, Juliette.'

Alex said, 'Juliette, I'll leave you with your family. But may I take

267

you and Daisy out tomorrow to celebrate?'

In the emotion of the moment, I agreed.

Alex kissed me on the cheek, hailed a cab and then he was gone.

'It's like having an assassin for your boyfriend,' Mum commented. 'One minute he's there, the next he vanishes.'

'He's not my boyfriend,' I said. 'We're just friends.'

'At least he dressed appropriately for court,' said Dad.

'But inappropriately for *Eurovision*,' Mum pointed out.

Maybe there's a message there.

Either way, I'm looking forward to seeing Alex tomorrow.

Wednesday, 6th December

Alex's driver picked up me and Daisy mid-morning and drove us to Nona's Italian in Kensington for lunch.

London was freezing, but Nona's was warm with steaming pasta and pizza.

Nona – a cuddly, smiley Italian lady – showed us to the table herself, then pinched Alex's cheeks and told him how he'd grown.

'Do you know *every* restaurant owner in London?' I asked Alex. 'Almost.'

Nona cooed and clucked over Daisy, lifting her to her huge bosom, then whisking her off to see pasta being made.

Wasn't sure Daisy would like being stolen, but she seemed fine in the open kitchen, stuffing fresh basil and pasta into her mouth.

Within minutes, a giant, hot pizza appeared at our table, and Alex asked: 'You know, my mother asked about you. She couldn't remember your name, but she remembered you had curly hair and a little girl.'

'Does your mother like children?'

'Actually, I have no idea. When Zach and I were growing up, we hardly saw her.'

'What about your dad?'

Alex laughed. 'My father? We saw him even less. Not that we minded. It saved us a beating.'

'That's horrible.'

'No worse than boarding school. But I suppose it gave me a certain determination. Toughness.' He smiled. 'And various psychological issues I'll never get over.'

After lunch, Alex suggested a trip to the Natural History Museum.

Daisy loved it.

The tiled floor kept her entertained for ages.

We had a walk around London, looking at the Christmas lights and the huge tree on Trafalgar Square, while Daisy stuffed her happy little face with hot chestnuts.

Then Alex hailed a cab, saying, 'Bond Street Dalton. Don't go via Oxford Street.'

'We're going to your hotel?' I asked.

'It's getting too cold for Daisy to be out,' Alex explained. 'She can sleep in a suite with a member of staff. And we can have supper.'

So that's what we did.

We drank wine, ate posh steak pie and talked.

Alex told me about his business this year and how difficult he's found it, being away from me.

'I understand my father more now,' he said. 'His mood swings and bad temper. Buying a business is one thing. Building one is quite another. There's a lot of responsibility.'

I asked if he regretted taking on such a big workload.

'I don't regret the business,' he said. 'I'm building something no one can ever take away. But I regret…other things.'

We held hands then, and I said, 'You never needed to be jealous of Nick. You do know that, don't you?'

'No,' he said. 'You have a child together. That's something I can't compete with. So of course I'm jealous.'

'What are you doing for Christmas?' I asked.

'Let me guess,' said Alex, giving me a meaningful look. 'You love Christmas.'

'Who doesn't love Christmas?'

'Lots of people. I don't.'

'Why on earth not?'

'In my family, celebrations are like dodging bullets,' said Alex.

'So, what will your family do at Christmas?'

Alex took a thoughtful sip of wine. 'Zach will go to his father's. I don't know what my mother has planned. And I'll be heading to the Bahamas with a laptop and ignoring all calls.' He put his wine glass down. 'Will you stay here tonight? With me?'

'You mean sleep over?' I asked, my voice all high-pitched.

Alex laughed. 'If you want to call it that.'

I fiddled with my napkin. 'I don't think that's a good idea, Alex. I mean, we're friends. Let's not muddy the water again.'

'I don't have an answer to that.' Alex took my hand across the table. 'But my whole family nearly died in a fire, once upon a time. It's given me a certain appreciation of the here and now.'

'Oh, I see,' I said. 'Let's have sex now, in case we die tomorrow.'

'This isn't about sex. There are hundreds of women I could have sex with.'

'How lovely for you.'

'You know what I mean.'

It's Christmas – a perfectly acceptable time of year to live in fantasyland.

Right?

Alex and I held hands all the way to the hotel suite, and then I ducked inside to check on Daisy.

She was sleeping in one of the four bedrooms, under the watchful eye of a cuddly female concierge (whom Alex had known for ten years).

Alex requested clothes for the morning and extra toiletries then dismissed the concierge.

The two of us watched twinkly, Christmas London through the panoramic window.

Then we decided which double bed we were going to sleep in.

Alex took keys, a little silver box, his wallet and mobile phone from his suit jacket and put them on the bedside table. Then he hung his jacket over a chair.

'You're beautiful,' he told me. 'Put your arms down.'

I did, and Alex walked around me, then picked me up and carried me to the bed.

As he lay me down, he said, 'This is another perfect moment. Don't you think?'

He kissed me, and it became impossible to think of the future. Right then, I wanted to be with him so much.

Sometimes, moments are all we have.

Thursday, 7th December

Woke up under big, billowy bedclothes to find Alex gone.

Of course.

There was a note written on buff hotel paper:

'Will call soon. Alex.'

Daisy was just waking up, so the two of us had room-service breakfast looking out over London.

'Where Rex?' Daisy wanted to know.

'Gone,' I told her. 'Rex is gone.'

Friday, 8th December

I have a house.

I have a job at my parent's pub that (just about) covers the bills.

I'm getting regular, court-ordered maintenance payments from Nick.

And I have sole residency of my little girl, which of course is the best Christmas present anyone could wish for.

But something is wrong.

Alex.

It's all wrong.

We can't go on like this.

Saturday, 9th December

Althea came over last night and did a tarot reading for me, while Wolfgang and Daisy slept upstairs.

She doesn't use the traditional deck, declaring it full of male symbolism. Instead, she used her Voodoo cards (purchased in New Orleans) covered in naked ladies wrestling ferocious animals.

We drank Althea's homemade Christmas sultana liqueur, which was strong enough to strip tooth enamel, and deliberated over my future.

'The cards say Alex has lion tendencies,' said Althea. 'And you're a raven goddess.'

'What does that mean?' I asked.

'In a nutshell, you've got no chance,' said Althea. 'But hey – they're only cards. It's all bullshit, isn't it?'

'Maybe.'

'Listen, Jules. Sod the cards – how do you feel?'

'I feel like we've got no chance.'

Sunday, 10th December

Called Alex this morning.

He was in the middle of some sink disaster, and shouting, 'No, I need one hundred white porcelain butler style 500mm, *plus* taps, and I need them TODAY.'

'Alex, that night in your hotel shouldn't have happened,' I said. 'No more being friends. It doesn't work. We really are over. You can't keep doing this to me, stringing me along.'

Silence.

Eventually, Alex said, 'Is this to do with Nick Spencer?'

'No,' I said. 'It's to do with wanting more.'

'Spencer wants you back,' said Alex. 'Doesn't he? You may as well admit it.'

'Yes,' I said. 'But it's not about Nick.'

More silence.

Then Alex said, 'I'm not going to argue with you.'

And hung up.

Monday, 11th December

Thought Alex might phone today. Begging me to reconsider and offering me the moon, like Nick used to do.

But that's not his style.

Is he upset? He didn't sound upset, but then again, he's very controlled.

I doubt he'd accidentally cry watching *Lassie Come Home* like John Boy did this afternoon.

Tuesday, 12th December

Sad today.

Am throwing all my energy into getting the house perfect for Christmas.

The painting is finished.

Kitchen looks brilliant.

Heating works.

And I have furniture.

Plus an aisle of Poundland Christmas decorations.

All that's missing are a few homey touches.

Took Daisy out to collect holly and ivy, and ended up bringing half the forest back.

I mean, it was all *free*.

We made some quite decent wreathes and swathes, using the stolen forest delights and an old glittery dress that doesn't fit me any more.

The house was full of woodlice by the time we'd finished, but Daisy enjoyed clearing them up with her little pink dustpan and brush.

She did quite a good job until she emptied the dustpan into the 'bin' (my underwear drawer).

Wednesday, 13th December

Made Christmas food today, and filled the house with cinnamon and orange fragrance.

This made me feel like a proper mother – if you ignore the fact that nothing Daisy and I cooked was edible.

It was my fault.

I decided Daisy and I should bake cinnamon biscuits, like the ones I used to do at school. The recipe is designed for heavy-fingered school children and theoretically impossible to mess up.

However, when I saw the amount of sugar called for, I panicked.

It equated to roughly four teaspoons of sugar per biscuit.

In the 1980s you could get away with that, but not these days.

Halved the sugar, and added sweetener, honey and extra flour.

The resulting biscuits tasted like sadness.

Daisy loved them. Not to eat, but to chuck on the floor and play at 'clearing up'.

I now have a load of broken, crap-tasting biscuits in my underwear drawer.

Thursday, 14th December

How can I be this fat? I've put on an inch around my middle, and the Christmas festivities have barely started.

Daisy asked about Alex today.

She saw me attempting to Facebook-spy on him, and asked, 'Where Rex?'

I said Mummy wasn't seeing Rex any more.

She looked sad, and said, 'Like Rex, Mummy. Let's see Rex Mummy!'

If only things were that simple.

I wonder if Alex is thinking about me.

Friday, 15th December

Expected Nick to have rung by now to organise visitation, but looking over the specific court orders, the new arrangements don't start until January.

I suppose we'll see Nick at the end of the month like we agreed before. But I'm not going to chase him up. Very possibly, he's sulking over losing residency.

SOOO happy all that court stuff is over.

I have MANY things to be grateful for.

The house is looking fabulous – really warm and cosy in time for Christmas.

Not so long ago, I never thought I'd be in this position.

My own *house*, for crying out loud. With a roof, toilet and running water!

And my little girl, warm upstairs in her own bed.

Althea is coming round soon with a bottle of homemade clove liqueur.

Everything is fantastic.

Who needs a boyfriend?

Saturday, 16th December

John Boy and I took Nana to Gala Bingo last night for the OAP Christmas Ball.

It was a big celebration – the OAP equivalent of prom night.

By 9 pm, Nana was so drunk she could hardly walk.

She was swaying on a stolen, tinsel-covered Zimmer frame and screeching the words to 'My Way', while occasionally lifting her glittery dress.

The bingo hall asked Nana to leave, so John Boy and I helped her into a taxi.

Lifting drunk, elderly people is extremely difficult. Nana's limbs moved in their sockets like cooked chicken. I was terrified we'd pull something loose.

Eventually, we got Nana back and into her bedroom.

Thank goodness the care home had a stair lift.

I think she had sobered up a bit as we were leaving, because she called John Boy and me 'dears' and gave us each a pound coin.

Now we just need to find out who owns that Zimmer frame.

Sunday, 17th December

It's a bloody nightmare now Daisy has started walking.

I've had to rehang Christmas tree decorations countless times, and every fragile bauble has been smashed.

People always talk about new-borns crying for hours, but at least they stay in one place and are therefore less likely to get killed.

Daisy roams the house seeking out danger and causing chaos.

She's like a little chubby-legged 'untidy' robot, programmed to destroy the lounge and chew germ-ridden items.

Monday, 18th December

Christmas treat for Daisy today – her winter flu vaccination.

We should have had it done in November, but surgery appointments were hard to get because so many old people die this time of year.

Doctor Slaughter always talks about the 'November rush'.

Daisy looked outraged when they sprayed the stuff up her nose. She cried and cried – it was horrible.

Althea was sympathetic. She always has a terrible time taking Wolfgang for his vaccinations.

The nurses refuse to see him at the local surgery because they don't have the staff to hold him down.

Tuesday, 19th December

Mum is receiving complaints about the pub's Christmas lights.

She's added blue and white flashing icicles to the mix, and the neighbours keep thinking there's an ambulance outside.

This is particularly distressing for the lady who lives opposite because her husband was hospitalised this time last year.

Mum was unsympathetic, saying, 'Serves him right for nicking all our pint glasses.'

Wednesday, 20th December

Spent today getting the house all spic and span for Christmas.

Theoretically, a newly refurbished house should be fairly clean. But nothing is clean when you have a two-year-old.

Daisy has biro-ed the new paintwork again and rubbed toothpaste into her teddy-bear curtains.

She *does* have a little toy dustpan and brush to 'help' me with the housework, but she uses it to bring dirt in from the garden.

Thursday, 21st December

After a few Christmas snowballs, I decided to do an online love test to assess my future relationship status.

I didn't like the first result, so kept doing it until it came out OK.

The outcome fluctuated between broken relationships and disappointment, to joyful families, love and happiness.

Friday, 22nd December

Callum's school Christmas Fair today.

It was anarchy.

Cake-fuelled children ran around the school hall, bellowing their heads off and climbing gym apparatus, while Daisy cried because Santa had gone home with a headache.

Thought I could pick up a few last-minute presents, but everything had been made by children.

I didn't think anyone would appreciate lolly sticks with felt tip and glued wool all over them.

One little kid ran into my (still) pre-menstrual boobs, and I nearly smacked him one.

Saturday, 23rd December

Have decided to brave Oxford Street for a few last-minute Christmas bits.

I know I'm an idiot, leaving things to Christmas Eve, but I really do have an excuse this year.

Court hearing. Huge house refurbishment. Boyfriend trouble. Ex-boyfriend trouble. Ex best-friend trouble.

I've had quite the time of it.

Have persuaded Mum to hit the shops with me.

She's a first-class accomplice in a crowd situation, due to hefty elbows and no manners.

Mum and I haven't shopped together for ages, so it could be a really nice day out.

You never know.

Althea refuses to come, calling it 'festive suicide'.

To be fair, she's busy packing for her Australia trip. She and Wolfgang fly to Perth tomorrow and will be heading into the bush for a survival experience.

Sunday, 24th December

Christmas Eve

It didn't start out as a nice day out. But it ended that way.

Am writing this in bed at nearly midnight, with Alex sleeping beside me.

Yes.

Alex.

Miracles really do happen at Christmas.

Of course, the last-minute Christmas shopping was a stupid idea. I should have known better.

The crowds were particularly vicious this year, clambering over old ladies to grab last-minute bargains.

You'd think people were grabbing food rations from UN helicopters.

I admit I did a little clambering myself. But any mother of a 'Daisy' would do the same when spotting the last half-priced Upsy Daisy doll.

Mum was fed up within half an hour, and claimed her diabetes was making her tired.

'I'm too old and fat for this,' she said. 'I'm going to Laura's for a mince pie, and a nice sit-down.'

Was sorry to see her go. She'd been useful muscle, parting the crowds with her big shoulders.

Loaded up the pram with bargains and escaped John Lewis in one piece, only to discover the bloody Central line was down.

Daisy said, 'Train Mummy. Home. Want home.'

I told her we were temporarily stranded in shopping mayhem and did she want a hot chocolate while we waited for the trains to work?

'*Unhealthy* Mummy,' said Daisy, parroting my own lectures back to me. 'TOO busy now. TOO MUCH boys and girls. Dange-*rous*.'

Remembered last Christmas, when I was stranded in London. And Alex rescued us.

Made me feel sad.

Had a mad Christmas moment and phoned him.

I didn't expect him to answer because I thought he'd be en route to the Bahamas.

But he did. On the first ring.

'Juliette,' he said. 'Is everything OK?'

'Happy Christmas,' I said.

Alex said, 'Happy Christmas to you too.'

'I miss you,' I said, feeling tears forming. 'I'm last-minute Christmas shopping. And I just remembered...oh never mind.'

'It sounds extremely rowdy,' said Alex, in a telling-off tone. 'No place for Daisy. You should get yourself home.'

'I'm trying to. The Central line is down.'

'You're in London? Get a connection from St Pancras. It's not far to walk.'

'Thanks for the transport advice.'

'We're friends, no matter what you say about that. Friends give advice.'

Then I said, 'Alex. Do you miss me too?'

'Don't let me keep you, Juliette,' Alex replied. 'Go now while those connections are still running. You don't want to get stranded again.'

Then he hung up.

Was a nightmare getting the pram to St Pancras with all my shopping.

Daisy dozed fitfully against the metal side of the Maclaren, frowning and making worried noises as I bounced her along the pavement.

People kept shouting about my 'bloody pram', but I couldn't shout back because Daisy was sleeping.

It lacks impact, *whispering* 'fuck off'.

Reached St Pancras, and pushed through the shopping mall bit towards the mainline train connections.

Daisy had woken up by then and had a big, red line down her cheek.

Someone was playing a jazzy version of 'White Christmas' on the public piano, which entranced Daisy for a moment. But as we took the lift to the concourse, she started to howl.

The next connection to Great Oakley was an hour away, so I walked Daisy around the cold concourse, willing her to fall asleep.

I took the route past the Meeting Place statue, and as we reached it, Daisy pointed and said, 'Rex. Mummy, Rex.'

A brown-haired man in a suit was a few feet away, talking to a police officer.

He did look a bit like Alex.

Then the man turned.

'REX,' Daisy yelled excitedly.

And it was. It was Alex.

I won't lie – I was happy to see him. Possibly, I may have smiled a bit.

'Juliette,' said Alex. 'There you are. I tried to call. Your phone went straight to voicemail.'

Just like that. As though it were perfectly normal for him to be waiting for me.

'What are you doing here?' I asked. 'I thought…shouldn't you be travelling to the Bahamas right now?'

'I changed my mind,' said Alex. He turned to the Meeting Place statue. 'I thought you might walk this way. Past this hideous display of sentiment. It occurred to me that this statue is about moments. Maybe we're more similar than you realise.'

'A moment isn't enough, Alex.'

'Will you come downstairs with me,' said Alex. 'For a moment?'

I shook my head, but Alex took my hand and said, 'Juliette. It's Christmas.'

Relented at the 'C' word, and we took the lift down to the main concourse.

'You say I'm too closed-off,' said Alex. 'I want to change that. So, I'm going to play something for you.'

Then Alex strolled right up to an unoccupied piano and sat down.

'It's not Dire Straits, is it?' I asked.

'No.' Alex removed sheet music from his laptop case. 'Elton John. "Step into Christmas". Because you like Christmas.'

'Um...' I thought for a moment.

'You *don't* like Elton John?'

'I mean, it's all right if he comes on the radio. But I wouldn't go out of my way...'

'He's an astonishing musician. Timeless.'

Daisy shouted, 'Sing Rudolph. RUDOLPH! REX! RUDOLPH'

Alex hesitated. 'Rudolph the Red-Nosed Reindeer?'

Daisy nodded.

'Are you sure you don't want "Step into Christmas" by Elton John? I have the music right here ...'

'RUDOLPH!'

Alex muttered something about it 'being short, at least', then rested fingers on the keys and played the opening chords.

Daisy clapped happily.

Soon a crowd gathered.

An elderly lady with armloads of shopping started singing along, and then half the crowd were joining in.

Surprisingly, this spurred Alex into showmanship. He hit the keys with panache and sang 'Rudolph the Red-Nosed Reindeer' with gusto.

When the song finished, everyone smiled and clapped.

Alex turned to me and asked, 'This is me, trying to be more open. For you. Have I embarrassed myself enough to meet your approval?'

'Almost. You need a pair of wobbly reindeer antlers.'

'We should be together at Christmas, don't you think?' said Alex. 'All of us. You, me and Daisy. Isn't that what this time of year is about?'

'It's about the birth of Jesus,' I said. 'But I suppose... I mean, there is a love aspect.'

'May I buy you a glass of Champagne?'

At the St Pancras champagne bar, Alex ordered a bottle of Louis Roederer, then messaged the King's Cross Dalton to bring Daisy a fleecy blanket.

Daisy fell straight to sleep under the blanket, which was a blessed relief. Although it was a delicate business, laying her down in the pram with all the shopping on the back – like a real-life game of buckaroo.

On the concourse below, a group of carol singers sang 'Silent Night'.

'They sang that on Christmas Eve you know,' said Alex. 'During World War One. And everyone understood – it meant truce.'

'Yes,' I said. 'But after Christmas, they carried on blowing each other to bits.'

When we finished our Champagne, Alex had a driver take us home.

The house was freezing, but I got the heating going with the hammer and Alex lit a fire.

'It's nice here, Juliette,' said Alex, after we'd put Daisy to bed. 'You've made it feel warm. Like a home should be.'

'Some of the furniture is stolen,' I said.

Alex laughed, unaware I wasn't joking.

'I don't have much to eat,' I admitted. 'We're at Mum and Dad's for Christmas dinner, so I didn't get any food in. Mum always sends me home with a fridge-load of leftovers.'

Alex investigated the fridge and cupboards. 'You have cheese. You have slightly stale bread. You have macaroni. Do you have garlic?'

I nodded, showing him a scarily gnarled lump at the bottom of my organic veg box.

Alex made macaroni cheese with garlic breadcrumbs.

We sat on the sofa, fire blazing, with Christmas music on the radio and lights twinkling on the tree.

It was pretty funny, hearing which songs Alex liked. I suppose that's the trouble with boarding school – you have no sense of what's socially acceptable.

I mean, Boney M isn't a band you *admit* to liking. Even if secretly, you want to sing along.

After we'd eaten, we drank sherry and talked.

Then we went to bed.

And yes.

We did.

Again.

I don't know what the New Year will hold, but Alex is right – sometimes, you just have to grab those perfect moments when they come along.

Sleep now.

Can't believe I'm going to wake up with Alex on Christmas Day.

Monday, 25th December
Christmas Day

Woke this morning to hear the shower running, and to see Alex's suit folded neatly on Daisy's toy kitchen. His suitcase and shoes were arranged neatly against the wall.

Daisy was calling, 'MUMMY. MUMMY. Get me UP. Get me UPPP!'

I put on my dressing gown and took Daisy downstairs for porridge and presents.

As I was sniffing the milk, Alex came down, hair wet from the shower. He wore the pressed suit his driver had packed him and carried an armful of gifts.

'Happy Christmas,' he said, kissing me on the cheek.

'Where did those presents come from?' I asked.

'Just call me Santa Claus,' said Alex. Then he felt the need to give a serious answer, and added, 'My driver packed them. Along with the clean clothes.'

As Alex arranged presents under the tree, there was a jaunty knock at the door.

Nick's voice called out: 'Yo ho ho! Merry Christmas!'

My heart sank.

Bloody Nick.

Alex sprang to his feet, looking furious. 'After all this talk of *me* changing, you've invited Nick Spencer around on Christmas Day.'

'No,' I said. 'He mentioned calling by Mum and Dad's place, but not here.'

'You know how I feel about *that man*. Could you be any more disrespectful? To have him arrive while I'm *still here?*'

'I didn't know he was going to come. And he's Daisy's father. You have to accept—'

'Goodbye, Juliette. Goodbye, Daisy. I wish you a happy Christmas and New Year.'

'Yo ho ho, Merry Christmas!' called Nick through the door.

'You're leaving?' I asked Alex.

'Of course I'm leaving. What do you expect, Juliette?' Alex ran a stressed hand through his hair. 'Listen. If you want us to have a chance, you have to make a choice. Him or me.'

'He's Daisy's father,' I said. 'I can't make that choice, and I shouldn't have to. The problem here is *your* jealousy. If you can't make your peace with Nick, then we have no chance.'

'Then we have no chance.'

I suppose that's the thing about moments. They don't last.

'What do you expect me to do?' I said. 'Turn Nick away on Christmas Day? Say he can't see his daughter?'

Alex looked at me. 'Yes. But you won't. I was foolish to think I could handle this. I can't.'

He stalked out the front door, past Nick and into the cold.

Nick watched him go.

'What was fancy-pants Dalton doing here so early?' Nick asked, sidestepping into the house and closing the door behind him.

Nick was wearing an ironic Christmas pom-pom jumper and snowman scarf and holding baby Horatio in a way that suggested he could projectile vomit any minute.

'I'm not sure about much, where Alex is concerned.'

'Where's my Daisy?' Nick bellowed. 'Where's Daisy boo? Daddy has presents!'

From the kitchen, Daisy clapped her hands together and shouted, 'Baddy present! Baddy present!'

'You should have phoned first,' I told Nick. 'You said you'd come to the pub. Not here.'

'Santa's sleigh got lost. Ho ho ho!' Nick set Horatio on the sofa, then picked up Daisy. 'Hey, Daisy boo! Happy Christmas.'

'Bloody hell, Nick,' I said. 'It's not OK to turn up unannounced. We have a visitation schedule.'

'Not until next year.' Nick put blue eyes on mine. 'And it's Christmas *Day*. Do you remember that first Christmas we were together?'

'Yes,' I said. 'At Louise's "It's shit being born on Christmas Eve" birthday party. You wore that skin-tight C3PO costume. No one knew where to look when you stood up.'

'Remember what I told you at that party? That I'd love you forever and ever?'

'That's not what I remember,' I said, 'I remember you going AWOL, then being delivered back by the police two hours later.'

'Oh yeah,' Nick laughed. 'I was so pissed! Don't you miss those times?'

'Some of them,' I admitted, taking Daisy. 'Others, less so. Listen – Daisy and I have to go to my parents soon. So…you need to leave. What are your plans?'

Nick glanced at Horatio, lying on the sofa. 'Take the little dude to Mum's house.'

'What about Sadie?'

'She's at her mum's.'

'Isn't she going to Helen and Henry's?'

'She and Mum had a screaming match over the Christmas Day dress code.' Nick caught his reflection in the oven and adjusted his snowman scarf. 'It's looking nice, this place. You did it, Jules. Country house. Garden. All that shit. Just like you always wanted. You won.'

'You think this is all I wanted?' I said. 'I wanted a *family*, Nick. For Daisy. It was never about a house OR winning. But it's OK. We'll be fine.'

Nick said, 'I've made a big fucking mess, haven't I?'

'Yes,' I said. 'You have. But it's OK. Honestly. I'm over it.'

And I am.

I just wish I could get over Alex.

Got to Mum and Dad's house just before midday.

Nana Joan was in the living room with Callum on her knee, drinking a sizeable glass of Bailey's.

Brandi was quiet for once, slotting Match Attax cards into Callum's new album.

Mum was in the kitchen, shouting, 'No one's going to bloody CARE if the plates don't match, Bob. This is a FAMILY MEAL, not *Come Dine with Me*.'

Dad was shouting back, 'I WASHED and WARMED eight plates that *do* match, Shirley. What have you *done* with them?'

'Those ones in the oven? I used them for the veg.'

'WHY WOULD YOU DO THAT, SHIRLEY?' Dad bellowed. 'WHEN I SAVED UP ALL THOSE CO-OP VOUCHERS FOR THREE BERNDES VEGETABLE PLATTERS.'

I sat on the sofa with Daisy and poured myself a much-needed Bailey's.

'Is that you, Juliette?' Mum shouted from the steam-filled kitchen. 'What took you so bloody long?'

'I had visitors,' I shouted back.

'What visitors?'

'Nick and Alex.'

'OOOoo!' said Nana Joan and Brandi.

'OOOoo!' Mum shouted from the kitchen.

'Well I know which one I'd choose,' said Nana Joan. 'That well-filled-out lad. The one that came over for lunch. That Nick is a wrong 'un.'

'Nick will be in my life forever,' I said flatly. 'Alex might not be.'

'Oh well,' said Nana Joan. 'Plenty of fish in the sea.'

Why do people always say that at precisely the time you only want one fish?

Skyped Laura before lunch, and we all held up snowballs and shouted 'Cheers!' at the computer screen.

Laura seemed a bit emotional. She was sitting in a cavernous drawing room with baby Bear on her lap. Every so often, a maid came into shot, then scurried out of view.

'Where is everyone?' Mum boomed.

'Having pre-dinner drinks in the parlour,' said Laura.

'Do they have real gold cutlery?' Mum wanted to know.

'No,' said Laura. 'But it's really ever so nice. Zach's family couldn't have been kinder. And we've already had Champagne and smoked salmon and all sorts.'

'Sounds cracking,' said Mum.

'But I just want to be with all of you.' Then Laura burst into tears, adding, 'Sorry. I think it's the hormones. I'm so *emotional*.'

'Oh, hormones will do that to you,' Mum agreed. 'Bob – do you remember that time I cried watching the *Only Fools and Horses Christmas Special*? You know, just after Juliette was born?'

Dad nodded sagely. 'And you were addicted to custard creams, even though they made you constipated. Common sense just went out the window.'

'Bring Zach to our house next year,' Mum told Laura. 'We'll show him a good time.'

Laura had to go then. They were serving dinner, and baby Bear needed dressing in a three-piece suit.

Mum cooked Christmas dinner this year because she thought Dad would serve up 'tiny fucking diet portions' on account of her diabetes.

On the positive side, there was plenty of food.

On the negative, Mum got distracted rowing with Dad, and some things were overcooked, some undercooked and some not cooked at all.

I got a completely raw chippolata, a mushy carrot and a burned parsnip. But the turkey was fine, as long as you only ate the outer edges.

After lunch, we settled Nana Joan in front of the TV, while Dad and I washed up.

Dad refuses to use the dishwasher, claiming tablets cost 'a king's ransom' at nearly forty pence apiece. He washes up the old-fashioned way, using lemon juice, vinegar and the rinsing sink.

We had buttered crumpets for tea, and after that, I wanted to take Daisy home.

'Don't you want to stay over, love?' Mum asked. 'It's cold out there.'

'I fancy an early night,' I said.

Truth be told, I was feeling really sad about Alex.

Was home by 7 pm, and put Daisy straight to bed.

Lit a fire, got into my pyjamas, warmed a mince pie and poured the last glass of sherry.

Then I fiddled around with my phone, deciding whether or not to call Alex.

Being half-drunk, I did.

Alex didn't answer.

Tried again.

He still didn't answer.

Felt stupid then.

He's already made his feelings perfectly clear.

Tuesday, 26th December
Boxing Day

No calls from Alex.

If he'd called back, that would cancel some of the two missed calls mentalness.

But he hasn't.

Wednesday, 27th December

Have put on a STONE over Christmas.

Half has gone to my boobs, the other half has gone straight to my tummy. That's disappointingly huge too.

Need to do weight loss in the New Year.

Mind you, I always think January is a stupid time to lose weight. It's such a miserable month.

Thursday, 28th December

Althea phoned this afternoon.

'G'day!' she shouted. 'It's nearly tomorrow here. How weird is that!'

She was at an outback pub, drinking Victoria Bitter from a stubbie holder, while Wolfgang arm-wrestled the regulars.

They were due to catch their flight soon, but Althea always leaves things to the last minute.

When I told her about Alex and Christmas Eve, she asked if I'd be going to the Dalton Ball.

It's at the Westminster Dalton Hotel this year, which Althea reckons will be really cool because it's right by Big Ben and the big party crowd.

'I doubt it,' I said.

'You should,' said Althea. 'Go to the ball and show him what he's missing, the jealous idiot.'

'If you mean a stone of Christmas weight, dry winter skin and spots from all the mince pies I've been eating,' I said, 'I think you may be off the mark.'

'But you go every year,' said Althea. 'It's tradition.'

'You hate tradition.'

'Only *traditional* tradition,' said Althea. 'Your own traditions are different. Like my David Bowie day.'

Friday, 29th December

Feel really tired today.

And fat.

Althea is en route from Australia to cheer me up. She and Wolfgang don't get jetlag because they don't have sleep schedules or set meal times.

Saturday, 30th December

Althea arrived on my doorstep looking tanned and wearing a straw hat decorated with real crocodile teeth.

Wolfgang held a didgeridoo.

They had gifts for us – some Aborigine artwork made from authentic tribal handprints and a box of assorted dried witchetty grubs.

'Your boobs look *massive*,' Althea announced, as we took up stools in the kitchen.

Told her I'd porked up over Christmas – which seems unfair considering all the manual labour I've done on the house.

Expected Althea to do her usual bit about fat being a feminist issue.

But she said, 'When was your last period? Your boobs look pre-menstrual.'

Told her not for ages.

'You should take a pregnancy test,' said Althea.

'I have,' I told her. 'Before Christmas. And *anyway*, Alex and I used condoms every time we slept together. Probably really expensive, rigorously tested condoms.'

But Althea was insistent.

'I can't be *pregnant*,' I said. 'I drank a pint of Bailey's on Christmas day. Surely my body wouldn't let those two things coincide?'

'I know a friend who got pregnant *without* having sex,' said Althea. 'Have you got any vinegar?'

She made me wee into a glass of Sarson's, then studied the mixture to see if it changed colour.

'How is that supposed to work?' I asked.

'The vinegar should get darker if you're pregnant,' said Althea. 'But it's not very accurate, so...'

Daisy kept trying to drink the urine and vinegar, saying, 'Apple

293

juice?'

'You shouldn't drink other *people's* urine, Daisy,' Althea advised. 'Only your own has health benefits.'

After ten minutes of coughing on urine fumes, Althea decided I should do a real test.

We drove to the pharmacy for what Althea called, 'one of those plastic, planet-destroying wee sticks.'

There were all sorts of tests on the shelves, including ovulation kits for foolish women who *wanted* to get pregnant.

Althea snorted at those, claiming the moon was the best indicator of fertility.

Ended up choosing a robust-looking test in a plastic case.

It was ten times more expensive than the little 99p wee sticks, but I felt safe with its solid pink packaging and hopeful-looking blonde model.

Got home.

Weed on stick.

Two lines appeared.

PREGNANT.

Didn't believe it at first. Still not sure I believe it.

'I *knew* it,' Althea bellowed.

Burst into tears.

'Oh my god,' I cried. 'What am I going to do?'

'Everything will be OK,' said Althea. 'The fertility goddess only blesses strong women.'

'It won't be OK, Althea,' I wailed. 'How can it be OK? I'm barely coping with one. The test has to be wrong.'

'You'll be *fine*,' said Althea. 'Everyone says two children are easier than one.'

'Who?' I demanded. 'Who says that?'

'I overheard a mother say it once,' said Althea. 'In India. At least, I think that's what she said. She was speaking Gujarati, so maybe there was another meaning.'

'I should talk to Alex,' I said.

'You don't need a *man*,' Althea bellowed. 'Come live with me. We can be single mums together.'

Then she sang an augmented version of Beyoncé's 'Single Ladies' song.

'All the single mums! *All the single mums*. All the single mums. Put your hands UP!'

But the thought of living in a single mum commune with Althea conjures up unpleasant images of fennel toothpaste and watery almond milk porridge.

Also, there's always a blowtorch or two hanging around Althea's place, which is not great now Daisy's into everything.

Sunday, 31st December
New Year's Eve
Morning

Holed up at Mum and Dad's house, with Daisy in the travel cot.

Can't be alone – I'm way too stressed.

Keep fiddling with my phone, wanting to call Alex, but not knowing how to phrase things.

Mum bought me up a pint of Guinness to calm my nerves, but obviously, being pregnant, I couldn't drink it.

'It'll be OK, love,' said Mum, sipping the rejected Guinness. 'You've got your own place now. Nick is finally paying up. We're down the road. You'll be fine. Two kids is easy.'

Doesn't she remember how horrific new-borns are?

When I think about the work involved caring for Daisy at one-month old, I feel physically sick. And that was with two parents in the same house.

All the crying and burping and feeding and crying and not

knowing what on earth was wrong.

To go through all that again on my own. And with Daisy too...

'How on *earth* did you have three kids, Mum?' I asked, in an awed whisper.

'You just get on with it,' said Mum. 'I wouldn't want to go back, though. Buckets of shitty water forever in your kitchen. You should thank God for Pampers. And those squeezy food pouches are a revelation.'

This brought back memories of messy early weaning, and grimy ice-cube trays of puréed carrot.

Started to sob.

Mum put a placating hand on my shoulder. 'It could be much worse love.'

'It could always be worse,' I said. 'But that doesn't make it good.'

'Oh, count your blessings,' said Mum. 'Some women can't even have kids. You'll love the baby when it arrives – wait and see. Who's the father, anyway?'

'No one I'm about to settle down with,' I told her.

'Fair enough,' said Mum cheerfully, downing the rest of the Guinness.

I suppose I have Brandi to thank for my family's casual approach to paternity.

Afternoon

Worked up the courage to phone Alex.

He didn't answer.

That made me furious because now he'll think I've called to 'live in the moment', when the moment has very much passed.

I can't *text* him to say I'm pregnant.

Will just have to try later.

Evening

Alex still not answering.

Can't wait any longer.

Am going to see him.

Late evening

Caught the train to London with a load of cheering, singing New Year's revellers.

Had to turn down a mini gin and tonic from a cackling group of girls, but out of gratitude for their kind offer, I shared the reason for my journey.

'What do you think he'll *say?*' they kept asking.

Told them I had absolutely no idea.

Made it to the Westminster Dalton Hotel without getting run over.

The security man wouldn't let me into the Dalton Ball at first though, because I didn't have a ticket and was 'flouting the dress code.'

'But I need to speak to Alex Dalton,' I insisted. 'It's important.'

The fat security man crossed his arms and said, 'If it were that important you would have stumped up fifty quid and put on a nice frock.'

But then a waiter recognised me as a 'friend' of Alex's and persuaded the security man to let me through.

The ball was packed, as usual.

I scoured the crowd for Alex, but in a sea of black suits, he was hard to spot.

Then I saw him near the auction stage, frowning, arms crossed.

Catrina Dalton was nearby, flamboyant in a canary-yellow bow-covered ball gown, laughing with gay abandon, bejewelled fingers flailing and pointing.

Silly hormonal tears welled up. I couldn't talk about this in front of Alex's *mother.*

Decided that now wasn't the best time to share my news after all.

Then Alex spotted me.

Our eyes met, and his frown deepened.

He pushed through the crowd. 'Juliette, what are you doing here? Where's Daisy? Did you come alone?'

'I need to tell you something,' I spluttered.

'Where *is* Daisy?' Alex asked.

'At the pub. Not *at* the pub, obviously. I mean, she's sleeping there.'

Alex's dark eyes held mine for a moment. 'I know what you're going to say. New Year, new start and so on. I've been thinking long and hard about the two of us, and—'

'Alex, I'm pregnant,' I blurted out.

The whole room seemed to stand still.

Alex put a hand to his forehead and said, 'You're… *Christ*. OK. I'll support you, Juliette. Maternity specialists. The very best care. Whatever you need.'

My stomach dropped to the floor. 'That's what you think I need? Private healthcare?'

'What else can I give you right now?'

'I need *you*. I need you to grow up, stop being jealous and step up to this relationship. Otherwise, you're no better than Nick.'

'Can we go somewhere private to talk about this?'

'There's nothing to talk about,' I said. 'Not unless you tell me right now that you can get over this jealousy.'

Alex didn't say anything.

I turned away before he could see my tears, and pushed back through the crowd.

Alex called after me, 'Juliette. *Juliette*.'

As the crowd began the midnight countdown, I started to run.

I hurried out of the ballroom, down the hotel steps and towards Westminster Bridge, just as Big Ben's chimes rang out across London.

If I were Cinderella, I'd have left a glass slipper behind.

But I'm just a normal person.

So, I left my hopes and dreams instead.

I pushed into the New Year's Eve crowd, as fireworks went off over the River Thames.

Everyone oohed and aahed, cramming themselves towards the water for a better view.

'Juliette,' I heard Alex shout. '*Wait.*'

I didn't wait.

'Juliette!' Suddenly Alex was beside me. 'I told you to wait.' He grabbed my wrist.

'No, Alex,' I said, snatching my hand back. 'I'm sick of waiting.'

'You're pregnant with my child. A crowded street on New Year's is no place to be.' Alex took my hand again and pulled me along the bridge.

'Bloody hell, Alex,' I shouted. 'Stop. What are you *doing?*'

'Taking you back to the hotel.' Alex pulled me through the crowd.

I was too dumbfounded to complain. And anyway, Alex was probably right – I shouldn't have been among all those people.

I let Alex lead me back over the bridge, along the Thames and into a private lounge at the Westminster Dalton Hotel.

'You can stay here until the crowds die down,' said Alex, showing me to an embroidered sofa.

He paced back and forth, hands in pockets. 'I'll look after you,' he said. 'Daisy too. You know that, don't you?'

'What if I don't want looking after?' I said. 'What if I've had enough of men who can't grow up?'

Alex sat beside me. 'Whether you like it or not, I will have a say in this child's future. And yours.' He took my hand. 'You know, when I first learned the piano, I could never quite grasp the harmonies. How different notes could work together. I understand them a little better now. Not completely, but better. It's New Year's Day. A time of new beginnings. New harmonies, wouldn't you say?'

He kissed my fingers and looked at me with intense, brown eyes. 'Juliette, let's start again.'

'Start again?'

'Yes. Completely start again. Do things the right way. I need to ask you something.' He dropped down onto one knee, still holding my hand. 'Juliette Duffy, will you marry me?'

I gave a shocked laugh. 'Are you serious?'

'Of course I'm serious. When am I not serious?'

'You think we should get married? After all the problems we've had this year?'

'Juliette, this isn't just about us. There's a child involved.'

'Having a child isn't a good reason to get married.'

'I love you. Is that a good reason?'

I felt myself smile. 'It's a reason.'

'But?'

'But...Alex, is it enough? We're so different. And there are so many problems.'

Alex's expression darkened. 'You were quick enough to walk down the aisle with Nick Spencer. Christ – there should be a law against men like that having children.'

'I've grown up since then, Alex,' I said. 'I'm not looking for the picture postcard any more. Reality isn't like that. I just want to do what's best for Daisy.'

'This *is* reality,' Alex insisted, gripping my fingers. 'We're having a baby together. And I want you to marry me. Because I love you.'

'You're a better man than Nick,' I said. 'I do know that.'

'I should hope you do.'

We looked at each other.

'I suppose...the new year is a new start,' I said.

Alex's lips twitched. 'Is that a yes?'

'One thing at a time,' I said. 'I'm not agreeing to marriage. But... I'm willing to give us another try.'

'I'm determined to marry you,' said Alex. 'And I can be *very* convincing. Just ask my investors.' He sat beside me, still holding my hand.

Outside, fireworks exploded over the Thames and Big Ben.

Thank you for finishing my book.
If you have a minute, please review
on Amazon and GoodReads.

Suzy xx

What to read next?

BOOK III:
The Bad Mother's Holiday

Here's a taster...

The
BAD
MOTHER'S
HOLIDAY

SUZY K QUINN

Lightning
Books ⚡

BAD
MOTHER'S
HOLIDAY

SUZY K QUINN

Lightning Books

Monday 1st January
New Year's Day

How do you measure a life in a year?

+ 416 fish fingers cooked for Daisy, but mostly eaten by me.
+ 244 loads of washing.
+ One stone lost, one gained.
+ Seven bottles of Calpol.
+ 364 nights of disturbed sleep.
+ Said 'no' approx. 5000 times, told no 50,000 times.
+ Two calls to 999 (Daisy glo-stick chewing incident and freaky green poo two days after).
+ One unexpected pregnancy.
+ One marriage proposal.
+ Told Daisy 'I love you' more times than I can possibly count.

This year? I would like fewer:

+ Custody battles with Nick, Daisy's feckless, irresponsible father.
+ Relationship uncertainties with Alex.
+ Stressful house renovations.
+ Mortgage, credit card and utility bills.

Finances are an uncomfortable subject right now.

I'd planned to get a proper grown-up job in London this year, but commuting will be tough now I'm pregnant.

I know employers aren't supposed to discriminate, but pregnancy mimics hangover symptoms – tiredness, sickness, bad memory, etc. – and lasts all day, every day. There's no afternoon respite after a restorative Big Mac.

Frankly, I wouldn't hire me.

Alex has offered to pay my bills during the pregnancy, but told him 'no thank you'.

Maybe I'm being an idiot, but it would just be too weird. Yes – we're having a baby together, but our relationship is extremely uncertain.

Have asked Alex to give me thinking space, re: his marriage proposal. I think he's a bit offended. Am imagining him drinking an expensive Southbank latte, watching the Thames, black hair romantically tousled, dark eyes flashing.

'Another coffee, Mr Dalton?'

'No thank you. I'm too furious.'

Tuesday 2nd January

It's only been four days since the positive pregnancy test result.

Four years wouldn't be enough to digest this information.

Two children.

How will I do it?

Have booked in to see Dr Slaughter tomorrow.

Called Alex to let him know.

Alex was silent for a moment, then said, 'Juliette – a very good doctor and family friend has agreed to see us too. I spoke to him this morning. He's called Dr Rupert Snape and has promised to take very good care of you.'

'I've known Dr Slaughter since I was a little girl,' I said. 'He's wonderful. Why would I see anyone else? Look, you don't have to come. First appointments are just routine, anyway. All they do is log you on the system and tell you not to eat Stilton.'

'Dr Snape also mentioned sushi,' said Alex.

Told Alex I don't like sushi, so Dr Snape's premium advice would be useless in my case.

Alex asked where I'd eaten sushi.

'Marks and Spencer,' I said.

Alex said Marks and Spencer doesn't do real sushi, because it's made from cooked tuna, mayonnaise and seafood sticks. Then he asked me to move into his Chelsea apartment.

'I can't move to London,' I said. 'I have a job here and a house. And a family.'

'If we're committing to a life together,' said Alex, 'we have to make compromises.'

'OK, Alex,' I said. 'Why don't you stop working a fourteen-hour day and move back to Great Oakley?'

Alex said moving out of London was impossible right now.

'I hate the city, but it's where the money is,' he said.

'You're obsessed with earning money,' I replied. 'Babies only need a cot, clothes and nappies. Most of the other baby gadgets I wasted my money on never got used. And you can get a lot of free stuff second-hand – people are always getting rid of baby things. Your business earns millions.'

Alex said that company profit and personal income were not the same, and anyone who said different didn't pay enough tax.

Told Alex he reminded me of an anorexic girl who thinks she's fat.

Alex didn't seem to understand the comparison, citing the fluctuating diet industry as an excellent example of boom and bust.

'And children are expensive,' Alex insisted. 'They need schooling, healthcare, good-quality ski equipment... The list is endless.'

'That's what you're working for?' I asked. 'Ski equipment?'

'Every child needs ski equipment,' said Alex.

It was another reminder that we're from different worlds.

'So are you coming with me tomorrow?' I asked.

'Yes, of course,' said Alex. 'I'll see this NHS doctor with you.'

I felt he said the word 'NHS' in a derisive tone.

'You'd better not be snobby about private healthcare if you come along,' I said. 'Dr Slaughter doesn't suffer fools gladly. He's one of the few people who's shouted at my mum and lived to tell the tale.'

'What did he shout at your mother for?' Alex asked.

'He caught her buying twelve custard-filled doughnuts in the Co-op,' I explained. 'The day after she'd been diagnosed with diabetes.'

Wednesday 3rd January

Appointment with Dr Slaughter.

Alex drove me to the doctor's surgery in his shiny MG.

It was unnecessary to be driven there, since the doctor's surgery is a five-minute walk from my house, but I think Alex wanted to feel useful.

Felt a bit conspicuous, getting out of Alex's fancy sports car.

It didn't help that Alex looks a bit like James Bond – black tailored suit, clean-shaven jaw, dark eyes scanning the surroundings for snipers.

An old lady, hobbling past on a Zimmer frame, whispered, 'Tosser'.

'This is the doctor's surgery?' Alex asked, looking over our village health centre. 'The medical facility where you'll be cared for? It looks like an insane old lady's house.'

It's true – our doctor's surgery is essentially a bungalow, complete with moss-covered roof and orange curtains. But it's very cosy inside, except for the damp.

We waited the usual half an hour (Dr Slaughter is always late, except for the rare occasions when I'm late, in which case he's always right on time and I miss my slot).

'This is unacceptable,' Alex announced, when we were finally called into Dr Slaughter's office. 'Juliette is pregnant. She's had to wait over thirty minutes.'

Dr Slaughter said it was impossible to run an over-stretched NHS medical facility on time.

'Most problems exceed the ten-minute appointment slot,' he explained. 'And the older patients like a bit of a chat.'

'Is this a health facility or a community centre for the elderly?' Alex challenged.

Dr Slaughter considered this for a moment, then replied, 'I suppose it's a little bit of both. Are we congratulating or commiserating?'

'Congratulating,' Alex barked.

'Wonderful,' said Dr Slaughter, pulling out a box of mint-chocolate sticks. 'Well help yourself to the leftover Christmas spoils. Since we're celebrating.'

Alex declined the chocolate, muttering something about purified water and hand-cut vegetable platters at Dr Rupert Snape's surgery.

'You've done all this maternity stuff before, Juliette,' said Dr Slaughter, munching on a mint chocolate stick. 'You know the drill. Don't eat Stilton. Stay away from raw egg. We'll do a glucose test next time you come in. Buy yourself a bottle of Lucozade and drink it one hour before.' Then he handed me a Bounty pack of maternity information and said, 'The midwife will see you from now on. I'd make the appointment today if I were you – she's booked up solid until March.'

'You're not going to carry out a pregnancy test?' Alex asked.

'A home test is sufficient,' said Dr Slaughter. 'You have done the wee on a stick test, haven't you Juliette?'

'Yes,' I said. 'I bought a kit from Boots.'

'But what about a proper pregnancy test?' said Alex.

'Pregnancy tests are all much of a muchness these days,' said Dr Slaughter. 'It's just absorbent paper at the end of the day. The home tests are no different from the NHS ones. If anything, they're more accurate.'

'Juliette.' Alex took my hands. 'I really think we should see Dr Rupert Snape.' Then he turned to Dr Slaughter, eyes blazing, and said, 'You haven't even mentioned sushi.'

Thursday 4th January

The morning sickness hit today – a sort of low-level, travel-sickness feeling.

Did watery, spitty sick in the toilet when I woke up and now feel both sick and starving hungry.

Long, curly hair is no friend of the nauseous, so I've tied it up in one of those messy top buns that make me look like a sumo wrestler.

Have spent the morning watching kids' TV with Daisy, delicately sipping teaspoons of Heinz Tomato Soup. We watched a *Mickey Mouse's Club House* episode all about hot dogs, which finished with the usual 'Hot Diggity Dog' song. It made me feel simultaneously sick and in need of a hot dog.

Phoned Mum for sympathy.

'Will you come over and help with Daisy?' I pleaded. 'I feel awful.'

Mum refused, telling me to walk or drive to the pub.

Told Mum I couldn't face getting Daisy dressed.

'Why not?' Mum asked.

Explained that dressing Daisy, now she's a wilful two-year-old, involves half an hour of stressful negotiating. Doing her hair is equally challenging, since she either refuses to have it brushed or asks for some elaborate Disney princess hairstyle that I can't do.

'Why don't you just leave her hair?' Mum asked.

'I can't do that,' I said. 'Daisy's hair grows forward over her face now. She looks like a Yeti cave girl until I get a hairband on her.'

Then I moaned some more about feeling hungry and sick.

'How about something light to eat?' Mum suggested. 'Like a nice thick slice of buttered toast with jam? You want to get some calories into you.'

The thought of anything buttered made me vomit into Daisy's half-eaten bowl of Shreddies.

Mum took pity on me then. 'Dad will come get you,' she decided. 'Let me shout at him a bit and he'll be on his way.'

Dad arrived twenty minutes later on his bicycle, wearing waterproofs, cycle clips and a red reflector pinned to the back of his green bobble hat. With his neatly clipped white beard and the single white curl escaping onto his forehead, Dad looked like a special-edition cyclist gnome. There was a cushion strapped to his bike rack with hooked elastic.

'Hop on love,' said Dad. 'I'll pedal you up the road. Daisy can sit on your lap.'

'I thought you'd be in the car,' I said. 'I can't sit on the back of your bike with Daisy. It's dangerous.'

'As if I'd waste the petrol on a three-minute journey!' Dad chortled. 'There's nothing dangerous about this bike – I've just given it a full service.'

Told Dad my instructions had been miscommunicated, and I required a nice, warm motor vehicle.

Dad said I was getting spoiled, and relayed (again) the story of his own father pedalling him and his brothers to school on his bicycle crossbar with no cushion or padding of any kind.

'Our testicles were black and blue by the time we reached the school gates,' Dad announced. 'But it toughened us up. Taught us not to complain about minor discomforts.'

Ended up walking to the pub with Daisy, while Dad pushed his bike.

The ten-minute walk took half an hour, because Daisy needed to investigate every leaf, bramble and potential dog poo.

Am now at Mum and Dad's, taking yet more delicate sips of Heinz tomato soup from a mug shaped like a pair of boobs.

Mum keeps trying to force Guinness on me, believing it to be some sort of health tonic for pregnant women.

Phoned Alex to complain about how sick I felt.

Alex suggested taking me to Accident and Emergency. I hope he's not going to be this paranoid for the whole pregnancy.

Friday 5th January

Still at the pub.

KEEP being sick. The only foods I can keep down are bland, yellow processed foods.

Thank god my cousin John Boy is staying at the pub. He's stocked up on white bread, Super Noodles and Monster Munch crisps.

It's incredible John Boy has such a muscular physique on an unbelievably crap diet. But he's some sort of genetic oddity. Apparently, he lived off corned beef, biscuits and vodka in the army and didn't put on an ounce of fat.

Maybe it comes down to exercise. Even with his prosthetic leg, John Boy does squat jumps, ten-mile runs and one-handed press ups – the latter with Callum on his back.

'What happened to your weird pencil moustache?' I asked John Boy. 'You've let it go all straggly. And are you growing your hair out too?'

John Boy explained that he is cultivating one of those overly long, fashionable beards and a man bun.

Mum keeps asking why he wants to look like the back-end of a Crufts champion. But she isn't one to talk about succumbing to silly fashions. In the 1980s, her hair was bleached, permed and feathered. She also still wears lots of neon Lycra, animal prints and lace, often together, and shops in New Look, Top Shop and Forever 21.

Nice being back at the pub.

Dad has made the bathroom a bit more fun, putting magazines, crossword puzzles and a radio in there, plus a vase containing hazel catkins he picked from the woods.

Alex has asked to come see me, but I don't want visitors while I'm pale and throwing up. This has put into stark relief the uncertain nature of our relationship, and the fact I don't know him well enough to be sick in front of him.

The undesirable effects of pregnancy are yet another reason to be in a proper relationship before you get knocked up.

Saturday 6th January

Still at the pub.

Saw my tired, pale face this morning, coupled with a giant mess of frizzy curly hair, and realised there's no way I can go home yet.

Having morning sickness with Daisy running around is impossible.

Toddlers have no respect for illness. While I'm vomiting into the toilet bowl, Daisy prods me and shouts 'cuddle, cuddle'.

Realised, between vomits, that Daisy looks more like Nick these days. Her fluffy blonde hair is brown and straight at the roots, her eyebrows are darkening and her eyes are bright blue.

I wonder whose nose Daisy will get – my roundy, squishy one, or Nick's long, straight, actor nose? Hard to know what to hope for. Nick's nose does look striking in his headshots, but extremely evil on his mother.

I suppose it doesn't matter if Daisy looks like Nick, as long as his selfishness isn't genetic.

Afternoon

It's nice being looked after at the pub, but Mum can't get her head around me feeling sick. She is certain she can 'cure' me with the right meal.

Today Mum bought a range of 'get-well food' from the Cash and Carry: a catering-sized 24-slice pepperoni pizza, a 2ft garlic baguette and 50 chocolate-covered profiteroles. She unloaded this nauseatingly calorific assortment onto the kitchen table and said, 'There you go love – there must be something in that lot you fancy.'

Tried to ignore the tower of cream-filled chocolate puffs and cheesy, oily pizza, but Dad drew attention to it by starting an argument.

'You've bought enough food for twenty people, Shirley,' Dad complained, wagging the Guinness pencil he was using for Sudoku. 'It's a waste.'

'Jules and Daisy are here,' said Mum. 'We need a bit extra.'

'Juliette is feeling nauseous,' Dad insisted. 'A huge garlic baguette dripping with greasy butter is hardly going to settle her stomach. Nor is a pizza with all that gelatinous, bright-yellow cheese and fatty sausage on top. And she won't want a dessert, filled with whipped double cream and covered in rich, chocolate sauce.'

Slunk off to be sick then, but could still hear the argument about 'oil' and 'grease' through the toilet door.

'How are we ever going to eat a pizza that size in two days?' Dad finally demanded.

'Oh, stop going on,' said Mum. 'If there's any food left over, I'll bring it downstairs for the regulars.'

Dad took out his calculator and totted up the cost of leftover food Mum brought down to the pub last year. He estimated at least three-hundred pounds worth of food had been 'lavished' on Yorkie and Mick the Hat. He also pointed out that Yorkie is always too drunk to appreciate what he's eating and thinks smoked salmon is ham.

Mum snatched the calculator and added up Yorkie and Mick the Hat's bar bills last year. They worked out at over £10,000.

Dad sloped off to his office, muttering about 'dubious calculation methods' and 'imprecise measures.'

After lunch, Alex rang. 'How are you feeling?' he asked.

'Like I'm on a bumpy, winding road in an old, petrol-reeking truck,' I replied.

'I'm sorry to hear that,' said Alex. 'I was hoping you'd be feeling better. And that I could see you.'

Said I still didn't feel up to visitors.

'I'm not just a visitor,' said Alex. 'I'm the father of your child.'

Relented, and said Alex could come over for tea, which he calls 'supper.'

Told Alex not to bring any food.

'Not even a dessert?' said Alex.

'Especially not a dessert,' I said. 'Absolutely nothing contained whipped double cream or rich chocolate sauce.'

Evening

Alex just left. He brought me fifty red roses and a large bottle of Perrier (his mother told him sparkling water was good for morning sickness).

Things were a bit awkward, with Alex giving me a very formal peck on the cheek, then embracing me like I was made of china.

'Are you OK?' he whispered. 'How is the nausea?'

'Honestly, I'm fine,' I insisted. 'Just not too up for physical contact.'

Alex nodded sagely, a concerned expression on his handsome face. 'Perhaps we could see Dr Rupert Snape after all. He could tell us if this sickness is anything to worry about.'

'Almost everyone gets morning sickness,' I said. 'It's more common in healthy pregnancies. The extra hormones are there to prevent miscarriage.'

Alex struggled to get his head around this biological design flaw.

'But if the baby is healthy, why would the human body create illness?'

'You want to know why women throw up, wee themselves and get indigestion, sciatica, constipation, migraines and brain-fuddling tiredness during pregnancy?' I asked. 'It's simple. Mother Nature is a psychopathic old hag.'

Asked Alex about his Christmas, and whether he'd got to see much of his family.

'Yes,' said Alex. 'I stayed with Anya in Kensington.'

Asked who Anya was.

'My mother,' said Alex.

Remembered that Anya is the Hungarian word for mother. Felt guilty for forgetting.

'She would have been alone otherwise,' Alex continued. 'Carlos went back to Spain.'

'So it was just the two of you on Christmas day?' I asked.

'Yes,' said Alex. 'Very quiet. I imagine your Christmas day was somewhat busier. Listen. Juliette – have you thought any more about moving to London?'

'I don't want to move to London,' I said. 'Daisy is two-and-a-half. She likes parks and swings and woods. London isn't the place for her.'

Alex claimed London had 'some of the best parks in the world'.

'But Daisy has grandparents here,' I said. 'They love her. They want to be with her.'

Mum bellowed from the kitchen: 'I assume you're talking about your father, not me. The best thing about being a grandparent is giving the kids back at the end of a long day.'

I closed the door, and Alex and I chatted about family versus hired childcare.

'Whatever Mum says, she truly cares about Daisy,' I insisted.

Alex conceded that one of his nannies, Tiggy Carmichael, smoked forty cigarettes a day, stole cigars from his father and encouraged Alex and Zach to smoke, telling them that the Marlborough cowboy never caught a cold. 'But we loved her, nonetheless.'

'I'm happy in Great Oakley,' I said. 'I'm not moving.'

Alex sighed, knelt down to my stomach and kissed my woolly jumper. 'Little one, your mother is very stubborn,' he said. 'But we'll make it work somehow.'

It was a sweet thing to say, but actually having Alex's hands on my stomach made me feel quite nauseous.

Sunday 7th January

Still at the pub.

Woke up this morning to find John Boy red-eyed and quiet, automatically spooning Frosties into his mouth between swigs from a giant tea mug.

John Boy's teeth were a weird grey-purple colour and he smelt like an old tramp. His attempted man bun was straggling over his face.

Daisy said, 'On Boy. Smelly like wee.'

Asked John Boy why he smelt of stale booze and had teeth like a Victorian chimney sweep.

John Boy said his new girlfriend, Gwen, had dumped him.

I learned the whole story, through big swigs of sugary tea.

Gwen texted John Boy yesterday and said she was seeing someone else – a mature student at her university.

John Boy called Gwen over twenty times, but she wouldn't answer her phone. Heartbroken, he bought a £4.99 bottle of King's Oak Crème sherry, drank the whole thing and fell asleep on a park bench.

The cheap, red sherry explained John Boy's purple teeth.

I put my arm around John Boy and told him it would be alright. Couldn't think of anything else to say, so opted for the cliché, 'There are plenty more fish in the sea.'

John Boy said he hated fish. He spent the morning watching Rocky I, II and III back-to-back, then strapped his prosthetic leg on and said he was off to the shops.

An hour later, John Boy returned with two bottles of King's Oak Crème, a huge bag of pick and mix sweets for Daisy and a Liverpool football kit for Callum.

Callum was delighted with the football kit, declaring it 'well ace' and borrowing my phone to take selfies. The age six-to-seven kit was a bit big for Callum, because he's small for his age, but Callum declared his baggy appearance to be, 'Growing room, innit? That's better value.'

Nice that he listens to Dad sometimes.

Callum admired his selfies, believing he looked like Jamie Foxx from the new Annie movie.

John Boy put him straight. 'You're just not black enough, mate. You're more a sort of milky tea colour.'

Callum was disappointed. 'But I've sort of got an afro, haven't I?'

'No, mate,' said John Boy. 'Having tramlines shaved on your head is not the same as an afro.'

Callum looked sad about that. His dad (whom he never sees) is mixed race – half Caribbean, half Norwich – and Callum has always hoped to become a black football player.

John Boy put jelly rings on Daisy's fingers and laced up Callum's football boots, saying, 'You kids are the only things keeping me going right now. If it weren't for you two, I'd never smile again.'

Felt hurt by this. After all, I'd comforted him earlier and made that caring 'plenty of fish in the sea' comment.

Evening

Popped out to the Co-op after tea for more cream crackers and tomato soup, while Mum and Dad watched Daisy.

While I was at the Co-op, Mum phoned with a 'bright idea' for curing morning sickness – an all-inclusive holiday to Greece.

'I've found a cracking deal for May,' Mum told me. 'The Teletext people are on the other line right now, ready to book us all in. Your Dad and I will pay. It's cheap as chips – only £180 per person, including flights. That's less than it costs to live at home.'

'How will an all-inclusive holiday help my morning sickness?' I asked.

'All the food,' said Mum. 'You get so much choice on those all-inclusive buffets. Fruit, cheese – the lot. You're bound to find something you can eat.'

'You can't cure morning sickness with food,' I said. 'Food is what makes me feel sick.'

'Well, a few Coca Colas in the sunshine won't hurt,' Mum reasoned. 'And it's something to look forward to. Pregnancy is so miserable. And at the end of it, all you get is a screaming baby.'

'All-inclusive holidays aren't the place for a pregnant person,' I said. 'I can't eat at normal capacity. I can't drink alcohol. It just isn't cost effective. I don't want to sit around, being big and pregnant, watching everyone else get pissed and enjoy themselves.'

Mum told me I was being 'bloody miserable'.

She's right. I am bloody miserable. But that's pregnancy for you.

The moment Mum hung up, I regretted my grumpy, snap decision. A holiday would be nice, even if I can't drink alcohol or overeat, and it's very generous of Mum to pay for me.

Phoned Mum back, but the line was engaged. By the time I got through, Mum had already booked the holiday for the rest of the family.

'It's fully booked now, love,' said Mum. 'There's always next year. Of course, by then you'll have a baby and a toddler. And don't forget you'll have to pay full whack for Daisy's flight when she turns three. But never mind.'

Dad came on the line and said, 'It's not all bad news, love. Your Mum has agreed to a family camping trip at the end of June. So you can have a lovely break with the Duffy clan in the great outdoors.'

'I have not bloody agreed,' Mum shouted in the background. 'It is very manipulative of you to say that, Bob. All I did was mention the dry-rot in the caravan.'

Thanked Dad for trying to cheer me up, but there's no way I'm going camping. And from Mum's shouting and swearing in the background, there's no way she's going either.

When I got back from the Co-op, Brandi and Mum were colouring their hair in the kitchen.

They were both wearing dressing gowns – Brandi's skinny figure and push-up bra were wrapped in monogrammed Barbie pink. Mum's bulging bosom and stomach sported her favoured leopard print.

Brandi had foils all over her head and a full face of makeup, including creamy foundation, thick false eyelashes, flashes of black eyeliner and matte red lipstick.

'Do you want me to give you some more blonde highlights?' Brandi asked me. 'Your roots are nearly an inch long. It looks like Daisy felt-tipped the top of your head.'

Thanked her, but I've learned from past mistakes. Brandi always gives me white-blonde hair, no matter what tasteful, subtle blonde shade I request.